THE BRANDON PAPERS

THE BRANDON PAPERS

QUENTIN BELL

A Harvest/HBJ Book
Harcourt Brace Jovanovich, Publishers
San Diego   New York   London

Library of Congress Cataloging in Publication Data,
Bell, Quentin.
The Brandon papers, collected and edited by
Maurice Evans, with a foreword.
I. Title.
PR6052.E445B7 1985   823'.914   85-8573
ISBN 0-15-113708-0

ISBN 0-15-614045-4 (Harvest/HBJ : pbk.)

Printed in the United States of America
First Harvest/HBJ edition 1986

A B C D E F G H I J

Contents

Foreword

When the postman brought me a parcel containing the typescript of *The Brandon Papers* my heart sank. I have learnt to fear such offerings. Nor was I reassured by a covering letter from Miss Marguerite Evans explaining that these were documents collected by her uncle, the late Maurice Evans, documents which she thought would be of interest to me, 'since Lady Brandon was a close friend of Virginia Woolf and a member of the Bloomsbury Group'.

Miss Evans is mistaken; perhaps she was misled by a passage in Professor Dawson's biography of Lady Brandon in which *The Rewards of Maternity* is compared with *Three Guineas*. In fact, although they must have had many friends in common, I can find no evidence that Lady Brandon ever knew or even corresponded either with Leonard or with Virginia Woolf. Readers may rest assured that those names will not reappear on these pages.

Perhaps the discovery that the documents were no concern of mine encouraged me to read them. At all events, I did so and with increasing interest. I am delighted to introduce them to the general public which, I hope, will share my enthusiasm.

When I first read these papers I knew very little of Lady Brandon. I had read reviews of Professor Dawson's monumental study; but that was all. I knew that the subject of her biography was a noted feminist and a patron of medical science. She was what people call a 'do-gooder'. But Maurice Evans has collected information concerning her early life which compels one to believe that her fault lay not so much in doing 'good' as in large-scale fraud, perversion and homicide.

Startled by what I read, I turned to the Professor's 480 pages of learned and edifying prose. I found there no hint of the melodramatic transgressions recorded by Mr Evans. For this there is a sufficient explanation. When his investigative task was done the editor gave his word that nothing should be published while one of his most important informants was alive. He was content to wait for he was not an old man, and she was a very old woman. Fate, however, disposed of the business in its own way: Mr Evans was killed in a motor accident before he could publish.

According to Miss Evans, neither she nor her relatives knew anything of Maurice Evans's discoveries; his manuscript was left unread and remained unfound until a few months ago, when it was sent to me. (I present it here in the form in which I received it although, to help the reader through the text, I have provided chapter headings of my own, together with a plan of Penny Villa and a Brandon family tree.)

The family had therefore no reason to approach Professor Dawson when she was collecting material for her biography. The Professor, for her part, relied upon Sir John Frend's somewhat inaccurate monograph.

This important lacuna does not invalidate the remarkable contribution of Elise P. Dawson. She describes, and describes in detail, the history of preventive medicine in Britain; she examines the development of the Brandonian Institute with care; and she deals at very great length with the part played by Lady Brandon in the fight for the suffrage. All this is surely useful and it would be impertinent of me to do more than express my admiration for her immense industry. It is only when she turns from narrative to general considerations that the new evidence becomes relevant and leads us to question some of her statements.

Take, for instance, the following passage from page 443:

Mary Brandon was able to not only explicate but also to expose and finally to utterly defeat the corrupt and effete structure of British medical practice and British science with its backward-looking materialism working within the obscurantist presuppositions of man-made disorders and man-made placebos, basically because she was the kind of woman who is able to totally reject patriarchal values in favour of a maternalist philosophy of healing. Thus her motivation was right through her life completely devoid of egotism and of sordid calculations of any kind. She was as far from paternalist cupidity as she was from paternalist aggressivity and was able to comprehend on a higher plane of existentiality the true character of both maladies and therapeutic concepts.

Brave words indeed, but if the following narrative be true they may have to be rewritten.

The Brandon Family

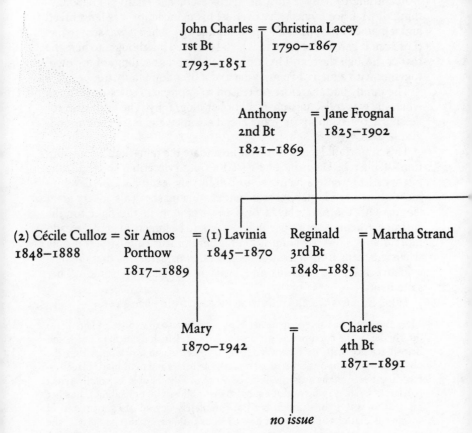

John Charles = Christina Lacey
1st Bt · 1790–1867
1793–1851

Anthony = Jane Frognal
2nd Bt · 1825–1902
1821–1869

(2) Cécile Culloz = Sir Amos = (1) Lavinia · Reginald = Martha Strand
1848–1888 · Porthow · 1845–1870 · 3rd Bt
1817–1889 · 1848–1885

Mary = Charles
1870–1942 · 4th Bt
1871–1891

no issue

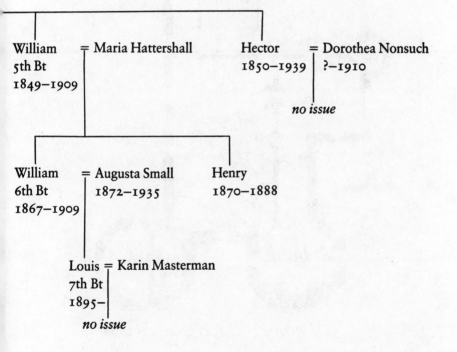

William = Maria Hattershall
5th Bt
1849–1909

Hector = Dorothea Nonsuch
1850–1939 | ?–1910

no issue

William = Augusta Small
6th Bt   1872–1935
1867–1909

Henry
1870–1888

Louis = Karin Masterman
7th Bt
1895–

no issue

ix

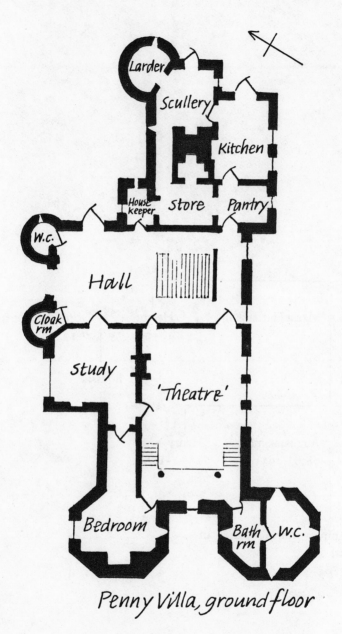

Penny Villa, ground floor

x

THE BRANDON PAPERS
Part I

CHAPTER I

[Maurice Evans's Investigation]

I suppose that the truth would never have been told, certainly I should have had no part in the telling of it, if I had not spent a part of my leave in October and November 1942 with my old friend and guardian, Hubert Mellish. Mellish was head of the justly respected firm of Mellish & Barker and had a secretary who, amongst other things, answered the telephone. Miss Postherne had 'flu; I volunteered to take her place. I sat in the office alone, Mr Mellish being late and the telephone silent. Presently my temporary boss arrived, hurried, distraught, and quite unlike his usual self.

'Margery!' he shouted. And then, 'Sorry, Maurice, can you get me Sir John Frend at the Ministry of Food?'

Sir John was guarded by secretaries, but eventually answered in person. I connected him with Mr Mellish and that should have been the end of the matter. There was a switch that made any outside call from Mr Mellish private. I could not find that switch; after a few seconds I ceased to look for it. I became, in fact, an eavesdropper. This is what I heard.

'Hello Sir John, this is Mellish. She's dead.'

'Sad, but not unexpected.'

'Look, the fool of a doctor whom they've called in won't give a certificate.'

'Damn!'

'I've used your name and he has agreed to hold his tongue; but he won't sign at any price. Look, you must come here at once.'

'You know there's a war on?'

'But think what will happen.'

'Oh, very well . . .'

At this point the other telephone rang. It was for me. I had to cut short my leave. It was something to do with the North African landings – what, I can't remember. But that conversation I did remember.

After the death of my father Hubert Mellish had become almost a second parent to me, one whom I loved. He was wise, benevolent, sometimes rather stern and always entirely honest, 'respectable' in the truest sense of the word. The idea that he might, for any reason whatsoever, falsify a statement, let alone a certificate of death, seemed both shocking and grotesque. Although I had never met Sir John Frend, I knew nothing to his discredit either.

I did not return to England until 1950. By then my guardian was dead. A V-1 had struck the fine old building in which he worked, killing him and destroying many documents that would have helped me later. But I could not lay his ghost. Perhaps because there was little else to occupy my mind at that time, I found myself reflecting more and more upon that perplexing conversation he had had with Sir John Frend. Then one afternoon, not long after my arrival, I went to visit James Mellish, my guardian's son and now senior partner of the firm, and I found Miss Postherne still at the switchboard. Seeing her there, deftly transferring calls one to another, revived still vivid memories in so forcible a manner that I felt I could no longer be silent and must confide my worry in James – perhaps he would be able to explain it.

Later that evening by his fireside the story began again, though even with James I was shy about mentioning the matter, and he seemed a little shy in answering.

'You knew the governor, he couldn't have done anything that wasn't straight.'

'That is one of the mysterious things about the business.'

'You could have misheard something, or again it could be some kind of illusion, some trick of memory.'

'I have asked myself those questions, and here I think you can help me. *If* it happened, it happened just before "Torch", that is the end of October or the beginning of November 1942. If my tale be true there ought to be some client of yours who died suddenly at that time. If there was no such person – and it had to be a woman – then we can really forget the whole business.'

'But if there is such a person?'

'Why, then we can decide whether it's worth pursuing the matter.'

'That sounds reasonable. I must admit that I would much rather put it all down to your fevered imagination running wild under the stress of war. The trouble,' here he smiled ruefully, 'is that we can so easily find out. We have a complete run of the *Sussex Mercury* in the office; if it's there, it will almost certainly have been marked.'

And so on the following morning Miss Postherne was sent to look for the relevant volume. And there it was, November 2nd, 1942:

DEATH OF LADY BRANDON

The editor of the *Mercury* announced with deep regret the death of Mary, widow of the late Sir Charles Brandon, Bt. She had died in her sleep at her home, India Lodge, Ramsgate; she was in her seventy-third year. The melancholy event had occurred during the night of October 31st; she had, for some time, been in a poor state of health.

Born in 1870, she was the only daughter of Sir Amos Porthow, the financier, by his first wife Lady Lavinia, *née* Brandon. She had been privately educated and spent much of her youth in Canada. In 1891 she married her cousin, Sir Charles Brandon, the fourth baronet; he died in tragic circumstances soon after the wedding. Thereafter, Lady Brandon devoted herself to social questions and to philanthropy. Older readers would remember her ardent, but non-militant support of the women's suffrage movement. Her greatest achievements, however, and her most generous offerings had been made in the cause of preventive medicine. She and her cousin Sir William, the fifth baronet, had between them created the Brandonian Institute. She had also been chairman of the Mid-Sussex Hospital Board, the South Coast Maternity Centre, the Sussex Welfare Association, etc. etc. She left no issue.

'That,' I said, 'clinches it. Sir John Frend was head of the Brandonian Institute.'

'I must admit that you were not dreaming,' said James. 'But the whole thing is crazy. Why should the head of the Brandonian Institute want to tamper with her death certificate? A harmless old lady dies, and dies liked by everyone. There is no reason to suppose she did not die a natural death. There was no inquest, no motive. It just doesn't make sense.'

'Did you know her?'

'A little. She was chairman, I was secretary of the Welfare Association. Like all the Brandons she was our client, they've all been our clients since the year dot. The idea of — what shall I call it? — irregularity? criminality? is grotesque.'

'Look,' I said, 'this is none of my business. It can't surely be illegal. But it might be painful. Shall I stop worrying? Shall I forget the whole thing?'

James considered this in silence, then he said, 'It may be painful, but yes, go ahead and find out. I shall give you all the help I can, but I don't want to know unless I have to. When you have finished your investigation tell me what you have discovered if it seems necessary.'

Thus it was settled, and James shall see this manuscript before it goes to the publisher.

I began there and then by asking what Lady Brandon had been like.

'A sweet old thing with a good brain and considerable diplomatic skill. She gave her money to medical science and was herself, to some extent, a scientist. A large social conscience: when I knew her she had for years been demanding that school children should be given free milk, long before it was government policy, and then she wanted them to have rose-hip syrup, blackcurrants, all those things. I suppose you might say she did a lot of good on the Welfare Association.

'I don't know whether you've ever had anything to do with a county welfare association. It is a rather saddening experience. Of course, everyone wants to help the needy and the unfortunate, but everyone has his own ideas as to how it should be done and Lord, how they fight!

'They co-opted Lady Brandon because they had to; she understood the business better than any of them. But they didn't like doing it. There had been a time when the "County" considered her a dangerous radical, a crank, a supporter of Lloyd George and Mrs Pankhurst. Some of the old animosity survived, but it was soon forgotten. She was irresistible. She did not sulk when checked, she did not triumph when victorious. If, as sometimes happened, she was inconsiderate, she apologised in a way that more than made amends. She ruled by persuasion. People called her "a socialist" but she used her class all right. She was never arrogant but she took it for granted, in the nicest possible way, that people would defer to a Brandon of Ramsgate. And they did. She had that gently imperious manner which becomes a habit in women who have been very beautiful and are very rich. Somehow she made people pleased to let her have her way. I remember one crusty old gentleman who had been worsted in an argument say after the meeting to another member, "It's impossible to deny oneself the pleasure of seeing that woman smile."

'Her fault was vanity, or rather mock modesty. She spoke of herself as an "ugly old woman" but she continued to dress very carefully and very well. She liked to be reminded that she had been beautiful. But her real weakness was a concern for her scientific reputation. Of her work at the Brandonian she would say, "Oh, I was just a dogsbody with a long purse and one who sometimes made a bright suggestion." But she purred like a Persian when people said that she had, in truth, done great things for science.

'The truth, I am told, is that she did play a most important part in the beginning but that later on the work went beyond her ken. She used to insist that, being a woman, she had been denied any proper education, but she loved to show off her scraps of Latin and Greek. I have never known any woman so fond of a classical tag.

'People told little stories about her vanity but they were not unkind stories; one could not dislike her. She found the Association bitter and left it sweet. I don't know that she had many intimate friends outside the Brandonian anyway. She certainly had no enemies.'

What else? Her father had been an engineer who enriched himself in rather queer ways. She lost her mother at birth and was reared by her stepmother in some remote part of Canada or Newfoundland – the stepmother was on bad terms with her father. She was quite young when she married her cousin and there had been some appalling tragedy soon after the wedding. She was a very rich young widow but never remarried; she spent the rest of her life at India Lodge. (A 'folly' built in the oriental style and much admired by aesthetic people, it now belongs to the Brandonian.) She lived quietly, collected pictures – her only extravagance; the rest of her money went to the Institute. She seems to have been popular in Ramsgate village.

There was no life of Lady Brandon, but Hesketh Pearson had made some preliminary studies and material was available. This enables me to say something about the history of the Brandon family without which the story of Mary Brandon can hardly be understood.

The Brandons used to describe their connection with the village of Ramsgate as though it had endured for many centuries. In fact, they had lived there only since the early 1800s when Sir John, the first baronet, had married an heiress and settled in Sussex; there he built Ramsgate House and also India Lodge, where he kept a mistress. Both he and his successor, Sir Anthony, had married and then dissipated a great fortune; and Sir Reginald, the third baronet [see family tree], was thus obliged to sell the estate.

But then for a short time (1869–70), the family prospects improved wonderfully. The purchaser of Ramsgate, Sir Amos Porthow (a man of humble origins but of great abilities) married Sir Reginald's sister, Lavinia Brandon. Although twenty-eight years her senior, he was a most 'desirable match', having crowned a successful career with the 'Liberty Sound Venture', an undertaking in which he had persuaded a great many people that the coast of Labrador was rich in gold. It was not, but by the end of the business Sir Amos was.

With such a brother-in-law, Sir Reginald himself was able to marry an heiress, Martha Strand. It did not take him long to spend all his wife's money. To make matters worse, he became deeply involved in the quarrel which had developed between Sir Amos and his young wife, thus making an enemy of his brother-in-law for life. Lavinia, however, died in giving birth to a daughter on May 7th, 1870; the child, Mary Porthow, is the subject of this study.

We have a description of the Brandon family at about this time from the pen of Maria Hattershall, the novelist, who was married to Sir Reginald's brother, William.

They were an astonishing race, as like each other as peas in a pod, small in stature, yet so well formed that one could have sworn that they were tall. They all had the same dark hair, the same grey-blue eyes, the same fair skins.

Their features seemed to exhibit natures of singular beauty: a group of them in a drawing room really did suggest a company of angels – I do not exaggerate. And yet, despite these captivating lineaments, in character they were at best feeble, at worst despicable. It was my good fortune to marry the worthiest of this race. My William has good principles and a most lovable disposition; his only fault is an entire incapacity for work of any kind. There never was a man so able to see what ought to be done in any situation or so entirely incapable, in any situation, of doing anything whatsoever. No one is more conscious than he of his own faults, no one less able to cure them. Of his elder brother, the present baronet, what can one say save that he is jealous of his honour and careful of his dignity? His wife, Martha Strand, brought him a great fortune which in a few years he has managed to dissipate. An admirable and religious woman, entirely devoted to his interests, he has made her cruelly unhappy. Himself he has beggared. Like all the rest he has done nothing to bring honour to his name and has in no way contributed to the greatness of his nation. He consumes but never produces wealth, he lives on his looks and on his title, and yet there never was a man so sure of his own rights. Of Hector, the youngest brother, I find it hard to write with patience. He is not ungifted, he is not indolent, neither is he unamiable. But he is without principles or pride, he chooses his companions amongst the basest of mankind, and, alas, of womankind. He seems to delight in vulgarity, he amuses himself in music halls and public houses with jockeys and professional entertainers of the lowest sort. He seems to have a natural taste for that which is common and meretricious.

If I were writing for the public eye I should not mention my sister-in-law, Lavinia Brandon, later Lady Porthow. She has gone to her Maker and one can only hope that Heaven will be merciful to her. Endowed with all and more than all the family beauty, she grew up to be a desperate flirt and, one fears, something worse than a flirt. In the end like all the rest she married for money, selling herself to a man of the vilest character, old enough to be her father. Sir Reginald has always declared that Sir Amos Porthow killed his wife. This is surely untrue, but there can be little doubt that he hated her.

About the time this was written, the Brandons were approaching the nadir of their fortunes. William, Maria's husband, tried in several ways to make money; but each time he encountered the same difficulty: people would not pay him a salary unless he actually did some work. He and his sons, William and Henry, were supported by Mrs William Brandon who, under her *nom de plume*, managed to write and sell three bad novels a year until, in 1886, she died.

Hector was the most resourceful of the three brothers. He was by turns a theatrical costumier, an agent, an impresario and the lessee of the Royal Cumberland Theatre. He was for a time married to a widow, Mrs Dorothy Nonsuch, better known to the public as Lulu Lavalse.

As for Sir Reginald, he lived on what remained of his wife's capital. His only solace was derived from a contemplation of the misfortunes of Sir Amos, which were indeed of a dramatic sort.

Six months after the death of his first wife, Sir Amos married again and even more disastrously. The second Lady Porthow had been a Mlle Culloz, employed to look after the baby. Sir Amos refused to look at the child but he must have seen a good deal of its nurse. She played her cards so well that her employer was entirely infatuated and made her one of the richest women in Europe.

Sir Reginald took this alliance as a personal insult. It was, he declared, a gross affront to the memory of his sister, and the notion that so plebeian a couple should inhabit Ramsgate House was outrageous.

But the year 1873 brought a rich consolation to Sir Reginald: Sir Amos was stricken by what seemed to his enemies to be the judgment of Heaven.

It happened thus. M. Guy Césaire, an insomniac living at No. 143 Avenue du Chevalier Trenca, Mentone, looked out of his bedroom window very early in the morning of January 3rd and observed a young man tying a rope to a balcony of the Hotel Splendide which faced M. Césaire's modest apartment. Presently, he was joined by a young woman wearing a very fashionable dressing-gown. The couple embraced, then, according to M. Césaire, the young man turned to make his descent down the rope; he leant over the balustrade and looked down at the pavement four storeys below, whereupon the lady, producing what appeared to be a poker from the folds of her gown, struck the young man on the back of the head with terrible force (*'avec une férocité indescriptible'*).

The victim uttered no cry. He fell lifeless to the street below, whereupon the lady unfastened the rope and threw it down after him. Taking the weapon with her, she retired to her room.

The police were summoned. It was discovered that the balcony from which the young man, a M. Jules Thouin of Tours, had been precipitated, served suite no. 2 in the hotel. It had that night been occupied by 'M. Sir Porthow and Milady Sir Porthow his wife' (I quote from the *Éclaireur de Nice*, January 4th, 1873).

Sir Amos declared that his wife had been in bed with him all night, that a slight internal disorder had kept him wakeful at the time when the alleged murder had taken place, and that he would have known if she had left him, even for a moment. No sign could be found of the weapon. The evidence of the medical men was inconclusive. It was said that the lady occupying the rooms above was of more than dubious character and, in short, everything that could be said or suggested in favour of Lady Porthow was put to the *juge d'instruction* by the ablest lawyers that money could buy. It may be doubted whether, for all their zeal, Sir Amos's representatives could have saved Lady Porthow from conviction if M. Césaire himself had not begun to express doubts about his own accuracy. It had been very early, the light was uncertain, he could not now swear that he had seen the blow struck or be certain from which balcony the victim fell. In fact, he could not be sure of anything. The prisoner was released and the case was closed.

But in the city of Tours the friends of M. Thouin were angry. They knew all about *La Belle Culloz*; they were credibly informed that M. Césaire was living in great style in the city of Valparaiso. There were some amongst them who swore that poor Jules should not go unavenged.

Sir Amos and his wife, although they were now united in little else, agreed in thinking that Lady Porthow should vanish, but whither? Sir Amos had the answer: Creek Castle stood empty and perfectly fit for habitation. Here we may again borrow from Maria Hattershall.

As a part of the monstrous fraud by which Sir Amos managed to impose upon a credulous public, an entire city, together with harbour works, dwelling-houses, ore-crushing machines and other industrial devices had been built beside the icy waters of Liberty Sound. Nearby stood Creek Castle, a lofty pile, solid, luxuriously appointed, ornate and, like everything else in that place, intended simply as an engine of deceit. But now it found an unexpected use; hither the erring wife and the innocent babe were conveyed and here they remained with nothing save a yearly supply-vessel to succour them, prisoners of that misguided woman's evil reputation and of the sempiternal frost.

With the departure of the stepmother and her charge, the life of Sir Amos becomes much less interesting. He settled at Ramsgate and tried to live the life of a country gentleman. The friends of Sir Reginald refused to have anything to say to him; but Sir Reginald had not very many friends and there were others who were ready to forgive the social faults of so rich a man. In this they were encouraged by old Lady

Brandon, who had been the wife of the second baronet and who had quarrelled bitterly with all her children. By settling at India Lodge she gave her landlord an air of respectability, made herself very comfortable and succeeded in infuriating her eldest son.

Sir Reginald died in 1885. Charles, the fourth baronet, was a schoolboy of fourteen; he inherited very little except the title, but his condition was greatly improved by his father's death. Indeed, no event could have been more fortunate for the Brandon family. Martha Brandon was now able, by strict economy, to arrest the decline of their fortunes; and, with a nice mixture of firmness and humility, came to terms with Sir Amos.

The owner of Ramsgate was now sixty-seven and he had reached a time of life when he wanted the affection of a family. He had no Porthow relations, he detested and hoped never again to see his second wife. He did, however, rely upon his solicitor, Robert Mellish, and so was ready to listen when that gentleman (the father of my guardian) urged that something might be done, at all events, for the children. Something was done: Martha and her son, the family of William, and even Hector, of whom Sir Amos did not approve, were subsidised. Sir Amos even talked about leaving Ramsgate itself to the Brandons – he talked, but he would not decide.

This was probably because he had begun to consider another direction in which he might look for love. Again it was the persuasive Mr Mellish who directed his attention. Mary Porthow had been three years old when her stepmother took her to Liberty Sound. She had had no education, no amusements, no friends of her own age. This seemed to Mr Mellish harsh treatment of a girl who had never, consciously, done her father any wrong. Now she was growing up; it was a scandalous thing that the daughter of one of the richest men in Europe should be deprived of all the advantages that might have been hers.

Arguments of this kind, tactfully but repeatedly advanced, had their effect. Sir Amos, writing through Mellish, suggested that the girl be sent to school in England and might, perhaps, enjoy a holiday at

Ramsgate. Lady Porthow replied, 'Yes, of course, but her stepmother must come with her.'

That price was too high for Sir Amos. He suggested that Lady Porthow's establishment might be improved and enlarged, she might have friends to stay, she might be satisfactorily mentioned in his will, if only Mary Porthow were sent back to England.

'When the girl leaves, I leave,' was the reply.

These negotiations were lengthened and made additionally frustrating by reason of the fact that it was only during the period from the beginning of June to the end of October that Liberty Sound was ice-free. When the summer's effort failed another winter had to be endured without messages or negotiations and, with every year that passed, Mary Porthow lost a little more of her girlhood and of her chance of being educated. In the summer of 1888, Captain Arthurs, an officer of one of Sir Amos's enterprises, was sent with fierce but vague instructions to bring Miss Porthow back 'by any means'. The instructions were too vague, the Captain was too weak. Lady Porthow outmanoeuvred him and he returned without even seeing the young lady for whom he had been sent. Sir Amos was now obsessed by the idea of regaining his daughter. He devised a new plan; there was just time to send someone to Liberty Sound before the season ended. He needed someone, as he put it to Mellish, 'who would be quite desperately anxious to succeed'. Fate supplied him with an envoy.

That summer, Mr Hector Brandon had a misadventure which nearly landed him in gaol, having visited a disreputable club just as it was being raided. It was not the first such incident, but on this occasion he involved his nephew Henry Brandon. The family was naturally in a dreadful state and Sir Amos, appalled by the merest hint of scandal, thought the boy had better leave the country. Believing he had some ability, he therefore sent him out to Liberty Sound with fresh instructions.

From a letter from Mr Mellish, Sr to Mr Mellish, Jr, July 1888:

Master Henry's task is to bring Miss Porthow and, if she insists, her stepmother out of Liberty Sound and to deposit them in Boston, Mass.

If he can manage it, Master Henry will proceed with them at once leaving the servants to look after Creek Castle until the winter is over; but if necessary Master Henry will remain throughout the winter and await Captain Arthurs who will be sent out as soon as the ice breaks. In Boston Master Henry and the ladies will find a Mr and Mrs George Pullman, Mrs Pullman and her daughter are friends of Lady Porthow and have, it seems, visited Liberty Sound. They will have been approached by us. In Boston Lady P. will benefit by a small quarterly payment, but only in Boston. Miss Mary will come to England as soon as a suitable chaperone can be dispatched.

If Lady P. makes any difficulties then Master Henry is empowered to say that she has several old friends in the city of Tours who are still anxious to renew her acquaintance. These people will be assisted and she may expect a visit from them. If Lady P. wishes to avoid such a reunion then she must write to Sir A. He will pay no attention to her letter unless it is brought by Miss Mary in person and she must, if she is to deliver it, leave her stepmother either in Creek or in Boston.

It will be seen that Sir Amos had provided his envoy with a formidable weapon. Henry Brandon did not, it was true, proceed immediately to Boston with the ladies and soon it was clear that he was remaining at Creek Castle for the winter. Sir Amos, however, had little doubt that when Captain Arthurs sailed for Liberty Sound in the summer he would be able to report success.

But on this occasion the financier's carefully laid plans came to grief. In February 1889 Sir Amos died, shortly after having made a will in which everything went, under careful safeguards, to his daughter, Robert Mellish being named as guardian.

Mr Mellish was left with plenty to think about but not very much to do for the next four months. Captain Arthurs set sail at the end of May but there was no news from America until June 8th when a cable despatched from Halifax, Nova Scotia, carried the following message:

REGRET LADY PORTHOW HENRY BRANDON ALL MENSERVANTS
LOST AT SEA STOP PROCEEDING BOSTON AWAIT INSTRUCTIONS
LETTER FOLLOWS

MARY PORTHOW

This was followed by Mary Porthow's letter which is a document of central importance in our story. It must be reproduced *in extenso*.

On Board SS Brunswick

June 7th, 1889
Honoured Sir,
You will already have my telegram from Halifax where we berth tomorrow. In this letter I must accomplish the sad duty of letting you know that my stepmother, Mr Henry Brandon, Mr Henry McGill, Mr Thomas Thurlow and Mr William Davies have been drowned at sea. I, for my part, have already learnt from Captain Arthurs that my father has expired. Alas, how many deaths!

It is with infinite regret that I learn that I have lost a parent whom I had hoped one day to embrace and to whom I owe so much. I am sure that I also owe much to you, sir. I know that you were my father's trusted and loyal advisor for many years. In that I am indeed fortunate, and it is with pleasure that I realise that it is to you, sir, that I must now turn for advice and that it is you to whom I now owe obedience.

I have made a full statement of the tragic circumstances in which so many of my friends disappeared and Captain Arthurs, who is goodness itself, will see that this is placed in the hands of the proper authorities. I give you the substance of the matter here.

You will know that Mr Henry Brandon arrived here on the evening of October 25th. It was the end of the season for revictualling but, as sometimes occurs, we were given a few days of Indian summer, calm, cloudless and sunny, the creek being as smooth as a mirror. Also, as sometimes happens, but seldom so late in the year, a vast shoal of fish made itself known in these waters. On such occasions we go fishing, for the meat is good when fresh and can be smoked against the winter. My stepmother proposed a party consisting of herself, who loved the chase of fish, my cousin who desired a better view of the country on so fine a day, and our three menservants to handle the nets. My servant Thérèse Boileau and myself remained high on the Castle to watch the sport – alas, what sport!

From the battlements we could easily observe what passed; the water

16

was full, it boiled with fish, and the nets being thrown out, a vast quantity was taken at once so as to fill the bottom of our little boat the *Caprice* to a great depth. The net was again thrown out and drawn to the side of the vessel, so full that it could not easily be lifted. All those on board began to help in pulling in the catch whereupon – I think – the big weight of caught fish shifted suddenly and in one instant the boat capsized (? – *chavira*) so that all were thrown into the water and the *Caprice* floated upside down. Thérèse and I cried out together and ran down to the boathouse (which was at some distance from where we had been standing). With difficulty we contrived to launch the sailing dinghy and thus sought to rescue our friends. But it took too long and all was useless. In another place the peril might not have been so great, for the victims were not very far from the shore; but here there is a very strong current running down towards the Sound and, off Labrador the cold water-melted ice comes from the Arctic regions and is soon fatal. We rowed out but could find nothing and returned in tears to the Castle.

I need not speak of the loss of my stepmother, the principal person in my life since I was of an age to remember, or to understand. My Cousin Henry seemed a person of charming disposition but was taken to Heaven before I had time to know him. Through the years I had got to know our servants well and they too were friends. Mr McGill, active, humorous and helpful in a thousand ways, I much regret. Old William Davies was not easy to get on with but had excellent qualities and, as Tom used to say: 'really he is a good old sod'.(!)* Now in an instant they were all gone.

Thérèse and I were left to face the winter alone and if Thérèse were not an angel of goodness and patience I think I should have lost my reason in that dark lonely place. I can never reward her enough.

When at length the relief boat arrived, Captain Arthurs explained your wishes and those of my late father. It seemed to me that I should be acting in accordance with your desires if I were to go at once to Boston and take up residence with the Pullman family, there to await your commands. These I shall of course obey whatever they may be, but I would plead for a little time in which to stay quiet and be as little observed as possible. You will know that I have always lived out of the world, as in a convent. I do not recollect ever seeing a horse and it was only for three brief days that I had the experience of conversing with a gentleman. I have though a certain knowledge of Miss Pullman, we have corresponded and I believe that she

---

* Thus marked in the hand of Mr Mellish. – M.E.

may be able to help me to prepare myself for a larger scene. There is a thing that gives me great uneasiness. With Maman and Thérèse I have always conversed in French. My English I have learnt from books and from the servants. I think that it is not gentlemen's English. With my Cousin Henry, and once or twice with Captain Arthurs, I have sometimes used words which made them look at me strangely and I suspect that these words are not *comme il faut*. With Miss Pullman, who has been educated as a lady in Boston and who, being of my own age could speak to me frankly, I could discover my errors in a way that might not otherwise be possible. I would not like to meet my relations in England without being sure that I am not guilty of improprieties in speech and perhaps in other things.

Before leaving Creek Castle I removed various objects which I thought to be of value and these will remain in the care of Captain Arthurs. Your letter to my stepmother I thought it wrong to open; it may contain matters not intended for my eyes and the Captain has it sealed. The Captain did inform me that provision had been made for me under my father's will. It seemed best that I should await information and instructions from you; but meanwhile I possess no money at all of my own. My stepmother did write a will, although I doubt whether it has legal value. I enclose it. You will see that she leaves me everything of her own at Creek. I have taken for safe keeping and immediate uses the £650 which she kept, together with a large amount of jewellery, most of it, I think, glass. Captain Arthurs did offer to lend me quite a large sum; but I feel that it is better to manage matters in this way until you tell me how to act. Until then I will keep these valuables.

In conclusion may I offer, through you, my respectful condolences to Mr William Brandon and to my Cousin William who I fear will be much afflicted; also my humble compliments to Lady Brandon and her son. And please, honoured sir, accept the assurance of my most respectful sentiments.

MARY PORTHOW

Part of a letter from his father to Mr Mellish, Jr, enclosed with the above:

... confirms our news and does help in establishing the circumstances of death. I think that this can now be proved without trouble.

Poor Master Henry a short but not a happy life, as for Lady P. *de mortuis*. But Miss Porthow is a real problem, reared amongst servants and foreigners, as you will see she writes like a foreigner and the English that she has picked up – oh dear. But she is our client's daughter and the heiress to an immense fortune. Actually, I think a decent enough girl but I would not like to ask her to tea with your sisters. By all means let the Americans keep her for the present; but there ought to be someone else; we can't leave her to be educated by people of whom, really, we know nothing. She ought to be put under the care of a governess, some sensible experienced woman who could teach her how to behave in the society to which her wealth entitles her. Do you think you could find someone with the necessary qualifications?

Please return her letter.

Yours etc.

CHAPTER 2

[Lady Alcester's Memoirs]

Extracts from the unpublished memoirs of Lady Alcester, now in the possession of her granddaughter, Mrs Charles Oxbrow, and reproduced with her kind permission. In 1889 Lady Alcester (then a young widow and known by her first married name of Cecily Gordon) became Mary Porthow's companion and closest friend.

LADY ALCESTER'S MEMOIRS: CHAPTER III
MARY PORTHOW

It was at a dinner party in 1889; I was sitting next to the younger Mr Mellish and he said to me, 'Would you like to be employed as a good fairy?'

'I hate to be gross, but what do good fairies earn?'

'Oh, about £700 a year plus expenses, fairly large expenses.'

'On those terms I wouldn't mind being an old witch.'

'It's all very romantic. We, our firm, I mean, have rescued a captive princess from an enchanted castle far in the frozen north. The old witch is dead, but before dying she cast a spell upon her captive; when she opens her mouth toads and adders fall from her pretty lips.'

'I have an uneasy feeling that the salary might turn out to be faery gold.'

It was with some such nonsense as this that I was launched upon an enterprise that was to change my life entirely. A fortnight later I was on board the *Hibernia*, bound for New York. I carried with me a trunk of new clothes (those thrice-blessed expenses), an English dictionary and list of the foulest expressions in the language compiled by the firm of Mellish & Barker, with some assistance from a naval friend.

My task was to educate a girl not much younger than I, a girl who had been brought up by servants and criminals. She knew nothing of decent society, probably she picked her teeth with a hairpin.

'What then am I to do with her?'

'Make her presentable. After all she's a great heiress, she ought, as far as possible, to be a lady.'

'And she may be quite horrible.'

'To judge from her letter I should say not, but even if she has two heads I know you will make something of her.'

She did not have two heads. In a manner of speaking she had three and, in a manner of speaking, one of them had to be removed. It was a very delicate and painful operation. I first saw Mary from the deck of a ship; she was on the quayside with two companions. The Venus of that trio was strikingly beautiful, what they used to call a 'Gibson Girl' and what I call 'cheap expensive', her looks quite spoilt by a lot of vulgar flounces. On the other hand, Juno (a youthful Juno who would become properly Junoesque one day) was clad soberly but with a good deal of style. Minerva, the plainest of the three but not ill-looking, was even worse dressed than Venus. There was a kind of feeble, artless frivolity about her, she held herself very badly, but the crowning disaster of her appearance arose from the fact that she was trying to be skittish in black crêpe. I realised that she was wearing what she supposed to be mourning and must therefore be my charge. My heart sank.

It was Venus who took the initiative. She scrambled aboard with an undignified rustle and tumble of petticoats, extended a gloved hand and exclaimed in much too loud a voice, 'Mrs Gordon, I'm Katie Pullman and I certainly am glad to make your acquaintance and to welcome you here in Boston. This is my friend Miss Porthow and this is Miss Boiler.'

Miss Porthow vouchsafed a smile – it certainly did a good deal to redeem her general aspect. Miss Boiler, who for a time remained unidentifiable, later found occasion to tell me that she was a Mlle

Boileau, *femme de chambre* to Mlle Porthow. If she had not done so I should have set her down as a casual friend of the other two, for they addressed and treated each other with democratic familiarity. Me they regarded with apprehension and curiosity.

The curiosity was, of course, mutual. Mary's two companions were quite easily understood. Miss Pullman was good-natured, vulgar, silly and vain; Mlle Boileau was taciturn, sullen and suspicious but might be curable. But Mary herself! The mere sight of her made me wince, she had no notion of how to dress, or move, or behave; and yet, from the outset, I was sure that she was splendid material. It was obvious at once that she was clever in a bookish sort of way and it very soon became evident that she had a remarkably sweet disposition and could be made perfectly charming. It was obvious that she would be a problem; but a problem well worth solving.

The three of them took me to the hotel where they had rooms reserved. The advantage of the place, as they saw it, was its proximity to the Pullman residence. It was in every way unsatisfactory. Then I had to meet Pa and Ma – a discouraging experience.

What one knows of Bostonians makes one think that they will, in their way, be respectable. What one overlooks is that nowadays most Bostonians are Polish or Irish, mostly Irish, mostly poor, very poor, although some have prospered exceedingly. The Pullmans had not done that, they had just scraped themselves out of the slums and into a decent but unfashionable part of town. Mr Pullman was something not very important in a bank or a business.

Mrs Pullman had met Mlle Culloz, as she then was, when one was a scullery-maid and the other a nurse-maid in someone's house in London. They must have been fast friends for when Mlle Culloz became Lady Porthow and immensely rich, her ex-colleague – if that be the word – was enabled to emigrate to Boston and provided with a fortune which took her and her husband out of the slums. After that appalling scandal, Lady Porthow was immured in Creek Castle, and Mrs Pullman became one of her very few links with the outer world.

The mothers arranged that the daughters should correspond so that Mary might improve her English (which she did) and Kate might learn some French, which she did not.

What kind of people were the Pullmans? Well, as Mary said, they were 'good people'. Mary was much too inclined to think well of everyone. But it was true; they were always kind, they were honest, they really loved Mary and they put up with me very well; they were enormously hospitable. Mr Pullman I came to know rather well before I left Boston and he certainly had some good qualities, he meant well; by and large, he behaved fairly well. He endured the company of his silly wife very patiently and, although honest and affectionate, she was almost unendurably silly; but then so, at times, was he. Kate was spoilt but did not show it in an unpleasant way, for she was capable of laughing at her own vanity; she was almost as stupid as her mother but she did not pretend to be clever. No, I can't find much to say against them except only this: they were hopelessly and incurably vulgar – vulgar in their speech, their manners, their dress and their ideas. The parents had no control over their daughter, she came and went as she pleased, she made excursions to the seaside with friends as vulgar as herself, she went out with young men unchaperoned and she returned at any hour and nothing was said. These young people with their loud voices, their screams of idiot laughter, their complete lack of propriety or dignity, were perhaps harmless enough. But as a school for manners nothing worse than their company could be imagined. It was into this group of rowdy, carefree juveniles that my charge had fallen. She thought them wonderful, she called upon me to admire their energy, their spontaneity, their democratic *sans gêne*. Poor innocent, coming from that isolated and squalid outpost in the Arctic – how was she to know better?

Mary had only been with them for a few weeks but already she had accepted their lax manners, their slovenly demeanour, their loutish speech and their impossible way of dressing. It was horrible, and was made even more horrible by reason of the fact that she thought that she had come to civilisation. They encouraged her to retain all that was crude, rough and unladylike in her barbarous upbringing. The really delicate and sensitive feelings which lay beneath her awkward boorish manners had no chance to emerge in such surroundings. One could see that she had a good mind and a beautiful nature, that despite all the overlying crudeness and roughness she had delicate instincts; she had even given herself a kind of education. Creek Castle had no teachers but it seems to have had a very good library; she had read enormously. She had taught herself Latin and English; she had indeed read many books which should not have been opened by a young lady. She was very intelligent (although not very clever) and she had a passion for science, not the most suitable thing in the world for a girl in her position, but it was better that she should spend her days in the Boston Library than with the imbecile youths and rowdy maidens who would otherwise have been her companions. And always, it must be said, she was quieter, more thoughtful and more sensitive than they. But it was plain that very severe treatment would almost certainly be necessary if Mary were to be made into a lady; the effect of years of neglect and years of self-indulgence had to be removed. That would be hard, and it would be no more than the beginning: it is never easy to break a lively filly and mine was still unbridled.

Fortunately we liked each other and, although she did not realise it, she sensed that I stood for a kind of life more dignified and more interesting than any she had known. This was so much the case that I was always confident that she could, in the end, be brought to see reason and to offer obedience. But it was a long and difficult task – not that she was actually defiant, but she was terribly hard to handle. If I so much as hinted that her beloved Kate was not a paragon of virtue, beauty and intelligence there would come into her face a miserable expression of wounded dismay which made it impossible to proceed. She would obey an order, and she would even attempt to obey cheerfully, but the attempt was so pathetic that it would have been hard, it would also have been unwise, to insist.

Everything seemed against me. The Pullman family by their mere

presence undermined my authority, Mary was ruled by Kate far more
than she was ruled by me, and Thérèse regarded me with suspicion and
dislike, a dislike which she scarcely bothered to conceal.

I could, of course, have used my power, I could have dismissed
Thérèse (I came very near to doing so), I could have taken Mary to
England, and I could have started severe training at once. It was a
tempting solution. But to have done that would have been to throw
away my one advantage: Mary's increasing affection for me. The work
that I had to do required not only that Mary should submit, but that she
should love me.

I decided that Thérèse must either be brought to heel or dismissed
and that Kate must be separated from Mary. I knew that this could be
done in Europe. Kate was quite willing to make the journey, but the
trouble lay with Mary herself; she seemed frightened of meeting her
English relations. And in this it must be admitted that she was not
unwise, indeed, wiser than she knew, for she would at that time have
made a very bad impression. But she was unwilling also to come with
me to Italy. The fact was that some tremendous scientific bigwig –
Charles Darwin himself, I dare say – was to deliver a series of lectures in
Boston that autumn. It had been agreed before I ever arrived that it
would be fun to travel to Europe, but not until the spring. But by the
spring too much mischief would have been done. I made up my mind
that the plan should be altered; but for the time being I had to wait – I
needed greater power and a good opportunity. My first task was to deal
with Thérèse.

Thérèse Boileau had been at Creek Castle for four years. At the end
she was all alone with her mistress and, because of that, they had
become more like friends and equals than mistress and maid. Thérèse,
I could see, was really a sensible girl and completely devoted to Mary;
she had the makings of an excellent servant, but only the makings. At
that time their familiarity showed far too much in public. Thérèse did
not know her place and neither did Mary. Worse still, Thérèse did not
know her job and, although vaguely aware that her mistress should not

have been allowed to wander around Boston looking like a tart in mourning, she, Thérèse, had no notion how to set matters right. I could have told her, but in those early weeks she would not listen to me. The plain fact of the matter was that Thérèse was not only deeply attached to her employer, but deeply jealous of me and, of course, because my only field of action lay in making Mary love me, this made Thérèse more jealous than ever, so that it became increasingly difficult to disregard her insolence and her incivility.

Matters were set right in a rather roundabout way and as the result of an incident in which I displayed some aplomb and from which nobody else emerges with any credit whatsoever.

The foyer of the Hotel Incredible, or whatever it called itself, was a bustling, overcrowded place full of newspaper stands, candy shops, spittoons, potted palms, etc. Usually I managed to pass through it rapidly but it was there one afternoon that I met, or rather that I was able to observe, Mr Pullman.

There is a certain look, half-smug, half-furtive, which one sees on the faces of gentlemen who have been *en bonne fortune*. I know it, alas I know it only too well; you could positively see it in the back of Mr Pullman's head. I was sure that he had been spending the past hour in charming company — but in whose? My charge, thank heavens, was safe in the library and would not be back for another two hours at least. But Thérèse? Thérèse was upstairs taking a rest or trimming a bonnet or — yes, it could be Thérèse.

It *was* Thérèse. Having been alerted I saw what was going on, and going on with very little discretion. Once I very nearly ran into him as he left her room. He came regularly between one and two.

I hate all meddlers and busybodies. So long as they conducted their little intrigue with tact it seemed entirely their affair. But, of course, it might become very much my business; I kept my weather eye open and waited for squalls. It was lucky for the Pullman family that I did so.

Let me set the scene, for the setting of it was important. It was our wont in those hot summer evenings to dine, if you could call it dining, with the Pullmans, then we would gather on their veranda. I was at one extremity of our semi-circle, so placed that I had a good view of all my companions, illumined as they were by the rays of a municipal street lamp. Next to me was Mr Pullman. Mary, sitting beside him, was in black *mousseline de soie*, the only one of us unable to greet the torrid summer in white; she divided her conversation between the politics of Mr Pullman's newspaper and the plans, which seemed to preoccupy the entire household, for Kate's birthday. This, no doubt, was the grand topic of Miss Pullman herself who sat at the centre of the arc, a little princess in a superabundance of cheap white machine-made lace. Her mother sat next, eagerly joining in the birthday plans, and Thérèse, a little removed from the rest, occupied herself in silence with some darning.

There was a pause in the chatter and then, speaking very clearly through her pretty little nose, Kate addressed her father. 'Say, Pa, what were you and Mary cooking up this afternoon? I happened to be in the hotel and saw you leaving her apartments.'

'But Kate, that's not possible. There was nobody there but Thérèse, Mrs Gordon and I were both out.' This was Mary, speaking with the artless clarity of innocent youth.

It was as though that starry summer sky were suddenly filled with thunderclouds. Mr Pullman reminded me of a man I once saw riding full tilt into wire. Mary and Kate were a little perplexed, just starting to be apprehensive. Mrs Pullman was passing from bewilderment to dread, seeing the coil that was being unwound. Thérèse suddenly became deeply interested in her work. As for me, as I have said, I had been keeping my weather eye open.

'You are wrong, Mary. I turned back to meet Mr Pullman and Thérèse. I shall not tell you why; young ladies who are going to have birthdays should not enquire too closely into the comings and goings of their elders and betters.'

There was some giggling, the girls returned to their usual topic and disaster was averted before most of the potential victims had had time to become aware of it. But when Mr Pullman, who had plunged his head into a newspaper, took a new cigar he lit it with a trembling hand, and it was quite a long time before Thérèse looked up from her work.

She came to see me as soon as she could. She had the wits to perceive that I had it in my power to destroy her. She had given me provocation enough in all conscience, and although I had saved her for the time being I had only to whisper a few words here and there in order to gain the perfect excuse for dismissing her without a character. All this she saw. She saw also that she must capitulate. She went down on her two knees and begged my pardon for everything. I made it clear that, in future, I should expect goodwill and perfect obedience; she promised that she would behave and was, on that firm understanding, forgiven. I questioned her about the affair and she answered that she had enjoyed having Mr Pullman for a lover but was not at all in love with him. Indeed she didn't understand more than half the things he said. As she put it in her rather earthy way, 'We just want to enjoy ourselves, what need have we of phrases?' He was handsome, he was strong, he was appreciative; it was enough; it had made her stay in Boston interesting. She could hardly be called a good girl, but there was something engaging about her frank simplicity. I told her that it must stop; she sighed but agreed.

Mr Pullman was rather more difficult to deal with. He was absurd but he was manageable, and the thing was brought to an end quietly.

The great gain was that Thérèse and I became friends and have indeed remained friends ever since. I was able forthwith to begin to train her as a lady's-maid and found, as I had expected, that she was quick to learn; also, and this was of immediate importance, she no longer had any motive for remaining in Boston. The place began to bore her and she was eager to return to Europe.

After about three weeks she handed me the lever that I needed. Her parents, narrow, acquisitive people who had not used her well, now lived in Paris writing letters every day to complain that her wages, which had hitherto gone directly to them, were now being sent to their daughter. In one letter Mme Boileau declared that Thérèse must return because her father was unwell.

'Unwell? Thérèse, how anxious you must be.'

'Anxious? Oh no, Madame, with them illness is a bad habit.'

'Thérèse, you ought to be anxious, please oblige me by being exceedingly anxious and, without saying very much, just hint at your anxiety in talking to Mademoiselle.'

Thérèse understood and produced a broad grin.

'Mary,' I said at breakfast, 'you are a fortunate girl. You are the only one of us who is happy in Boston.'

She expressed surprise.

'It's true. The rest of us want to go to Europe. Not England – England can wait – but Europe. I know that you have your lectures to think of and of course it's right that your education should come first, whatever the rest of us may feel.'

'But what do you feel? I thought we were all so happy here.'

'We are happy if you are happy, my dear; but it must be confessed that we do have selfish feelings. Still, as I say, you have your lectures to consider.'

'Please tell me about the selfish feelings, Mrs Gordon.'

'Well, there is Kate. She is supposed to be learning French and Renaissance history at the Ladies' College. She's much too intelligent to suppose that they can teach her anything and in truth she pines for Europe, where in fact she might learn a good deal. Also there's Thérèse; I am sure she would not tell you, she would think it wrong to do so, but it seems that her father is very ill.'

'She did say something.'

'I am sure she did not add that she is longing to see him, perhaps for the last time; but that is in fact the situation.'

'And you, Mrs Gordon?'

'I don't matter. But I must admit that there are times when I think how perfect Rome can be in the autumn; and then America is really too strenuous for me. Also I would suggest, merely suggest, that science, unlike art, can travel easily from continent to continent. Surely you can learn as much, or almost as much, in Paris or in Berlin as you can in Boston, whereas for Kate, Europe is really a necessity.'

'Oh, Mrs Gordon, how horribly selfish I have been.'

It was not quite fair to appeal to Mary's better feelings. She hadn't any others.

And so it was settled. In the second week of September we set sail for Cherbourg. I cannot resist, in this place, telling a story about Thérèse. She packed all Mary's worst sartorial indiscretions into one large bag and then contrived, very cleverly, to get it stolen from her at the quayside.

From all of which it will be manifest that Thérèse and I were not only friends, we were allies. We had struck a bargain and it was none the less binding upon us both for the fact that it was signed, sealed and ratified without a single word spoken. Thérèse would help me to make a lady of Mary. She would set herself, under my orders, to become a really good, respectful and efficient lady's-maid, and she would do this on two conditions. First, it was understood that we always had Mary's best interests at heart, even if she had, in some manner, to be coerced – that important condition was never to be forgotten. Secondly, I was not to be too curious; I was to refrain from asking questions.

Something had happened at Creek Castle, something that was not to be discussed. Mary would say nothing. She would not talk and preferred not to think about her life in that place – and indeed she was so piteous in her plea to be allowed to forget her sad girlhood that it would have been inhuman to make her talk.

When once we had become friends, Thérèse was far less discreet; but although she blamed herself for saying too much and was furious with me for 'leading her on', in fact she told me very little. I began, however, to get a picture – and it was not a pretty picture – of a house full of hatreds and persecutions, a prison. Lady Porthow was a horror and the other servants were brutes. But there was something else, a spectre which came and vanished in conversation, a monster. Sometimes I felt sure that this must be Lady Porthow, but at other times I got the impression that Mary herself, acting under I know not what provocation, had been guilty of some crime, that in the strain and misery of that lonely existence she might have done things which a loyal friend would wish to forget. I have heard stories of men sent out on solitary missions in the Himalayas who have experienced a sudden breakdown of the moral personality. Or again, Thérèse herself might have suffered some kind of breakdown and imagined things. I was content to leave it at that, there was a tacit agreement between us that the past should be forgotten.

LADY ALCESTER'S MEMOIRS: CHAPTER IV
IN EUROPE WITH MARY

(The greater part of Lady Alcester's fourth chapter is irrelevant to our enquiry and may be summarised in a few paragraphs.

The four ladies travelled first to Paris, where Mrs Gordon was amazed by the moderation of Mary Porthow's demands as a shopper, and from thence to Rome. Here Mary developed a taste for art and Kate found what was almost a home from home in the company of a group of young men, American, English and Italian, who were very ready to flirt and to make themselves useful. Of these there were two who succeeded in alarming the chaperone. One, known only as Ettore, was so discreet that Mrs Gordon only came to know of his existence at a later date; the other, a Prince of Negroponte, a charming but penniless young man, began by paying his addresses to Kate. When he transferred his attention to Mary, Mrs Gordon intervened and brought the flirtation to an end. The young man then returned to Kate and succeeded in making her fall very much in love with him. Mrs Gordon attempted to use this infidelity in order to make mischief between the two girls – with Mary she failed completely. Mary seemed incapable of jealousy and even went so far as to furnish her triumphant rival with a dowry. This transaction had to be kept a secret from Kate herself. Mrs Gordon was, however, much more successful in making Kate jealous. She waged an adroit campaign of suggestion and innuendo which in the end produced a violent, though one-sided quarrel between the friends. This ended with Kate's marriage and her permanent separation from Mary.

These machinations began in Rome and ended in Florence and it was here, Mary now being isolated and Thérèse entirely won over, that Mrs Gordon obliged her charge to agree to what she called 'a severe course' and Mary herself described as 'Prussian tyranny'. In spite of her pupil's acquiescence and her willingness to work all day and every day at the business of learning to be a lady of fashion, progress was very slow. Chapter IV of Lady Alcester's Memoirs continues.)

. . . all the little graces and deft habits that girls of good family pick up in the nursery had been denied her, she had been reared amongst servants, her stepmother was a servant, and she knew nothing that was not in books. You can't become a lady by reading books. All that was bad. But in some ways worse was her utter lack of ordinary tact, her seeming indifference to good form and good manners. She was too nice a person to be consciously rude to anyone, but her social vagueness could be disastrous.

Her one social asset, apart from her face, and of course her money, was her voice; she had a very sweet and beautiful contralto but oh, the use that she made of it! I shall never forget listening to her clear, well-educated accents, distinct and lovely as a bell, in the Marchesa Rasponi's drawing room during a pause in the conversation.

'But Mrs Benson, consider the anatomical evidence; the genitals of the primates are almost indistinguishable from yours or mine.'

This to the wife of an archbishop. But worst of all was Mary's behaviour when she realised that she had made a gaffe. She was seized with a fit of the giggles which she found it very hard to contain. At that moment I could willingly have struck her.

(The educational process continued through November and December 1889 and well into 1890. The unhappy party – they were all made miserable by the course – went from Florence to Venice and from Venice to Vienna. It was in Vienna, when Mrs Gordon had begun to despair, that Mary suddenly began to make progress and thereafter improved with such assurance and such rapidity that in June they proceeded to Paris. The Faubourg, in Mrs Gordon's estimation, provided the acid test of deportment. Here again it seems that Mary was a great success. But, as Lady Alcester's Memoirs show, there was a severe reaction.)

. . . when she ought to have been rejoicing in her victory she became listless and miserable. It was clear to me, although she would not admit it and would not see a doctor, that she was unwell. Fortunately, a doctor was provided in the person of her cousin William Brandon, Jr, who had come to Paris on family business. Mary did not seem anxious to meet him and, in fact, the morning before he arrived she looked so pale and woebegone that I had to order her to tell me what was wrong.

She reminded me that Mr William's brother Henry had been drowned before her eyes at Creek. It had come back to her quite by chance that Mr Brandon believed that she, Mary, had not behaved well. Given a little more time, she was sure that she could exonerate herself, that she could put matters right, but it would be an immense comfort if she might meet her cousin tête-a-tête when he arrived.

This seemed to me reasonable and after all he was a cousin, so I gave my permission. She then told me what had happened on that fatal day at Creek.*

When, late in the afternoon, Mr William Brandon was announced, I was surprised – he had so completely escaped the Brandon good looks. And although he was, and really looked like a gentleman, he looked

---

* This account agrees so nearly with that in Mary Porthow's letter of June 7th, 1889 that it may be omitted. – M.E.

like a gentleman whose strange ambition it was to pass himself off as a seedy commercial traveller. He said practically nothing to me and was at once taken to Mary's suite by Thérèse. If I had been Thérèse I should have found it hard to stay away from the keyhole. As it was, we both waited in my room. It was very like waiting outside an operating theatre.

When they rejoined us, I could see at a glance that she had persuaded him of her innocence; she came in on his arm, walking on air. When I had last seen her, half an hour earlier, she had been ill and tired. Now she was at some pains to restrain the exuberance of her high spirits. She had done much more than prove her innocence: she had made a friend, and it was as though they had known and loved each other for years. For the rest of his visit they were inseparable. At meals he was, in a clumsy way, gallant; she received his advances with explosions of friendly laughter and he laughed back, almost as happy as she. Her eyes, when she looked at him, danced with affectionate amusement; he grinned back, twinkling through his spectacles with the kindliest good humour.

It seemed that she had made a sudden conquest, that they had fallen into each other's arms. And yet I could not quite believe that that was the case. There was much of the friend but nothing of the lover in his manner, or in hers, and I could not really believe that this stammering, uncouth, bespectacled cousin was an object of romantic interest. She saw him leave with calm goodwill. He wrote her letters on scientific subjects and in one he announced his engagement to a Miss Small; she received this news with sympathetic amusement.

I asked her what had passed between them when they met and she replied that she had been stupid and that he was not the kind of person who could believe evil of anyone without very strong evidence.

That was true enough. We set off for a holiday at Etretat in good spirits and good health.

LADY ALCESTER'S MEMOIRS: CHAPTER V
INDIA LODGE

We reclined inert in white muslin upon the beach at Etretat. Mary took a holiday (her way of taking it was to read some horribly boring scientific books), complete rest having been prescribed by Dr William Brandon. But it was also he who induced us to break our regime.

Billy had settled near Ramsgate where he had a practice and he had some charitable scheme in which Mary was interested; he invited us to stay. At the same time, Mellish needed Mary's presence. As they were just across the Channel, it seemed proper to pay a flying visit. By then Mary had ceased to be afraid of meeting her English relations – she was quite right, she was now entirely presentable.

We saw Ramsgate House (Mary did not think much of it) and we saw India Lodge. We spent an afternoon there and Mary fell hopelessly in love with it. It seemed to me an outlandish place. Mellish told us that the Brandons had decided that it was not worth the upkeep and should be demolished. Mary at once offered to rent it and got it for a peppercorn. It was all settled very quickly. This must have been at the beginning of August, by the middle of September it was ready to receive us. Mary wanted to live near William and his charitable schemes, which meant that we became close neighbours of the Brandons. At that time we did not know the Brandons; if we had I think I might have persuaded Mary to settle in London.

Lady Brandon was the best of them, a neat composed woman with a sort of style. She and her son called, then they dined; while Sir Charles was talking about art to Mary we chattered and grew intimate.

'Mrs Gordon, how fortunate we are; fortunate in our cousin, I mean. It's not just that she's pretty and intelligent and modest, though she is all that, but she is – well, how shall I put it? We came half-expecting to eat off gold plate.'

'Certainly she's not ostentatious.'

'Nor parsimonious. We've eaten well, the wine was good, her dress is from Paris, but no one would suppose she's a millionairess. Now, Mrs Gordon, I do like that.' She sighed. 'It's so different from some people.'

I liked her for saying that. A less intelligent woman might have been disappointed or even have complained of pitiful doings. She knew better. For years she had had to scrape and save and charm away duns and deal with angry tradesmen. Now she had a good income, thanks to old Sir Amos, and also the Ramsgate Estate, thanks to his daughter. But already it was obvious that she was desperately worried about her son who had shown that he could be reckless about money – and other things.

She had her schemes for Mary. No mother of an unmarried son finding a great heiress at her gate could fail to have schemes. Mary's prudence – for indeed it was she who urged moderation in money matters – was an additional recommendation. She seemed a most eligible daughter-in-law, and Lady Brandon clearly hoped to enlist me in the campaign that was to give young Sir Charles a suitable wife.

I was sorry that I could not oblige her. One had to remember that Charlie was only a boy, a boy playing at being a man. It was possible, as his mother insisted, that a good wife would be the making of him, but I did not think that this was the task for Mary. Mary needed an older man, a man with intelligence and authority whom she could recognise as a superior. Charles Brandon was not such a man.

He told me that he was 'a man of the Renaissance', which meant that he could turn his hand to anything from poetry to pugilism and was quite above 'ordinary morality'. In practice this meant that he missed birds, shirked fences, frequented the Café Royal, read French poetry of the more disgusting kind, smoked scented cigarettes and loafed about with a gardenia in his button-hole. Also he had a number of third-hand stories about 'Jimmy' and 'Algernon' and 'Oscar', characters whom he knew by sight but who, I fancy, hardly knew him. He kept two spaniels, one was a golden cocker called Fifi, the other was called Saxton Filbert-White, Esq. He kicked them both without mercy, and Saxton Filbert-White seemed positively to enjoy it. He was an odious little man – we suffered from him throughout the whole of a long week-end. It was, thank heaven, his first and last appearance, for his parents had had the sense to send him off to Natal. He and Charles had been rusticated after some unusually outrageous piece of silliness at Oxford.

No, I didn't like them in the least and was very sorry when Mary said that she found Charles 'amusing', which he was not, and very handsome, which admittedly he was, for he had inherited all the Brandon good looks, together with a stature which most of them lacked.

As for the rest of the Brandons, Mr William was in a 'home' for the incurably insane and Billy was our neighbour. That Mary should like Billy was to be expected, they shared an interest in science. But Mary went further; she positively liked Mrs Billy, a mousey little thing without wits, or manners, or looks. We, of course, saw a good deal of them, and it was I who had to do the polite with Mrs B. while Billy and Mary discussed the frequency of mumps amongst board-school boys, this being the kind of topic which they found enthralling and just the sort of thing to make a dinner party go with a swing. Oh, those long, long evenings with the Billy Brandons.

Picture us then, about three weeks after our arrival, breakfasting at India Lodge. A cheerful room, despite its grotesque oriental fittings, a blazing fire. Continental breakfast – coffee, toast and *The Times* for Mary, tea, toast and the *Morning Post* for me. Letters on the table; one from Italy, a little Negroponte now expected; a lot of begging letters – I had at last taught Mary to throw them away. We chatter, we discuss the family at the Great House.

'I have seen all the Brandons,' says Mary, 'and that is more than you have done.'

I stared. 'You don't mean to say.'

'Yes, I saw Uncle Hector yesterday. I ran into him in the National Gallery. He recognised me at once. We had a cup of tea and a chat.'

'Oh, Mary, you're not going to say you liked him too?'

'Very much, he was delightful.'

'But Mary, surely I have told you: we don't see Uncle Hector.'

'It was he who saw me. Was I to cut my own uncle?'

'Well, yes.'

'But why? What has he done?'

'He's not respectable.'

'So I am told, but I am told nothing else. Am I to be rude to my own blood relation?'

'Mary, are you turning into one of those tiresome young women who go about being impossible in Scandinavian plays?'

'I don't know,' she answered stoutly. 'But if they are people who refuse to be unkind unless they are given a good reason for it, then I think I may be.'

I saw that I had adopted the wrong approach. Moreover, I was hampered by the fact that I myself had been told nothing save that the family refused to know Uncle Hector.

'Mary,' I said, 'I think that you can keep out of his way without being unkind and that he would realise why you have to do so and not be offended. When you come of age you can make enquiries and decide what to do. At present I am still your governess, in name at all events, and I am responsible for your conduct and have to answer for it. When you go up to the Great House and say, "Uncle Hector is coming to stay," Mr Mellish will change his opinion of you and also of me – and I shall be looking for another employment.'

Mary was at once repentant, kissed me and begged to be forgiven; no, Uncle Hector certainly shouldn't come to India Lodge, and, she added, 'If I should run into him again I shall certainly forget to tell you.'

With that I had to be content. It will be seen that the days of my Prussian tyranny were over.

To tell the truth, I was not greatly worried about Uncle Hector. He and she would have the sense to be discreet. What did worry me, increasingly, was young Sir Charles. I became more and more convinced that he was utterly detestable; but he was immensely handsome, and handsome in a way that young girls find particularly attractive.

'Michelangelo's David, just as handsome and almost as large,' was Mary's opinion. And she added, 'I've always felt that it would be rather nice to be kissed by that particular piece of sculpture.'

'But you wouldn't want to marry him?'

'He wouldn't want to marry me. But no, honestly no, he frightens me.'

Which to my mind was much too equivocal. Not that I then thought her at all in love; but at first she had laughed at him, then she had found him amusing; if now she was frightened, she was taking him much too seriously. These things are hard to manage: one cannot be too frank about someone who may become one's dearest friend's husband.

It would be easy to hint that I had some premonition, that I somehow knew that that marriage would end in horror – easy, but untruthful. I simply felt that he was not good enough for Mary, I could not anticipate the final tragedy. Of the mysterious proceedings which led up to it I did, however, get the merest hint. It happened thus.

It was just after that tiresome week-end when Sir Charles and Mr Filbert-White were in and out of the Lodge continually, seeking refuge, I suppose, from Lady Brandon's icy disapproval. Sir Charles had treated the wretched young man with arrogant brutality and I felt that it was legitimate to point this out to Mary.

'Yes, I was sorry for the Flibert,' replied Mary, 'but chiefly because he was being sent off to Pongo Land where no doubt he will be very miserable amongst all those strenuous empire-builders. But I don't think he was so very miserable while he was staying here.'

'Not even when Charlie made him walk back in the rain to the Great House?'

'Not even then. Flibert was made to be miserable. He knows it, Charles knows it; it's an understood thing between them, and because it's understood it is to some extent forgivable.'

'Mary, you're trying to be subtle.'

'Perhaps I am. But I think that what I say is true. You know the world much better than I but wouldn't you say that it contains a certain number of – what shall we call them – natural slaves? People who are not really happy without their chains? Also a certain number of natural slave-drivers?'

'Possibly.'

'Well, that's the way I see it and I think that Flibert is a natural slave and that Charles sees himself as a natural slave-driver. In that I believe him to be mistaken. He is still very juvenile and has not made a success of anything – how could he so soon? But he believes that he should have. Flibert and other toadies play up to him and make him feel very imperial. But because he is at bottom a perfectly nice character, he can only crack the whip on the backs of people like Flibert who rather enjoy it.'

'You may be right Mary, but to me it all seems rather nasty and unhealthy.'

'That is because, like me, you find Flibert a rather disgusting creature; he is a man, and our convention is that a man should be manly. Flibert is not, so we shun him; but it may be his misfortune rather than his fault. Nature makes us what we are.'

'And where, Mary, in this grand classification, do you place yourself?'

'Oh what a base and peasant slave am I.'

'Mary, you don't really mean that!'

'No, not altogether. Still, if you come to think of it, when you were the Queen of Prussia I succeeded in making myself quite a convincing Prussian soldier.'

I was to remember that conversation.

I think that it was about the middle of November that I began to become really worried. Sir Charles was laying himself out to charm and it had to be admitted that he could be charming. I tried to get Mary to London, but she had become very involved in her charities. I tried to find other young men in the neighbourhood but the field was not strong. And then a serious rival did appear. Another friend of Charlie's,

Richard Buxton Russell, was staying at the Great House. I knew him well from the days before I had met Mary and asked him to dinner.

At first everything went according to plan. Mary set him down as one of my ignorant stupid soldier friends; she decided to shock him and demolish him. Much to her astonishment, she was worsted in argument and had to capitulate. He, being a gentleman, was magnanimous. She, being a dear creature and honest as the day, was grateful to him for treating her as a serious opponent. They became sparring partners, both being argumentative and very well read; they enjoyed their bouts, became friends and soon something more than friends. He sent for his horses and prolonged his stay, and Sir Charles was furious.

And then, when everything was going swimmingly and I gave them a good opportunity to settle the business, something went wrong. For reasons which I never quite discovered she refused him. I hoped that it was not a final refusal, and certainly they remained on very good terms.

At Christmas there was a family gathering at Ramsgate. It would have been a dull affair if during the course of the evening Charlie had not managed to get Mary alone. I think that she was then able to find out what it was like to be kissed by Michelangelo's David. But perhaps he was too monumental; at all events, Charlie sulked for the rest of the evening.

But altogether, it was a gloomy Christmas. I was depressed and so was Mary. A day or two after the family gathering I found Thérèse in tears – one of the servants in the Great House had been faithless, a commonplace tragedy, to be sure, and her grief was very understandable. What I found less understandable was Mary's reaction. She loved Thérèse and, of course, it was natural that she should be sorry for her, but I had not seen her so cast down since that time in Paris.

And then a few days later when we were talking about the furniture at India Lodge she remarked, in the most matter of fact tone, 'Of course, none of these arrangements will much matter when I go to the Great House.' And then, blushing furiously and correcting herself awkwardly, 'Always supposing I were to do anything so reckless.'

I could see that I must in some way rally my troops. I had to urge Richard to return to the fray. He had, I am sure, been too easily repulsed; he was too modest, too diffident. And then Mary was so obliging: he had only to ask her in such a way that it would seem very unkind in her to refuse, for him to be accepted. And unless he did something I felt sure that there would be no stopping Charlie. Two days after Christmas I had for some reason to be in London. I arranged to have tea with Richard.

It was a momentous conversation but I can't remember all of it and there were parts which I do remember, but will not record. I told Richard that I believed that Sir Charles had proposed and had been rejected, but I thought that if he proposed again Mary would accept him and that would, from every point of view, be a disaster.

'Yes, I suppose it might be,' agreed Richard. 'Charles takes a long time to grow up. He is still at a stage where dreams are confused with reality. When he is thirty he may do something remarkable. He has some really valuable qualities . . .'

'For heaven's sake, stop being so beastly fair-minded. He may be what he likes at thirty; being what he is now we must not let him marry Mary.'

'If they both want to marry we might find that a rather difficult operation.'

'I don't think she really does want to marry him and I believe that if a proper man were to speak to her urgently she would change her mind.'

Richard smiled, shook his head, and began to examine a macaroon with unnecessary attention.

'Look Richard, is there any chance that you will marry her?'

'Simply in order to disoblige Charles?'

'She's a sweet girl, a rich girl, a clever girl, just the wife for you.'

Richard continued to inspect the macaroon. Then he looked up and said, very gently, 'There are girls who demand that their husbands shall be able to offer them love, indeed they go further – they want to be able to offer that strange commodity themselves.'

'And you say that Mary neither loves nor is loved by you?'

Richard put down the macaroon very gingerly – one would have thought that it contained high explosive. 'I am sure of it. As you probably know, we had an interview and discussed the matter quite thoroughly.'

' "Probably know" indeed! I took such pains to arrange it.'

'That was considerate, but then you always are considerate. It is one of your numerous perfections. Also, you are abominably persuasive. You persuaded me that it was, in effect, my duty to marry her and of course she does look and really is rather nice and has lots of money and so on. One evening when she was looking really charming I did propose, and was most civilly rejected. In rejecting me she managed to point out that in fact I was not in the least in love with her, a fact which I had not fully realised until that moment. There seemed to be everything in favour of our union except for that. We are such very good friends, and nothing else, nothing else at all.'

'This is indeed frank.'

'It is my purpose to be frank, shall I go on being so?'

At this point I feel that I ought to go back to the beginning and rewrite everything with me in the middle. Mary has been the centre; I was her minister, her mistress, her confidante. I was not yet thirty; old in experience but not in years; not an old maid, or any other kind of maid; and I had my feelings, my hopes. Therefore, when Richard spoke as he did some remarkable things began to happen. There was a distant sound of trumpets, the potted palms in the tearoom burgeoned with flowers, and I felt slightly faint.

If this were a novel I should lead up to this point with great care. It was like that wonderful passage in *Persuasion* when Captain Wentworth gives Anne a letter and everything is changed to happiness. Oh Lord though, like Anne Elliot I had suffered. This business of being the governess of a girl hardly younger than myself. It had its pleasures and I did, I do love Mary, but it was becoming terribly hard to bear.

I had, I swear, been quite honestly intent on seeing Mary properly married. As God is my witness, I fought tooth and nail to see her married to Richard. I was like Shakespeare's woman, 'like Patience on a monument smiling at pain'. The only person who could deter me from doing what I felt that I had to do was Richard himself, and now he was releasing me from my torture.

I put down my cup, lifted my veil and said, 'Yes, if you wish it, let us be frank.'

Having said which we found, of course, that there was nothing to be said. He took my hand and I had to remind him that we were in a public place.

There was a moment of embarrassment when I explained to Mary that I had to resign my post, but that did not last long. Mary was one of those people who can, in a completely disinterested way, rejoice in the good fortune of others. She was far too happy in my happiness to have any thoughts for herself. Of course, I had in no way taken him from her; there was nothing to resent. But I know some people who would have been resentful. Not Mary. If there is a heaven hereafter Mary will be there, considerably confused and confounded, naughty unbeliever that she is, to find herself so oddly situated.

So at the time it was all joy and loving kindness. Later on, when we were parted and her marriage had ended so horribly it was impossible not to feel a kind of guilt – my own immense happiness was founded upon her misery – but, in truth, that was morbid and absurd.

Then came the New Year party. There was some family tradition about celebrating the New Year, or Martha Brandon had invented one. At any rate, this was to be a very special occasion with guests from all over the county and musicians from London. And there was Mary, quite lovely in white, and Richard with whom I danced more often than was proper – but it was all right for the engagement was to be announced in two days' time.

The band stopped, Sir Charles mounted the conductor's podium and tapped on a glass.

'Gentlemen, I have to tell you that if the name of Miss Porthow is on your programmes you must cross it out. She is dancing with me for the rest of the evening and has consented to be my wife.'

It was just like Sir Charles to announce his engagement by being uncivil to everyone else. Still, there was applause and Billy got up on the podium and made a wholly unnecessary speech. I am not sure that he did not refer to the marriage as this 'interesting experiment'. There was a little knot of well-wishers around the happy pair, Lady Brandon was in heaven and I heard Mary's clear voice saying, 'Oh yes, I am a most fortunate girl but I deserve no credit; Charles simply carried me off and ordered me to marry him.' And I saw the happy smirk on Charlie's face and longed to take it off with the back of my hand. But that was to be her account of the matter and she stuck to it.

After my formal and public congratulations in the ballroom it was not so easy, in the carriage going home, to renew the usual happy, intimate exchange which was one of the pleasures of going to a party with Mary. It was she who, with a kind of sweet boldness said, 'Cecily, I know you can't approve now of what I have done. One day I believe that you will. Charles is a better and greater man than you suppose. Even if he were not, I find it impossible to resist him.'

There was very little that I could say in answer to that and she hardly gave me a chance to do so for she turned the conversation on to Richard's merits and my happiness. But I found it hard to see Mary capitulate to so poor a fellow and I could not see in him the young god who had carried her away in his chariot.

Both the young men, as accepted lovers, were constantly at the Lodge. When both were present it was easy – we split up, pleasantly enough, into two pairs and wandered into different rooms or upon different paths. But when I was alone with her and her beau it was impossible not to watch, to listen, and to wonder.

Mary had indeed surrendered completely to her lover. Until they were engaged she had been quite ready to argue with him, to tease him and, where her pride or principles were involved, to resist him. Now she deferred to him, accepted his orders, acknowledged his superiority in everything. I have never had any sympathy, as Mary was to have later, with all this women's rights business: no woman should need an Act of Parliament to help her to get her own way. But Mary in the first weeks of 1891 seemed perfectly content to be a doormat – really there is no other word for it. She was abject. And this made Charles even more intolerable than he usually was: never before in his life had he met anyone, not even Filbert-White, who accepted him so completely at his own valuation. His arrogance, his conceit, his self-satisfaction drove me mad with irritation. I was exasperated by her submission to his tyranny. 'Oh what a base and peasant slave' indeed!

Richard, who did not altogether agree with me, made nevertheless an acute observation. 'She has found the way to make her lover happy and after all that's not a bad thing to do and she is by nature a most obliging person who will always seek the happiness of others. None the less,' he added, 'she has to make an effort to do it, and because it does involve an effort I don't think it can last for ever.'

Like so many of Richard's sayings this was profoundly true. But although it may sound like perversity in me, I must admit that my irritation at seeing Mary so enslaved was increased by my doubt as to whether her servitude were not really a sham. There are girls, even intelligent, rebellious-minded girls like Mary, who do suddenly accept their lovers as absolute rulers and are happy to be subjects. It is not, I think, a very happy situation, but it is understandable. They surrender because they do honestly feel that their lovers are perfect and they rejoice in that perfection. But with Mary, watching her closely and knowing her as well as I did, I felt that although this did form a part of her feelings, and of course Sir Charles was a splendid brute of a man, still there was a tiny element of play-acting. At times, when he made some monstrous demand and she yielded, as she always did, she seemed almost to be saying, 'See how well I do this' – and that, in my view, was more disquieting than anything. That she should behave as she did because she loved him passionately was bad enough, but if she were not, after all, so deeply in love with him as her subjection seemed to indicate then it was even worse.

This feeling was very much in my mind when we went off to Paris together to buy her trousseau. Sir Charles had another engagement, some tremendous stag-party at Penny Villa just outside Brighton, so we went off without him, taking Thérèse of course. And that visit worried me almost more than anything. Mary was in such tearing spirits, so manifestly glad – yes, I must write it – to be no longer playing a part.

In retrospect I feel sure that, although she saw far more in Sir Charles than I could, and did really find him very attractive, it was impossible to imagine so great a change in anyone as that in which she tried to make us believe. The rest of the world, including, of course, Lady Brandon and Sir Charles himself, took it all at face value. Richard and I, seeing more of her and knowing her better, did not. He made her do things which were unbelievable in her. If he had asked it she would have stolen from the poor-box; she actually did stop visiting the hospital – that does not sound like a big demand, but if you had known Mary you would have known that it was an utterly monstrous thing to ask of her. Her timidity was understandable, he was a man who could be moved to sudden frightening anger when checked, but even so, the completeness of her docility was barely credible.

That Paris holiday was our last really good time together. She bought recklessly both for me and for herself. My wedding present was sensational.

We came back to the same outwardly pleasant, inwardly anxious life at India Lodge. Soon enough Richard and I were married. His leave was up and my last sight of Mary Porthow, like my first, was looking across the water from the deck of a ship.

CHAPTER 3

[Maurice Evans's Investigation
continued]

Sir Charles Brandon married Mary Porthow in Ramsgate Church on April 7th, 1891. After the wedding, which was celebrated with some pomp, the young couple drove to Penny Villa on the outskirts of Brighton, having been preceded by Thérèse Boileau and George Arthur Selmersham, valet to Sir Charles, who were to accompany their employers, on the evening of the 8th, to Newhaven and thence to Paris and Madrid.

Penny Villa, Sir Charles's bachelor establishment, was used for parties composed mainly of people interested in racing and unlikely to be welcome at Ramsgate House. The villa was three storeys high: on the ground floor it contained a room which had once been a private theatre and which connected with Sir Charles's bedroom and with a lavatory [see plan on page x]; there was also a hall, domestic offices and Sir Charles's study; above were guest rooms, and above these the servants' bedrooms. The house was screened from the highway by a garden and rhododendrons.

The sequel, as it first became known to me, may be told by the *Sussex Mercury*; this account has been corrected at some points by reference to the report in *The Times* of April 13th, 1891.

THE PENNY VILLA TRAGEDY

This morning, at the Coroner's Court in Brighton, an inquest was held on the bodies of Sir Charles Brandon, aged twenty, fourth baronet Brandon of Ramsgate House, Sussex, and of George Arthur Selmersham, aged forty-six, domestic servant of the late baronet. Mr Roderick Smith presided. The Brandon family was represented by the firm of Mellish & Barker. The courtroom was filled by a quiet and attentive crowd.

P C Whitlock of the Brighton Constabulary gave evidence.

At 11.15 on the morning of April 8th he was summoned from his beat by a tapster of the Favourite Inn who reported a fatal accident at Penny Villa, a property belonging to the late Sir Charles. Hastening thither he found Lady Brandon, widow of the deceased, together with her maid, Miss Thérèse Boileau.

'They were in a proper state and no wonder,' observed the witness.

In the dining room on the ground floor the witness was shown the body of Mr Selmersham, in the adjoining bedroom, lying on the bed, was the body of Sir Charles. Both had received gunshot wounds and it was evident that both gentlemen were dead. The body of Mr Selmersham had been turned on its back; both bodies were covered with sheets taken from an upstairs bedroom.

A two-barrelled duelling pistol lay on the floor beside the bed. The remains of a breakfast and a bottle of brandy were also on the floor. They had not been placed there; they had been upset onto the floor. Both barrels of the duelling pistol were empty, they were fouled, and it was evident that they had recently been discharged. The witness discovered one bullet; it was lodged in the pillow on which Sir Charles's head had been resting. It was clear, from the angle at which the missile had entered the pillow, that the weapon had been discharged at almost point-blank range. The triggers of the weapon were very light.

The Coroner: By that do you mean that it was easy to fire?

Witness: Yes, sir. A very slight pressure was sufficient to discharge the weapon.

The Coroner: So that, with a weapon of this kind, an accident can easily occur?

Witness: Yes, sir. (continuing)

There were traces of blood leading from the bedroom to the place where Mr Selmersham had fallen. It was clear, in his opinion, that the deceased had been attempting to get away when he fell. Sir Charles was not dressed; Mr Selmersham was fully clothed for the domestic work of the day. The windows were closed and fastened, there was no sign of any intruder. The witness had made a thorough examination of the garden.

Dr Eric Lumly, the police surgeon, then gave evidence. He had arrived at 12.15 p.m., having been preceded by Dr Firminster of No. 33 Black Rock Terrace. Together they had examined the bodies *in situ* and had later conducted an autopsy. They were unanimous in their conclusions. In the case of Sir Charles, death had been caused by a bullet fired at very close range; there were powder burns on the neck and chin. The bullet had entered through the jaw penetrating the base of the skull and passing out through the cranium. Death would have been instantaneous. In the case of Mr Selmersham the same type of bullet was fired from a rather greater distance; it had lodged in the pelvis, having grazed, but not severed, the femoral artery. The wound would certainly have been fatal but not immediately so, the deceased might have survived for several minutes. He might even have been unaware of his wound.

The Coroner: Can you, from the nature of the wounds, form any hypothesis as to the manner in which they were inflicted?

Witness: It is obvious, sir, that the first shot must have been fired by Sir Charles. It is impossible, from the evidence, to form any theory as to why it was fired.

The Coroner: But would the evidence forbid us to suppose that the first shot might have been fired by accident?

Witness: Oh no, sir, it might have been fired for any reason.

The Coroner: Thank you, Dr Lumly. And the second shot?

Witness: The second shot must have been fired with the barrel of the pistol lying against, or almost against, the deceased's chest. Its direction was parallel to that of the body and if the head had not been supported by a pillow, a bullet might merely have grazed the nose or chin of the deceased, or even have passed harmlessly above his head.

The Coroner: If you were deliberately trying to kill someone is it likely that you would fire at him from such an angle as this?

Witness: Well sir, it would have been a foolish way to set about it. It would have been very easy to miss.

The Coroner: Is the evidence consistent with the hypothesis that the second shot was fired by accident while the deceased persons were struggling for possession of the weapon?

Witness: On the evidence that we have, this is perfectly possible.

Lady Brandon, the widow of the deceased, was then called. She was assisted by her maid, was in deep mourning and heavily veiled. She lifted the veil to give evidence. She was greeted with a murmur of sympathy. The coroner gave permission for her maid to remain in attendance while she gave evidence.

The Coroner: It grieves me very much, Lady Brandon, to subject you to such an ordeal at such a time; but it is my duty to ask you certain questions.

Witness: Of course, sir.

The Coroner: Can you describe the events of the morning of April 8th as you witnessed them?

Witness: I will try, sir. I rose at about eight o'clock, and left my husband sleeping. I had a few words with my maid. She then summoned the servants normally resident at Penny Villa. I interviewed these servants and paid them their wages, which were some weeks in arrears. Several, it seemed, were anxious to settle debts in the town; I therefore gave them all leave of absence until 4.30 that afternoon. Mr Selmersham was not at that meeting, but I saw him later when I was making a tour of inspection with Thérèse. In the course of this I came across him preparing my husband's breakfast. He told me that it was ordered for 10.30; it was 10.25 by the kitchen clock; I therefore bade him continue his preparations and went upstairs to inspect the servants' bedrooms on the top floor, the other servants had already left the house.

We were there, at the top of the house, when we heard the first shot. I said something about it being an odd time of year for shooting. Then came the second shot and I realized that the shooting was in the house. I hurried downstairs.

In the dining room which adjoins our bedroom there is a step. Mr Selmersham had fallen from it. He was lying on his face. I could see no sign of a wound so I turned him over on his back. There was a lot of blood and I could see that he was dead. Then I ran into the bedroom and saw – I saw enough. I think I fainted. I spent some time in a chair unable to call Thérèse, actually she was already on her way. I heard her scream when she came across the body of Mr Selmersham.

It was some time before I could think of what ought to be done. Thérèse made me drink a glass full of brandy. I sent her to the Favourite to summon the police and a doctor. While she was away I took two sheets from an upstairs bedroom and covered the bodies. Then I waited. I think you know the rest.

The Coroner: Lady Brandon, thank you for giving your evidence so clearly. I have only two more questions to ask. Were your late husband and his valet on good terms?

Witness: I never knew them exchange an unkind word. My husband had a very high opinion of Mr Selmersham, so far as I know Mr Selmersham was devoted to his master. I think that all his servants and friends . . . Please may I sit down?

The Coroner: Of course, Lady Brandon. Sit down and take your time.

Witness: Thank you, sir. I was only going to say that, so far as I know, all his servants were devoted to my husband and that he had no enemies.

The Coroner: Lady Brandon, are you aware that Sir Charles kept a loaded weapon by his bedside?

Witness: I ought to have been aware of it, for indeed he did tell me that he did so, but until after the tragedy I forgot. I then remembered that he had told me and that I had protested.

The Coroner: Lady Brandon, why did you protest?

Witness: I thought he was too fond of frightening people, he did so in order to tease them. He once persuaded some visitors from London that a perfectly harmless cow was in fact a dangerous bull (laughter). On another occasion he pretended to put a lighted match to my curtains.

The Coroner: Lady Brandon, do you think that he might, in a playful fashion and without meaning any mischief, have brandished a loaded pistol?

Witness: Yes sir, I can well imagine it.

The Coroner: Thank you Lady Brandon, that will be all.

Thérèse Boileau was then called and an interpreter sworn in. The *Sussex Mercury* did not report her evidence, which indeed added little to that of her mistress. But *The Times* did report one exchange which may be worth recording.

The Coroner: Was Mr Selmersham on good terms with his master?

Witness: I am sure they were on excellent terms. Sir Charles had every confidence in Mr Selmersham. In my opinion it was misplaced.

The Coroner: Should I be right in supposing that Mr Selmersham was not popular with all the other servants?

Witness: Yes, sir.

No further witnesses were called. The coroner addressed the jury. His remarks are greatly condensed.

It was a lamentable affair and everyone must have the greatest sympathy for a bride so tragically bereaved. Clearly Sir Charles had fired the first shot. Witnesses agreed that he had no quarrel with Mr

Selmersham; it might be added that he had every reason, at the time of his death, to be pleased with everyone and everything. He was a very happy man; it was even possible that the pistol had been fired in sheer high spirits. After that fatal first shot it would have been natural for Mr Selmersham to have sought to gain possession of the weapon. Witnesses have shown that the second shot was almost certainly accidental; it would have been the natural consequence of the struggle for a weapon which, as they have heard, it was fatally easy to discharge by accident. There was no evidence of any kind to suggest foul play. It was for the jury to decide whether to bring in an open verdict or one of death by misadventure.

After a few minutes, and without leaving the room, the jury gave a verdict of misadventure on both victims. The coroner expressed his agreement, offered his condolences to Lady Brandon and warned the public against playing with loaded weapons.

Even at first reading the proceedings of this court fail to inspire confidence. The suggestion that Sir Charles shot his valet out of pure *joie de vivre* is implausible. The fact that there was a struggle for possession of the pistol makes one suppose that Selmersham feared that it would be fired again. The reader may feel that the coroner was looking for a desirable verdict rather than for the whole truth and may wonder, as I did, why none of the servants was called. It is true that they were away at the crucial moment, but they might well have known why Sir Charles used his weapon. Surely they should have been heard. Mr Robert Mellish, the father of my guardian, knew why they were not.

The story, it seems, runs thus. Mr Mellish had been summoned to Penny Villa on the morning of the 8th and, in fact, arrived only a few minutes after the police. As soon as he could he sent the two ladies back to Ramsgate. He himself did not return until he had seen the doctors, the servants and the chief constable. On the following day he 'happened' to be lunching with the coroner. They were old friends and it was natural that, like everyone else in Brighton, they should discuss the Penny Villa tragedy. At this meeting Mr Mellish told the coroner that he was very worried by what he had discovered and was afraid that things might come to light at the inquest which would have a shattering effect upon the Brandon family. The servants had hinted darkly that there had been 'funny goings-on' at the wedding feast and that the bridegroom had been dead drunk; they thought it likely that he was still half-drunk the following morning. He had also heard, but did not tell the coroner, that one of the servants had said that Mr Selmersham had insulted the bride in a very gross manner. They were all frightened and reluctant to say very much, but – and this he did say to the coroner – they might easily blunder into a scandalous indiscretion.

What Mr Mellish learnt from the police was in some ways even more disturbing. They had little doubt that they were dealing with an accident, but pointed to the bottle of brandy beside Sir Charles's bed. They knew a good deal about the valet, Selmersham, and about two of the other servants. Selmersham was a blackmailer who fleeced homosexuals; he had 'done time' and had been saved from doing it again by turning Queen's Evidence. The cook had worked in a brothel, the boy in buttons was a male prostitute.

They had no real evidence concerning the events of the 8th but they were capable of saying anything and probably had old scores to settle which could make them indiscreet. The police did not want their evidence.

All this was put by Mr Mellish to the coroner. No good end would be served by calling these servants and no one would profit by their evidence save the gutter press – they would have a rich feast and the Brandons would be destroyed.

It has to be remembered that there was a great wave of sympathy for the unhappy bride, so swiftly and so cruelly widowed. She was a lady of title which, in Sussex in the year 1891, counted for a good deal. She had been generous in her dealings with the Brandons, she was young, beautiful and unhappy. No official who wanted to be popular – and Mr Roderick Smith wanted very much to be popular – would inflict further miseries upon this poor lady and her powerful relations unless it was his plain duty to do so. Mr Smith did not think that it was his plain duty. The witnesses were not called.

Mr Mellish felt that his action had been justified: even supposing the worst, supposing that Sir Charles had murdered his valet, the crime had at once been expiated. This, at least, is what I supposed for the story came to me from James Mellish who had had it from my guardian, but in a tactful disguise, no names being mentioned. Indeed it was not until I had it from him that I realised that the story must surely relate to the tragedy at Penny Villa.

CHAPTER 4

[Maurice Evans's Investigation
continued]

My enquiries into the youth of Lady Brandon were conducted simultaneously with my other researches. I went to Ramsgate House and India Lodge. I interviewed the servants who had been present when Lady Brandon died. I talked to undertakers' men in Lewes. I went to Amboise to see Mlle Boileau and to Suffolk to interview Sir John Frend. Also I spent a lot of time in the office of Messrs Mellish & Barker.

Of the documents held by Mellish & Barker I need say no more; they have already been used in the writing of these pages. They took me to Somerset House where I was able to read Lady Brandon's will. She had remembered her servants and a few friends, including Sir John; the biggest legacy to any individual went to Thérèse Boileau – she inherited a fortune. Everything else went to the Brandonian Institute, including a 999-year lease on India Lodge. This, however, was not her entire fortune. It was discovered that she had opened an account with a Dutch bank in 1891. In making her will she seems to have forgotten about it.

The Brandonian was helpful and I was able for several months to work at India Lodge.

The Lodge has one room entirely devoted to the two founders of the Institute; it had been Lady Brandon's study. It, and indeed the entire Lodge, is an interesting monument. Lady Brandon had furnished it with historical propriety, marrying the purest 'grecian' taste with oriental and orientalising work. Flaxman, Clodion, Manfredini, Chippendale and Wedgwood, a few drawings by Ingres and a good copy of his *Thetis and Jupiter* together with a David were set side by side with Manchu porcelain, furniture by Frederick Crace and William Porden, water-colours by Chinnery and the big portrait of Mary herself, *Harmony in Silver and Blue*. There was also a little Monet, a lithograph by Corot and a great many Japanese prints. When it came to her youngest contemporaries Lady Brandon's taste was more timid, Sargent, McEvoy, Wilson Steer and Lavery were as far as she would go in the direction of modernity.

The Brandon Room, as might have been expected, had much the appearance of a library. There were solid ranks of blue-books, together with *Nature*, the *Journal of the International Society for Dietetic Studies* and the *Lancet*; these filled one wall from floor to ceiling. On another wall were bound volumes of the *Women's Cause*, the *Suffrage Journal* and the *New Age*, and one shelf was devoted to crime, that is to say accounts of celebrated trials: Tichborne, Crippen, Wilde, Mrs Maybrick, Boulton and Park, Bywaters and Thompson, and so on. I also noticed the complete works of Maria Hattershall and, perhaps more surprisingly, Ovid, Livy, Suetonius and Tacitus together with Gibbon, Voltaire, Stendhal and Flaubert. There were a few framed photographs on the walls, most of them inscribed and including President Hoover, Nansen, Sir Frederick Gowland Hopkins, Mrs Pethwick Lawrence, Lloyd George and Metchnikov. More revealing was a large album of family photographs. Mary as a baby with her stepmother, Mary in Boston with Kate Pullman (she *was* a stunner), Mary with Mrs Gordon in Rome, Mary in a gondola, Mary in her wedding-dress with her Michelangelesque husband. Billy disguised as a Shakespearean character inscribed on the back '*Merchant of Venice*, July '85', Mrs Gordon looking charming in the preposterous draperies of the 1890s, Colonel Buxton Russell, the imbecile Sir William with a zany version of the Brandon good looks, Martha Strand as an equestrienne, portraits of Mary and Billy at the British Association meeting of 1908, Mary at a suffrage rally in 1912, the same, still handsome but growing stout, receiving an honorary degree at Johns Hopkins in 1925.

Perhaps the most amusing item was a photograph of a painting, the unfortunate Sir Charles as Hylas, being dragged down by a posse of water nymphs, all quite naked, but the water was discreet. I think that this might have been the work of Sidney Meteyard.

There were of course letters: letters from Beatrice Webb, from Jaurès and from Bernard Shaw; the letters from scientists were filed elsewhere. Also a box of MSS which showed that Mary had tried her hand at fiction. She loved to use the definite article in her titles: *The Heiress*, *The Rebel*, *The Sisters*, *The Changeling*, *The Casualty*. To many she had attached a rejection slip from a publisher. One couldn't blame the publishers. Despite her handwriting, I did manage to struggle through *The Rebel* and *The Casualty*. They were full of admirable sentiments, sentiments which did their author credit and which, at the time they were written, could only be expressed by a courageous person. But she seemed to have no gift at all for creating characters or for inventing situations. She wrote in decent English, but the reader is distracted by the lofty moral tone, the statistics and the classical quotations. Her polemical works are much more readable, even though most of the causes for which she fought are now victorious. Here she writes with much greater pungency and real feeling. She had a genuine enthusiasm for sexual equality, the toleration of deviants and, of course, the welfare of the unfortunate.

There was plenty at the Lodge to interest a biographer who was studying her later life. But of her activities before marriage there was really nothing, save the items which I have listed. A pair of elegant satin slippers, a dance programme, some feeble sketches made in Rome dated probably from those early years.

However, I was getting a fairly complete picture of the events of October and November 1942.

There were three servants in the house in addition to Thérèse Boileau. All of them, clearly, were devoted to their mistress and all those whom I could interview told much the same story of her end. But there was one who knew far more than all the rest and was very ready to talk.

Mrs Stacey, *née* Copthorne, had been employed for less than a year at India Lodge when Lady Brandon died. She had not seen very much of her mistress, everything was ordered and arranged by Thérèse. The other servants were used to this and did not resent it; Miss Copthorne was not used to it and did. 'A stuck-up French woman, very bossy and thought she could run everything.'

Miss Copthorne was, it seems, a very punctual and efficient person; she sought ways of vexing Thérèse and found one which worked exceedingly well. With advancing years Thérèse had taken to over-sleeping in the morning; one of her duties was to bring Lady Brandon a cup of tea. When Thérèse overslept Miss Copthorne took her place. 'She (Thérèse) had told me I must not; but I says Her Ladyship wants her cup of tea on the dot at 7.45, why shouldn't she have it?'

On the morning of November 1st, 1942 Thérèse overslept. Miss Copthorne made a pot of china tea and brought it up on a tray with two digestive biscuits, she rapped on the door and, without waiting for an answer, set the tea by the bed, drew the curtains and said, 'Good morning, Milady.' She then realised that Lady Brandon was dead.

'She looked peaceful enough and everything in the room was nor-mal, but her jaw was fallen. I knew at once that she was gone.'

Miss Copthorne shut the door and ran downstairs to ring a doctor. She knew that Lady Brandon's physician was Sir John Frend and knew also that he was in London, but there was old Dr Mayne at Whitecross, so she rang him and he said he would come over at once. She had just finished telephoning when Thérèse appeared.

There was a tremendous row. Thérèse was in tears, but she was also in a violent temper. 'Sore as a bad leg she was, shouted at me, jabbering in French half the time, as though that was any use. I thought she might get downright physical. But I just stood there and smiled. Lord, she wasn't half ratty.'

Thérèse did not become 'downright physical', but the extremity of her anger and her grief drove Miss Copthorne downstairs to the kitchen. We may infer that Thérèse at once phoned Hubert Mellish.

It was Dr Mayne who arrived first – but he was soon followed by the solicitor who immediately joined him as he examined the corpse.

Thérèse stationed herself on the stairs, so that Miss Copthorne could not hear what the two professional men had to say to each other; but at one point voices were raised and presently Dr Mayne drove away 'black as thunder'. Mr Mellish came downstairs and spoke to all the servants. Her Ladyship had died in her sleep of heart failure. She had left instructions as to what was to be done if she were suddenly to die. He was sure that no one would wish to disobey Her Ladyship's last orders. The room where she lay must be sealed. Sir John Frend would have to be summoned. He left Thérèse in charge. He spoke very seriously and very kindly, everyone liked Mr Mellish. He tried to ring Sir John, but Sir John had not yet arrived at the place where he worked. For the rest of the morning Thérèse sat outside her mistress's bedroom 'crying as though her heart would break'.

Thérèse remained at her post until about two o'clock when Mr Mellish returned with Sir John. They were joined about half an hour later by the undertakers' men who brought a coffin. Almost at once the undertakers came downstairs again and spent about a quarter of an hour in the drawing room before being summoned up again. According to Mrs Stacey, and her account has been corroborated by two of the 'mutes', Mr Mellish asked the men to place the coffin by the bed. Lady Brandon had asked to be put in her coffin by her old friend, Sir John and himself; certain books and letters were to be placed beside her.

'So the undertakers' men left them to it,' said my informant. 'And when they returned there she was in her coffin with the letters, and of course there was no knowing what they might be. I dare say she had some romance when she was a girl, poor lady, so all the men had to do was to screw up the lid and take her round to the mortuary. It was a lovely funeral and people came from all over, even with petrol on the ration.

'You couldn't have met a better-hearted lady and not stuck up like some of them I know. I could tell you . . .'

And indeed she did.

The next thing was to try and interview Dr Mayne. He had retired and lived at some very imposing address in Scotland. I wrote, received no answer, and went to the very imposing address, which turned out to be that of a lunatic asylum. The doctor could not help me.

An equally long excursion took me to the Château d'Ormeille, near Amboise. It was not a very large building, more like a farm than a castle. But it was the very comfortable home of a jolly old lady, very spry, full of jokes and delighted to talk about her old employer.

'Monsieur, you are writing the life of Lady Brandon? Bravo! It should be done for she was, I mean it, the best woman in the whole world. I think perhaps I was the happiest, in that destiny made me her servant and her friend for so many years.'

How happy they had been. The jokes, the kindness and never a quarrel, or if there had been a few little disputes, they had never lasted more than half an hour. No, she had nothing to complain of. Yes, they had been at Creek together, that was not so agreeable. But even there they had had each other's company and it had been a great consolation; her stepmother was not an amiable woman, but Milady was an angel. She could not bear that others should be unhappy. And then they had made such journeys: America, Italy, India, Egypt – oh yes, they had seen the world and laughed at it. And she was never cross, out of spirits perhaps, but never ill-tempered and she never forbade me what shall I say – my 'little adventures'. That poor Sir Charles – still he was married to her for a day, many men would have given a lifetime for that, not that he deserved her, who did?

And so she rattled on, full of praise and rather earthy jokes, certainly she was no prude. She spoke with evident complacency about her 'little adventures', but her whole life had been built around Lady Brandon. Even now, she liked more than anything to talk about her, her beauty and her many perfections and she did so in accents of real, deep affection. I suppose they were united by their common experience at Creek and then a long partnership which was a partnership of employer and employee, but also an alliance of very dear friends. But there was something more, a long, lasting tenderness which suggested passion. I felt this so strongly that I could not but suspect a Diana/Callisto relationship. But no, that was not her style. Then I made some tentative enquiries about the circumstances of Lady Brandon's death.

It was like stepping on the teeth of a rake. She had thought I was a serious biographer; she did not want to talk about her late mistress with a vulgar prying journalist. Suddenly she turned to stone.

I saw that I should get nowhere, apologised, declared that the matter was of no importance and in a few minutes she was again all smiles. She gave me a quite amazing dinner, we parted on good terms and I promised to return.

There remained Sir John Frend. I had left him to the last, partly because I was rather scared of him, partly because I wanted to approach him with as full a dossier as possible. I wrote and he invited me to stay the night with him in his Suffolk home.

Sir John was a short, stout, highly energetic man in his late sixties. He had grizzled crinkly hair, friendly brown eyes and a face which seemed to have been constructed to house a vast and cheerful grin. He seized my bag and threw it recklessly into the back of his aged but powerful car. We set off at a smart pace, smashing our rear light against a fence. This done, we set off in the right direction but on the wrong side of Hattendon High Street; we just missed a bus. I have never known a worse or a more dangerous driver. Getting clear of the little town and on to the straight road, where the car would do a comfortable eighty, Sir John began to talk.

'How much do you know about medicine? Pity. You need to know how pitifully ignorant we were fifty years ago to understand Mary's greatness. Yes, hers. She was much more brilliant than her cousin. Not a bad team though; she came across the big ideas, he found out why they were right. But Billy would have got nowhere without her. It was she who deserved the FRS. I told 'em so – bloody fools wouldn't listen. Pity she had no initial training, always an amateur. But what an

amateur! Too modest, perfect lady, raised in Canada, never gave
herself airs, gave Billy all the glory without thought of her own repu –
Bloody oaf! [This to a cyclist who had just avoided being destroyed.]

'Tell me now, you must have seen all sorts of people who knew her.
Has any one of them found a word to say against her? Was there
anyone so nearly sub-human as to dislike Mary Brandon? Of course
not. People couldn't help liking her. And it's not as though she played
safe with the world. The Brandonian was a struggle – bitter, ignorant,
stupid people tried to kill it. All the time, right up to the year of her
death, she had to fight for us; we still hadn't got chartered when she
died. She was a bonny fighter. And yet you know, no hard feelings, even
the worst of them ended by liking her.'

Thus he rattled on and somehow managed to bring us to his very
comfortable home. After dinner there was music in the next room and
we were left to ourselves. It was not until then, when I had been
emboldened by his excellent port, that I dared to let fly.

I told him all that I knew about the funeral arrangements; I told him
about the telephone conversation; I told him how Thérèse had taken
my enquiries; and I asked him whether he had any comment.

For the first time since we had met he fell silent. Then, rousing
himself with a smile, 'Oh, so that's it? Poor old John. Justice catches up
with him at last. Bring on the Eumenides. And supposing I refuse to
talk? What then, eh?'

'Well, Sir, I can only write what I know – that is to say, what I have
just told you. I am quite sure that nothing really wicked is being
concealed. But something is being concealed, so I shall have no
hesitation about going to the public.'

He was silent again but then began to talk, rather to himself than to
me. 'You can't hurt the Institute: it's too well established now. You
can't hurt poor old Mellish; he's dead. You can hurt me a little, but I'm
so old and so very distinguished, and will so soon be dead. But you
could hurt someone who doesn't deserve to be hurt.'

'Thérèse?'

'Of course. She must be nearly eighty. Let her die in peace; it's not so very much to ask.'

'I give you my word of honour, Sir John, and I'll put it in writing. While she lives I will publish nothing.'

'I have to be quite sure of that, my boy.'

'Dictate the terms, Sir John. I like her and don't want to hurt her.'

He insisted on having a written promise there and then; and it was not until he had folded it, and put it into an inner pocket, that he was ready to say: 'All right, here goes.

'As you know, it was I who signed the death certificate. In it I told a deliberate lie. Oh no, not about the cause of death – that was coronary and we'd been expecting it and tried to take precautions against when it happened. We had a bit of bad luck. No, I simply wrote one false word.'

'A word?'

'Yes. You know there is a place where it says male or female? Well, I said female. It was untrue – he, or if you like she, was a man.

'Yes, she – I can't break the habit – was a male with no breasts and with all the usual trimmings. She did not like talking about it, and she being remarkably healthy I didn't see much of her body until the end. Her cousin knew and was her physician for years. When he died I was let into the secret. I don't practise, but I am a doctor. I gather it was when she was quite young, when it usually happens in fact, there was a sex change – not quite so unusual a thing as most people think. But imagine the horror of it for a well-brought-up Victorian young lady living out in the wilds of Canada and no physician, no experience, just a wicked stepmother and some brutal servants. I can't think how the poor thing managed not to go mad. Thérèse knew from the beginning and must have been a great help.

'When she died, there were Thérèse and Mellish and myself who knew. We realised that she might go suddenly and tried to take precautions, but some fool of a parlourmaid rang some fool of a doctor and he, of course, examined the body and insisted on being pedantic about the death certificate. Mellish persuaded the idiot to hold his tongue and I was sent for. He and I put poor Mary into her coffin. Mellish, splendid old liar that he was, invented some cock-and-bull story for the servants. Most fortunately for us the local doctor was already known to be going off his head so that anything he said was likely to be discounted. We thought that the whole thing was neatly covered up. We didn't know about you, you bloody eavesdropper.

'But it was urgent you know. It wasn't just the scandal that worried us. For fifty years we'd been building up the Institute and Mary had signed her name thousands of times to documents without which we should have been penniless. It might have been all right if the Institute had been safe. But at that time it was not, and there were parties out gunning for us. We should have been destroyed.

' "Lady Brandon"! She was nothing of the kind. How could Sir Charles have married a man? Poor old Mellish, he used to be worried pink by the complications of scandals which would fall upon his head if the truth were known. Every single legal instrument that we had used, right from the very beginning in the 1890s, could be invalidated. The finest research instrument in the world, a thing which was saving millions from death and deformity could be brought down in ruins because some two-penny-halfpenny-half-wit of a GP refused to sign what was, except in one tiny irrelevant detail, a perfectly true statement.

'And then, what about Thérèse? Technically, she was an accomplice in what legal people would, I suppose, have called a fraud. I don't know what they might have done to her but she would have hated any scandal about Mary, and of course she would have been cheated out of a well-earned inheritance. My conscience is perfectly clear.'

'Yes,' I replied, 'I can see your point of view. The Institute had to be saved, Thérèse had to be protected. But why did Mary Brandon act as she did, as he did? How could she go through a form of marriage and why, when she did, was the result so terrible? One can't help feeling that it had something to do with the fact that Sir Charles had married a young man.'

'All that is long before my time. Mary did not like to talk about her marriage and I didn't like to ask; I did once in a roundabout sort of way, but I could see it hurt her terribly even to talk about the matter. I did not feel that it was really my business and I could not, cannot, see Mary doing anything dishonourable. I dropped the subject and never raised it again.'

'Perhaps you did not want to?'

'I certainly did not.'

In my bedroom, I began to meditate over what I had heard.

Was this, then, the final truth of the matter? Here, indeed, was a complete answer to my original question: now I knew for sure why it was necessary to falsify a death certificate. But was it the answer to all the questions that had been raised in the pursuit of that first enquiry? To some of them certainly, but there were loose ends. I felt as one feels when one finds a jigsaw piece which fits quite convincingly and then, as one begins uncomfortably to see, does not quite fit after all.

Getting into bed I laughed. I had remembered the story of Mary's gaffe with Mrs Benson in the Marchesa Rasponi's drawing room and realised now what a complication of improprieties was involved. But there was something else about that story, something I ought to have noticed. I remembered that Lady Alcester had said something about Mary's 'clear well-educated voice'. Well educated by whom? Not by Lady Porthow. She spoke French. Certainly not by her servants. Books would not have helped. The Pullmans? Lady Alcester would not have approved of their accent. It could only be Lady Alcester – but so soon? The Rasponis were in Florence. Mary seemed to have been learning very unexpected things at Creek Castle, but this was not unexpected, it was downright impossible. I puzzled at the thing and fell asleep over it.

Sir John was very affable over breakfast which was comfortably leisurely until, looking at his watch he cried out, 'Golly, we'll have to move fast to catch your train. Won't be a moment.' He dashed out of the room, slamming the door violently and bringing a picture off the wall.

It was a framed photograph, clearly a photograph of Mary as a young girl. Somehow it was familiar. It must have been made when she was about fifteen. She was wearing a high-waisted, square-necked, large-sleeved gown with pleats running down the bodice. It was trimmed with fur. She stood in front of a bookcase and it was this that interested me. The lettering on the books, the highlights on the leather bindings were familiar. I knew that background! It was the background of another photograph, a photograph at India Lodge.

Sir John burst in. 'Come on old chap, no time for wool-gathering.'

'Sir John, forgive me, but this could be important.'

'You will miss your train.'

'It's more important than my train.'

He was a bit nettled. I think he had been looking forward to showing me just what that car could do. I apologised. But it really was important. Could he remember anything about this photograph?

'Oh, it's a picture of Mary taken when she was a girl, the only one she had.'

'You are sure of that?'

'Of course I am sure, I'm not senile. I wanted a picture of her as a girl. She took it out of a drawer and laughed, "Me at Creek, aged fifteen – the only one I have." Those were her very words. There is still just time to catch that train.'

'Look, I know that I am being tiresome but I would like to see the back of that picture.'

'You are being rather tiresome. Oh, all right, take it out of its frame if you must.'

With trembling hands I cut the *passe-partout* from behind, opened up the mount, and there, sure enough, scrawled on the back was '*Merchant of Venice*, July 1885'.

'Sir John, there was no sex change.'

'Eh?'

'This photograph was taken in London. It makes a pair with another, a photograph of Sir William Brandon, your late colleague, when he was a boy. Same lens, same exposure, same background, even to the details. Same inscription on the back in the same hand. When this was taken Mary Porthow was two thousand miles away. It is impossible that it should be of her.'

'Who then?'

'Henry Brandon.'

'But he died didn't he?'

'I think that we shall find that it was Mary Porthow who died.'

'Can you be sure?'

'With that inscription, yes, I think we can be sure.'

'Henry Brandon dressed as a girl?'

'Not for the last time by any means – cripes yes, Boulton and Park.'

'I don't follow you.'

'It's only a tiny clue: Lady Brandon had an account of the Boulton and Park case on her bookshelf, I thought it rather odd at the time but then forgot.'

'But who were Boulton and Park?'

'Two men arrested for impersonating women; Rossetti and Swinburne were interested in the case. Why didn't I notice? It gives us a motive, a psychological motive – Henry Brandon's reason for becoming Mary Porthow, quite apart from the fact that she was an heiress.'

'Perversion? Fraud? You didn't know Mary, and you can't know just how disagreeable it is to have to consider such possibilities. I can't bear to think of her as being some kind of imposter, a sham, a changeling.'

'*The Changeling*, that's it!'

'Young man, do you have to be so elliptical?'

'I beg your pardon. It's just that I have been thinking of everything in a new light and I begin to see all the evidence that I have been missing.'

He produced a wan smile. 'Yes, I have had that experience. And what have you missed this time?'

'Lady Brandon wrote novels, unpublished, unreadable. I glanced at them at India Lodge, but did no more than glance. There is one which begins with a rather tedious defence of sexual perversion – I only read a few pages. It's called *The Changeling*, and it may contain Henry Brandon's story.'

'And the manuscript is at India Lodge?'

'Yes.'

'You have certainly missed the 9.45 and must catch the 10.52. Go straight to India Lodge and tell me what you find. I like to think that she may still be able to defend herself. Poor Mary.'

I had a compartment to myself. Sir John had entrusted me with that ancient and revealing photograph. Alone and at leisure I took it out and re-examined it. I felt absolutely certain that I had seen its fellow and that with it I had an unbreakable case against Henry Brandon.

What could he have been like? How does one live so monstrous a lie for fifty years? I supposed that the beginning would have been the worst part of it; after a time the lie would have become second nature. But there would always have been the possibility of some catastrophe, some dreadful exposure. And then there would have been that awkward hiatus, the missing story of his 'girlhood' in Creek, about which he would never talk. The world had to take that part of his life on trust. But then, all the witnesses were dead, all save Thérèse who loved him. But the photograph must have seemed a godsend. Looking at it now it was easy to see that Henry Brandon was dressed for theatricals, probably to play Portia since this was *The Merchant of Venice*. It is not easy, when you look at the clothes of another age, to know what is and what is not fancy dress. The distinction would not have been noticed and, in fact, Sir John never had noticed it, so it could be used to show that the Mary Porthow whom the world knew was visibly and identifiably wearing petticoats at the age of fifteen.

He couldn't wave it in triumph – the very nature of his fraud lay in the assumption that there was nothing to prove. But he could give the thing to a friend who might display it and, in so doing, give solidity to the myth.

But then, if this were fiction, hubris would be followed by Nemesis.

The other photograph would come to light, someone would compare the two, and would arrive at the inescapable conclusion. Once suspicion had been aroused all sorts of hitherto unnoticed things would have become apparent and years of dishonesty would suddenly have ended. Eventually Henry Brandon, *alias* Mary Porthow, *alias* Lady Brandon, that paragon of social conscience, civic virtue and public benevolence, would have been obliged to explain what had become of the real Mary Porthow and why it was that the false Mary had 'married' her cousin and how it was that that cousin, together with his valet, had met a violent death.

But Nemesis arrived too late. Henry Brandon died in his bed wealthy, secure and unsuspected even by those who knew the truth about his sex. Probably he never knew of that other photograph which, in the end, found its way to India Lodge. He believed that he had made himself perfectly safe and even now, I surmised, any attempt to expose him would encounter strong resistance.

That he should now be unmasked seemed to me right and proper – there were two, probably three deaths to be explained. I felt the excitement of the chase, the scent was warm for now I knew where to look.

Indeed, at the end it was almost too easy. A nine o'clock on the following morning when India Lodge opened its doors I was waiting. I set the photographs side by side and my last doubts vanished.

Then I returned to *The Changeling*. I struggled through that first long dreary chapter and, having mastered Mr Brandon's illegible hand, read on.

THE BRANDON PAPERS
Part II

CHAPTER I

[Maurice Evans's Investigation
continued]

The Changeling was written about 1930, in the pages of a minute-
book. It purports to be a novel. If it had been offered to a publisher
there can be no doubt that much would have been excised and much
rewritten. Already the manuscript is heavily and sometimes illegibly
corrected. I have been as faithful as possible to the original punctuation
and paragraphing and to what seem to have been the author's intentions; but in places silent correction has been necessary. Henry Brandon gave imaginary names to his characters but after the third chapter
he forgets them and uses real names. These true names have been
supplied throughout.

The first chapter has been omitted: it has little bearing on Henry
Brandon's story and consists mainly of a plea for toleration, compassion and a change in the laws as they relate to sexual deviation of all
kinds. It would command the assent but not the attention of liberal-
minded people today. But at one point the author does consider the
peculiar situation of the transvestite (or as he, following Havelock
Ellis, says 'the eonist') and what was, manifestly, his own case.

The eonist is so strangely constituted that he or she finds deep
satisfaction simply in wearing clothes appropriate to the opposite sex.
The great majority of 'normal' people do not seem to understand this;
they see in the travesty (I am thinking here of the male rather than the
female eonist) a means to an end, in fact a form of homosexual
courtship. This is an oversimplification. Such a disguise can, given the
appropriate circumstances, be a part of the apparatus of pederasty but

it need not be, and in fact many homosexuals find such masquerading distasteful. On the other hand, many eonists find an intense and sufficient pleasure in disguising themselves behind locked doors, greatly daring they may venture into the streets or visit some public place where they may display their borrowed finery and deceive the world; but this, for most, is the limit of adventure. A mild flirtation with a man would be adventure indeed. It must often be the case that the eonist finds his pleasure, not only from or, indeed, not at all from, the achievement of intimate relations with another man (in fact, this would be a most unreasonable ambition for homosexuals are the last people to be interested in those whom the eonists counterfeit) but rather from the satisfaction of a kind of envious admiration of women. In our society women suffer under cruel and unjust disabilities. Nevertheless they, and they alone, are permitted the full luxury of self-adornment, they enjoy social privileges which appeal deeply to those who are content to play a passive role in life, they are the guardians of the social graces and the erotic cynosure of the world. It is not unreasonable to envy their unassertive pre-eminence and to seek to identify with them.

Ordinary citizens have no more to fear from the simulated youth or girl than from those of both sexes who enjoy the preliminaries of courtship while avoiding its conclusion – not always an agreeable role, but not necessarily base if such flirtations are kindly and cautiously managed, and certainly not illegal in any way.

On the face of it, the eonist appears to be a harmless and decidedly ineffective person. His is usually a solitary vice, he affects others only in rather unusual circumstances. Usually, if he be let alone, he is his own worst enemy.

But he is not let alone. If his secret be made public he is a target for hatred, scorn and abuse. True, the law cannot hurt him, but there are plenty of people who can and will. I have been told, and it would not be astonishing if true, that Lord Clinton, who was involved in the Boulton and Park business, was driven to take his own life rather than face a court of law, the press and society. In that affair the summing up of the

Lord Chief Justice provides a remarkable instance both of the fairness
and of the barbarity of the British Themis. Lord Cockburn told the jury
that it must not convict the defendants simply because they dressed as
women: here the law could not touch them. Only if it could be shown
that this aberration was the prelude or the means to other acts, criminal
acts, did the accused stand in peril of the law. In fact, this could not be
proved and the men were acquitted. But in a momentous *obiter dictum*
Lord Cockburn lamented the fact that he had no power to hurt the
prisoners who stood before him. There *ought* to be a law, the thing was
'an outrage upon public decency'. The men should be flogged.

But an outrage upon public decency was exactly what it was not, not
at all events until the police made it so.

There were righteous legislators who would have been only too glad
to pass draconian laws to oblige Lord Cockburn. But as will be seen,
they faced a perplexing task. How shall we define female dress? 'Easy,'
says the righteous legislator. 'Skirts, bright colours, lace and ruffles,
long hair, simulated maybe by a wig.' Stop, righteous legislator, you
know not what you do: you are describing His Lordship as he appears
in court.

In fact, no law has been or could be drafted. But 'virtue' has other
ways of persecuting those who have been unfortunate.

I will mention one case concerning which I am well informed. A
youth of seventeen was persuaded 'for a lark' to visit what was called 'a
club' but which, according to the police, was a 'disorderly house'. He
had never been there before; in fact, he never did go there: when he and
his companion arrived they found that the place was being raided.
They were frightened, they made the stupid mistake of running and
were apprehended. The youth was disguised as a lady. He was made to
undress, to undergo a humiliating examination and to endure a
bullying inquisition which just stopped short of actual violence by
constables eager to extract a confession of sodomy and a denunciation
of his companion. He stuck to his story: he had been told that his
disguise committed him to nothing; he had been persuaded to visit the

club with promises that he would be no more than a spectator. In the end he was released and no charge was made.

It was then that his punishment started. Not unnaturally he felt ridiculous and ashamed. With righteous anger and savage ingenuity, friends, relations, teachers and guardians did everything they could to heighten this sentiment. He was browbeaten and abused, mocked at as a poltroon, shamed as a criminal. In the end he was expelled from his home and sent to a remote quarter of the globe. Only one member of his family, his brother, uttered a word of sympathy. The rest missed no occasion to express their disgust, their hatred and their contempt. When he attempted to defend himself, those in authority shouted him down. They provided a reasonably adequate substitute for the flogging block of Lord Cockburn's imagination.

It will be noticed that Henry Brandon here speaks of himself in the third person. In his second chapter he becomes frankly autobiographical. At the same time his style becomes less ponderous, his use of classical quotations less frequent and his prose altogether more fluid. His text, begins to read more like a memoir than a novel.

To what extent, therefore, should we regard *The Changeling* as a true record of the author's early life? In substance his account does agree pretty well with that of Lady Alcester. Nevertheless, it may be as well to remember that this version did begin as a work of fiction and certain passages may have been highly coloured for artistic reasons. Also, in so far as it is autobiographical *The Changeling* may be seen as an apology, a plea by someone who, on his own admission, was a thief – even though the money may have been well spent – and who admits to responsibility for the death of two of his fellow men. It may be felt that Henry Brandon cannot be trusted when he is attempting to explain and to attenuate his own crimes.

The existence of motives such as these may lead us to read the following pages with a critical eye. Nor perhaps are they the only motives which may have led to a distortion of the truth. Henry Brandon may be said to have lived a lie. Some of his motives were sordid, perhaps masochistic; he was also living a fantasy and clearly he was very much pleased by his success in that undertaking. The temptation to exaggerate his own achievements as a transvestite must have been strong; it has I think left its mark upon his text. *The Changeling* is indeed a sufficiently curious mixture of exhibitionism and reticence.

But here it may be that I myself am reading more into the text than a fair-minded critic would discover. I will leave the work of assessment to others.

CHAPTER 2

[The Changeling]

It was a miserable, lonely and almost hopeless boy who stood on the deck of the *Empress of Canada* and journeyed westwards during those dark windy days of October 1888. The storms were, in fact, his main comfort; they drove the other passengers below decks and made it unnecessary to imagine that they were all the time looking at him and saying to one another, 'There is the outcast. There is the wretch who has disgraced himself for ever. Poor little rotter.'

I had been told that people always would say that and I believed it. People would always hate and despise me. Oh, how I hated and despised 'people'! I prayed for some tyrant, some Nero who would overawe them as they overawed me. What did they think, what did they say, those stuffy old prudes of the Republic, when, as Suetonius puts it, he threw away all concealment and, with all due forms and ceremonies, married Sporus?

*Hunc Sporum, Augustarum ornamentis excultum lecticaque vectum, et circa conventus mercatusque Graeciae ac mox Romae circa Sigillaria comitatus est identidem exosculans.**

Later, Nero himself was given as a bride to Doryphorus and in that bed went so far as to simulate the cries of a deflowered virgin. And what did the Aunt Marthas of the Palatine say to that? 'My dear, one has to

---

* And this Sporus was drawn in a litter through the courts and markets of Greece and later, in Rome, through the art-dealers' shops, his body lapped in the finery of an empress and passionately embraced by his husband (Suetonius, *Lives of the Caesars* VI. 28). – M.E.

make allowances for an artist, plays quite beautifully I am told.' Just for once the social bullies were powerless, just for once it was they who had to cringe and to dissemble. When he was safely dead they could be publicly virtuous and tell lies about the man who had brought them to heel. 'People' were horrible. They made me ashamed of the weakness with which I accepted their cruelty and their injustice. For I was brave only in imagination. Courage is not one of my virtues. It would have helped me then, for I had been told – and again I had believed – that I had destroyed my life almost before I had begun it.

'Education,' said my mother, 'education is everything. You boys must educate yourselves out of poverty.'

And so, not being stupid, we had both won scholarships to Cordwainers where they taught us Latin and a little mathematics and science and no modern languages (but we got these at home). It was a day school and we were unpopular but not too unhappy. Billy went ahead and studied at Bart's while I was accepted by Trinity Hall, not doubting that through education I should make a decent living, wondering only whether I should not have gone to Imperial College and trained as a scientist. The prospect looked fair.

I should have hated a public school but I suppose it would have saved me from Uncle Hector and his 'larks' and my own silly attempts to be 'decadent'. But in the end it was just a stupid accident that brought the steel spring down upon the back of this foolish mouse and broke him.

It was so sudden, so complete. One day I was a brilliant young man and all the world before me. The next I was something to be hidden and hushed-up and swept out of sight.

Because one must hope for *something*, I hoped that I might accomplish my mission – my 'last chance' Uncle Amos called it: I was to confront the formidable Lady Porthow, to bring her and her daughter to Boston, to wheedle, to threaten and, if successful, to be rewarded with the dingiest of tasks in Melbourne. Mr Mellish had given me written instructions. I spent a lot of time studying them and making myself thoroughly acquainted with the coming task. It was all to prove completely useless, but it served to distract my mind at a time when it was sorely in need of distraction.

Finally, one misty morning I disembarked at St John's, Newfoundland. A small, slight, unimpressive figure, a schoolboy with a heavy suitcase and in the eyes of my interlocutor, Captain Henry McDee of the *Hudson Victory*, a confounded nuisance. Still, he need not have been quite so discouraging.

'Want to go to Liberty Sound, eh? Letters from Uncle and all that, eh? Well, yer can't, yer too late. The season's over.' He paused to spit copiously on Newfoundland. 'Yer think because Uncle's a wealthy baronite and all that yer can come and go as yer please. Well yer can't, Mr High and Mighty. Yer at the wrong address.'

So that was that. I turned mournfully away.

'Hey, where are yer goin'?'

'I'm going to see if some other boat will take me.'

'Ther ain't nothin' else – only fishermen.'

'Then perhaps a fisherman will take me.'

'Sink yer more like.'

'That's my affair.'

'No, it ain't,' replied Captain McDee with evident alarm. 'If you go off and get sunk by someone else it's I'll be in trouble.'

'Since you won't take me we must risk that.'

'Who said I won't take you? Look here Mr High and Mighty, can you be on board in half an hour?'

'Yes.'

'Then just you wait there where yer are and don't try bargaining with no fishermen. Half an hour I give yer.'

The ship was noisome, the food almost uneatable, the Captain did not improve on closer acquaintance. The officers and men were unfriendly; they did not conceal their contempt for so effeminate a landsman. I have never been made more unwelcome anywhere. Admittedly, the situation of my companions was unenviable. They had a cargo of rails to deliver at Port Nelson, Hudson Bay and it would be hard for them to complete their voyage before the sea froze. To land me at Creek would be an additional delay; but if they failed to do so they would have to reckon with the owner. The Captain compromised by taking risks upon a dangerous shore. He vented his ill humour on the crew, and the crew took it out on me.

At the close of a very fine still afternoon we sailed, much too fast I am sure, up Liberty Sound. Swift and silent we steamed past the ruins of the city that Sir Amos had built twenty years before. Then we executed a strange manoeuvre. The ship headed for the jetty, then turned away and fetched a circle in the fiord so that she came to the landing place at a tangent. A ladder was thrown over the bulwarks and I was bidden to go down until I had reached what was judged to be a correct position.

'Stop there,' growled the Captain. 'Jump when I tell you. Don't wait or you'll fall in and be sucked under by my propellers.'

There was a long, frightening interval while the stream between me and the jetty grew slower and narrower. I was very scared.

'Jump.'

I fell, barking my hands and knees. A projectile flew past my head. It was my suitcase. A bottle of scent, a present for my hostess, was smashed by the impact.

When I had picked myself up and looked about me I saw that the *Hudson Victory* was already gathering speed as she steamed up the Sound.

I had longed for solitude. Now I certainly had it. To my right was the grey, mournful, still-born city, a silent company of empty buildings with gaping windows. Above them stood the unused cranes, some of them still standing and rusting high in the air above me. To my left, looming enormous in the failing light was Creek Castle, an architectural monstrosity—Scottish baronial with crenellations, machicolations, turrets, towers and gargoyles – and no sign of life in all its many windows. All around me were the vast unfriendly mountains and everything as quiet as the grave.

The Castle lay about a mile away. Thither I walked, increasingly conscious of the weight of my luggage, increasingly inclined to halt, but increasingly aware that the night was descending fast and bitter cold.

At last I struggled up a long flight of steps and faced a great iron-bound, nail-studded door. There was a bell, an iron ring, rusty but usable; it produced a faint tinkle somewhere, far above me. But that was all. No one came to that ancient door. I rang and knocked and rang again and shouted. Still there was no sign of life in that cold desolate place. It was getting quite dark.

Desperately I flung myself against the shabby portal. With a hideous shriek it gave a couple of inches. I renewed my attack but it would give no further. I noticed a stout broom fallen by the doorway, thrust it into the gap and pulled violently against that fulcrum. My lever snapped in half but the door had yielded so that I could just squeeze my way in. Then I was in a great hall, but it was black as the tomb. I had a box of fusees, not enough to waste but enough to discover an enormous staircase before me. I ascended, stumbling up from landing to landing. My last fusee was gone, and with it what little courage I had, when I came to the fifth landing and perceived the very faintest suggestion of artificial light at the end of a long corridor. It led me, with mounting spirits, to a big interior window through which shone a light. Beneath it was a door. I knocked; there was no answer.

I knocked again and entered.

What I saw was strange beyond words. Let me try to be prosaic. It was a small, comfortable, overdecorated room, very warm, brilliantly lit by gas. A table was laid for a solitary banquet; there was an abundance of good things to eat and to drink. There were two young women; one, obviously a servant, stood, no, supported herself, against a wall. The other was seated, dressed for a party, dressed as though to dine with the Emperor Napoleon III, but loaded, blazing, incandescent with jewellery festive as a Christmas tree. But festive is the wrong word. The room was as festive as the Morgue.

The seated girl was just not fainting. Her maid was less completely terrified, but as they glared at me they might, either of them, have been facing a firing squad.

Their terror and my bewilderment robbed me of speech. But at last I contrived a few banalities: I was very sorry to have disturbed them; sorry that I was unable to give warning; hoped I was not causing too much inconvenience; perhaps I might explain myself to Lady Porthow?

'She's dead! She's dead!' cried the seated girl and chortling like a startled pheasant, fell out of her chair.

It was a help to have practical things to do. The maid and I set Miss Porthow upon a sofa, found brandy, found sal volatile and gradually life became a little less insane.

While her mistress revived, the maid told me that all the other members of the household had been drowned, there had been a fishing party, an accident, and now they two were alone. They had not heard the *Hudson Victory*'s siren; ships always announced themselves with sirens. They had heard me ring and knock and break in; they were afraid of marauders, Esquimaux perhaps, and they were defenceless. She had begun in bad English but then, finding herself understood, continued in French.

'What we must know,' said the reviving Miss Porthow, 'is how soon can we leave?'

'As soon as the ice beaks.'

'Another nine months! You fool, why hadn't you the sense to make the boat stay for us? We could have left at once.'

'I am very sorry about that. My instructions did not envisage the situation that has occurred. Even if I had known how matters stood the Captain of the *Hudson Victory* would I am sure have refused to wait. I am very sorry that you should be disappointed in this way. I never wanted to intrude in this manner, I will try not to disturb you.'

'You must look after the chickens,' replied Miss Porthow cryptically.

I ate the best dinner I had had for a long time. I told my story, they retold theirs. Miss Porthow was not communicative, she made it plain that I was an unwelcome intruder. Also she was still feeling very unwell and soon retired to bed – there she remained for the next forty-eight hours. It was left to her servant, now introduced as Mlle Thérèse Boileau, to do the honours of the Castle. She, who was clearly delighted to have company, obliged readily.

Creek Castle was as grotesque inside as out. A triumph of imaginative engineering and misapplied ingenuity. There were halls, galleries, ballrooms, sitting rooms, a library and bathrooms. There were stairs grandiose, like the one I had used, modest, like the one I ought to have used. There was a vast greenhouse from which the household drew its fresh vegetables and an aviary populated by Rhode Island reds. There were storerooms, gasometers, fuel tanks, emergency heating systems and so on. There was even a picture gallery, of some horror. Only a small section of the house was inhabited. Thérèse herself could get lost in the palatial suites that remained cold and boarded up. She made an excellent *cicerone*, chattering, exclaiming, laughing a great deal. From the first we got on very well indeed.

Of her mistress I saw less. She seemed anxious, unhappy and suspicious. She made no effort to conceal her dislike of me and she still blamed me for letting the *Hudson Victory* slip away without her.

How shall I describe that unhappy girl? We were first cousins, we had the Brandon looks, but there I hope, the resemblance ends. Her skin was spotty and sallow, her eyes weak and colourless; she had a stooping, peering gait which suggested an actual malformation of the spine. I suspect that there had been deficiencies in her diet – there was no fresh milk at Creek. She had been led a wretched life by her stepmother. At eighteen she had never had any fun, any friends or any education worth speaking of; she had great expectations which had repeatedly been disappointed. One could not blame her for being peevish, worried and aggrieved.

But why did she hate me so much? True, I had not brought immediate release, but eventual liberation was promised. I did my best to be friendly, I even tried to be entertaining; but usually she did not talk to me. She did, it is true, offer long, rambling and inconsistent

accounts of the boating accident. At times she was very savage with
poor Thérèse, who clearly was terrified of her. She wandered about the
house talking to herself in French; her English was bad and she had
picked up some startlingly coarse expressions from the servants. It was
like living with some hostile and miserable spectre. I looked forward to
the winter months with natural anxiety.

Then one morning the weather, which had been dull and very cold,
brightened wonderfully and so did my cousin. She seemed a new
person, gay, smiling, sociable.

'Here,' she exclaimed, 'is our Indian summer. We always get a few
days at the end of the season. Wrap up warm and come out with me in
the skiff – you ought to see the creek now, when it is beautiful.'

I made no difficulties. I found a warm coat and disguised myself as a
sailor. She asked me to go down to the boat-house and make the skiff
ready. She would join me in a few minutes. I had to wait a very long
time and was just turning back to the Castle when she appeared,
muffled in a great coat and carrying a very big basket.

'Can you sail a boat?'

I replied, not very truthfully, that I could. But it was not hard. A lively
breeze carried us forward at a fine rate. There is nothing so pleasant as
handling a sailing boat on a fine morning, the water beneath us gurgled
merrily; Mary sat there smiling, happier than I had ever seen her.

'Where are we going?'

'To Gull Island to collect eggs. They are delicious.'

'But what kind of bird lays eggs at this time of year in these latitudes?'

'Gulls. If you knew anything about the sub-Arctic you would know
that.'

There was a pause, I was watching the sail, then: 'Cousin, I think you
must be mistaken.'

'You are very ignorant, Cousin Henry. I know what I'm doing.'

'But how is it possible?'

'You will do as I tell you.' She spoke in quite a new tone of voice. I turned to look at her and found myself staring down the twin barrels of a carbine. I knew that she was quite mad and would kill me.

I made a grab at the gun, heard an explosion, fell with a hideous shock and felt the breath leaving my body.

So this is death, I thought, or will be when she fires again. Slowly, with enormous pain, my breath returned. Cautiously, I lifted my head. I was alone.

I thought it out later. When I tried to seize the gun I fell heavily against the thwart. I suppose Mary thought that she had killed me; I was prone. She must have stood up and paused – to have shot me again from above might have knocked a hole in the bottom of the boat. She must have forgotten that the vessel was out of control; with the tiller released and sail free, she would have gybed. The boom, which was quite heavy, would have swung back viciously, catching Mary below the knees, sweeping her and her weapon into the sea.

As I say, I thought this out later. At the time I was simply aware that she was gone and the skiff had to be brought under control. With trembling hands and little seamanship I managed it and set a course for home. I scanned the sea and called out, but we had drifted far from the scene of the accident. I take no credit for this futile effort. I was still amazed and half stunned.

After what seemed an age I was back at Creek Castle. No trace of Thérèse, breakfast had not been cleared, in the kitchen a kettle was red hot. I called and called. Then, very faintly from somewhere above, came an answering cry.

In the room where she habitually slept, Thérèse lay on an iron bed. Her hands and feet had been cruelly bound, her body was strapped to the bed itself. She had been gagged but had managed to free herself of that bond. She wept as I set her free and began to rub some life back into her tortured wrists and ankles.

'Mademoiselle?'

'Gone to join the rest. She fell overboard trying to kill me.'

'Thank God. I believed you dead and my turn coming.'

What followed seemed almost a matter of course, something entirely natural. She needed to be helped downstairs, she needed comfort and food and wine, she needed to weep in my arms and gradually, as that resilient creature returned to life, she sought for greater sympathy and for all that life might yet offer to one who had been so near to death. We had all the time in the world to pass from healing to comforting and from comfort to more positive joys.

'You poor dears, what a dreadful time you must have had all alone together in Creek Castle.' Kind people have said that so many times that I have come almost to believe them. Of course there were moments of less than perfect bliss. But in that first unpremeditated encounter, those two or three days when we lost count of time so that we nearly starved our poor poultry to death, Thérèse and I were about as happy as it is possible to be in this life.

For me there was a special happiness. I reflected, when the first lovely explosions of joy had given way to quiet serenity, that this had been my red-letter day. It had so nearly been my last day, now it seemed to be my first.

The reader, if he has followed me so far, will realise that I am by no means a strong person and one of my weaknesses arose from a very natural doubt as to my own abilities as a lover. Now, for the first time, I had been given the strength which I had so often feared would not, if called for, be granted. For the first time I felt myself to be a real man. I had, I supposed, turned over a new leaf, a normal straightforward life lay ahead of me and I was not, as I had feared, a bather in Salmacis.* I was inexpressibly happy. I believe that she and I were the two happiest people in the western hemisphere.

Soon enough there were to be new problems and discreditable solutions. But before examining them I must discuss some of the events at Creek of which I had known nothing.

---

* In Lake Salmacis Hermaphroditus was pursued by a nymph with whom he became physically united, the youth and the girl sharing one body. Henceforth those who bathed in Salmacis became impotent (*see* Ovid *Metamorphosis* 4.388). – M.E.

Thérèse had, in effect, been sold to the agents of Sir Amos by her parents. At Creek she was miserable, friendless and unpaid. Of the menservants, old William tried to rape her and young Tom to seduce her. She resisted and escaped and thanked the blessed Virgin for her deliverance. But from her employers there was no deliverance. The wretched Mary bullied her unceasingly; Lady Porthow bullied everyone but particularly Mary. Mary was to be kept as a bargaining counter in the contest with Sir Amos. Lady Porthow went so far as to have her stepdaughter locked in an upper room of the Castle when Captain Arthurs came in May '88.

The boating accident took place in July of that year. Lady Porthow was not involved except as a spectator – she was never in any danger.

Lady Porthow met her death in another manner. Miss Mary had told her stepmother that she was going to take the skiff to a place called Gull Island, there to collect eggs. Lady Porthow suspected that Mary might attempt to sail away and escape altogether (it would hardly have been possible); she therefore insisted on coming too. From what Thérèse could gather Lady Porthow stepped on shore, whereupon Mary cast off the painter and sailed back to Creek. Lady Porthow was a thoroughly unpleasant character, selfish, cruel, obstinate, probably a murderess. She had driven her stepdaughter mad. But I cannot think of her marooned on those barren rocks and the cold night gathering without feelings of horror. It was a fearful end.

Mary had no such feelings. What she regretted was that she had been unable to shoot the old lady down as she stood screaming on the rocks. She was plagued by a fearful doubt as to whether, by some almost impossible fluke, Lady Porthow might not have been saved after all. Some passing vessel, a party of Esquimaux might have ventured into the Sound. As the days passed she became more and more obsessed by the idea. At last she sailed back to the island and had the great satisfaction of seeing her stepmother's body floating by the shore. Then indeed, she exulted, and ordered Thérèse to prepare what she called her *'rejouissance'*. The best wine was brought up from the cellars and the best preserves, a pullet was killed in honour of the occasion. In fulfilment of a long-cherished desire she put on her stepmother's grandest dress and every scrap of jewellery she could find in the safe. Thérèse, in her best cap and apron, waited on her new mistress and was permitted a glass of champagne. She was told what fine things Mary would do. She would travel back to England in glorious state, she would be a great heiress, she would have a palace, a yacht, and prodigious finery. She would marry some great nobleman. Thérèse must drink with her. 'To a glorious future, and let the dead bury their dead!' And then the front doorbell began to ring.

It had not been used for many years, it was utterly inexplicable. Then someone was pounding on it. They heard the hinges shriek. Then, very slowly, step by step, someone was coming up the stairs.

No wonder those poor girls were frightened.

I, the banal reality, was of course a relief. But the shock had been terrible and Mary was, it seems, literally frightened out of her senses. New suspicions entered her poor, crazed head. I was too curious. I had seen her wearing all those jewels and must guess at the truth. I was much too friendly with Thérèse and Thérèse was much too talkative. She even fancied that I had been sent by her stepmother, a messenger from the unburied dead who would again cheat her of her rights.

She was stronger and more determined than Thérèse. When one morning she tied the poor girl to her bed it was no surprise, this had happened before. But when she said, 'I am taking your pretty friend to Gull Island,' Thérèse knew exactly what she meant and believed that she herself would be the next victim.

And all that time I was waiting patiently by the skiff.

The relief of having escaped from that tyranny, of being loved and valued, of enjoying the animal pleasures of affection, made her enormously happy. But the human conscience is a strange thing. Thérèse had been strictly brought up, she knew what happened to girls who 'fell'. Why she should suddenly have realised that she was living a life of sin while she was gathering lettuces in the greenhouse I cannot say. But she did and the results were appalling. She dropped the lettuces, broke two eggs and declared that she was damned to all eternity; then she burst into floods of tears which neither she nor I could check.

All that day she was in tears and would listen to no argument. It was not simply that she was damned, she was also disgraced and dishonoured. Even, and this seemed to affect her greatly, even if she had remained chaste, the mere fact that she had been living alone with a man, and would for months continue to do so, would be enough permanently to sully her good name. Her case was indeed lamentable.

She had, in fact, three reasons for being distressed. She had lost her virginity. She might be got with child. She was hopelessly and inevitably compromised.

I tried to meet her difficulties. A forceful agnostic of seventeen, vice-president of the school debating society and a follower of Huxley had, you may be sure, no trouble at all in proving by the most perfectly logical arguments that the doctrine of eternal damnation was a monstrous absurdity. Much to my astonishment I found that my reasoning had no effect whatsoever. It was met with the simple reply: 'I know that I have sinned. I know that I shall be punished.'

Her second trouble I disposed of with a confidence which today amazes me. Just as I had told my cousin that I could sail a boat, so I told Thérèse that I could terminate a pregnancy. My brother was a doctor, he had told me all about it, it was perfectly simple and she had nothing to worry about. Heaven knows what would have happened if my boasting had been put to the test. This assertion she accepted without hesitation. She was quite sure that I was a wonderful gynaecologist.

Her third trouble was the most intractable. I suppose that the reader will already have guessed at my solution and may well smile at my attempt to justify my conduct. Nevertheless, let me enter a plea on my own behalf.

A normal man might probably have met the girl's fear for her reputation by saying 'Thérèse, I will marry you.' And he might or he might not have kept his word. I am not a particularly moral person – in fact, most people would call me a criminal – but I did hesitate before making an offer of marriage with 'mental reservations'. For the reservations were inevitable.

In the first place, what had I to offer a wife? Love? No, not if you mean that all-consuming passion which makes lovers defy the very Fates. Loving kindness, congenial tenderness, extreme good humour on both sides, that we both had and that might have been sufficient for quite a good marriage if the circumstances had been propitious. But were they? What had I to offer in material terms? At the very best a steerage ticket to Melbourne, a job in a bank beginning at the bottom, a dishonoured name. Was I likely to rise in the world of finance? No. Was Thérèse likely to be happy under such circumstances? I did not know.

But that was the best imaginable situation. I could imagine others only too easily. Sir Amos had concluded his homily thus: 'I want my daughter, that's what matters. I don't want to be bothered with her stepmother. Get my daughter and there's a job waiting for you. Fail, and I don't want to see you again.'

Well, he wouldn't be worried by Lady Porthow again, but I could claim no credit for that, and as for the rest! 'I'm sorry Sir, I couldn't bring back your daughter. The fact is she's dead. No, I didn't actually kill her, you see she was insane.' I felt that the interview with Sir Amos might not be very easy and I did not think that it would lead to a job in Melbourne. What then? I was penniless. I had no qualifications, no influence, no reputation. I should starve or live on charity. And my wife?

But there was a much grimmer possibility. Supposing, when the ice broke, Captain McDee, or someone like him, were to be sent to Creek. Imagine his report.

'I found that of the seven people whom I expected to take on board, five were dead. Three menservants, who it was said died in an accident. Lady Porthow, supposedly killed by her stepdaughter. Miss Porthow, killed under very strange circumstances which involved Mr Brandon. Mr Brandon is well known to the police, he is a man of vicious character; he has seduced Miss Porthow's personal maid and she will say nothing, but the circumstances suggest foul play. Mr Brandon will be sent to St John's in irons.'

'You are permanently dishonoured. There can be no end to your disgrace.' That I had heard many times, and now I had failed in my mission. My cousin's death was the crowning disaster of my short, unlucky life and no one would sympathise with me. In the race for survival I was a non-starter.

From the beginning of my trouble it had been clear to everyone, nearly everyone, that the best thing, perhaps the only thing that I could do was to disappear. Everyone would be relieved, it would suit my family perfectly. It would suit me also. Already I had begun to meditate disappearance. If only I could save enough in Melbourne I might start somewhere new and with a new name. I had welcomed the solitude of Creek because that too enabled me temporarily to disappear. I had not thought of it as a place where one might disappear altogether. I now saw that I had been wrong. The greater part of the population had vanished and only two people knew how they had gone. Might I not arrange matters, seeing that I myself was so very much *de trop*, so that one of them would go on my behalf?

There was one person exactly suited to this office. When the summer came Sir Amos would expect to see a daughter, by which he meant not an actual person, but an abstraction. Of any real flesh-and-blood daughter he knew nothing; the child whom he wanted had been taken away when she was three years old to a place where she was invisible and inaudible; he had not so much as a photograph, Lady Porthow had seen to that. The specifications for this child were therefore extremely vague. A young person about eighteen years old, one who, probably, would look like a Brandon. I have described myself; all that was needed was to change trousers for petticoats, and I knew how that was done . . . *Ecce virgo*.

Henry Brandon would have sunk to a watery grave (hurrah). Sir Amos would have the daughter whom he desired (hooray). Thérèse would have been living in a state of exemplary, indeed of enforced chastity. It was only necessary that, at an appropriate moment, Mary too should disappear – but not before she had comforted the declining years of an old man who loved the idea of her. It seemed the perfect solution.

Still, I have some kind of a conscience. My plan was ingenious, but it was not honest. I did not know what Sir Amos would do with his money but I was pretty sure that his daughter would be much better provided for than his nephew. It was theft, theft from the dead, but still theft. Also, what had become of that new and normal life? I discovered, not without shame and dismay, that the old Adam, say rather the old Eve was still very much alive in me. Finally, and this was the blackest thing, Thérèse would become my accomplice; it was a mean evasion of my duty to her.

Let this much be said to my credit. I did propose.

My wooing, I admit, was neither eloquent nor passionate. I told her my whole story, I described my fears for the future. I did not mention my alternative plan.

She listened very quietly and attentively and at the end she said that I was the kindest person imaginable. She doubted whether she would be a good person to marry, I should be marrying out of pity and that did not seem to her a good beginning. Let us wait until we knew each other better. Let no one be bound by anything that had been said. If I still wanted to do so I might propose again in six months' time.

I replied that this was a very intelligent and kindly answer. The difficulty was that I had another plan which, if we adopted it, would have to be set on foot at once. If she had any doubts about this plan we would dismiss it and forget about it. I proceeded to unfold my criminal design. It took me some time to make it perfectly clear to Thérèse and to explain why a substitution of this kind was easier in these circumstances and at Liberty Sound than anywhere else in the world.

Her reaction took me by surprise. 'You would do this for me?

Masquerade as a woman simply in order to protect me from scandal? It is the noblest thing I ever heard of.'

> Sardana, flower of chivalry,
> Who conquered Crete with horn and cry
> For this was fain a maid to be
> And learn with girls the thread to ply.*

I suppose she did not actually quote Villon at me, although memory insists that she did. At all events that was about the size of it. She could see nothing but gallantry and advantage in my suggestion. It pleased her enormously.

'But you must understand, Thérèse, that it would be dishonest, it would be a matter of getting money under false pretences. I am the penniless nephew of a rich man. I have no rights, no prospects. If I were to impersonate Mary I should, for a time at all events, be a wealthy heiress with enormous prospects. There's no way round it – it's theft.'

'Pooh! It's not stealing, it's commerce. Sir Amos wants a daughter; he is already in your debt, for it is owing to you that he won't get the horror that he might have got. If he has no daughter he will despair. But you can save him, you can make his old age happy. I dare say you will find it hard work – almost impossibly hard unless you bring me along as your lady's-maid – but between us we can give him happiness. And who will be hurt by it? Your relations? What do you owe them? You, who have risked so much, done so much for Sir Amos, are to get absolutely nothing and all for a schoolboy frolic? It is quite unfair and you have every right to take something for yourself.'

Such were the arguments of Thérèse. I ought to have resisted them no doubt but, not for the last time, she conquered me by sheer persistent, good-humoured obstinacy. From the first she was all in favour of the resuscitation of Mary Porthow. She was not in the least shocked by my

---

* H.B. quotes the original; Swinburne's translation seems adequate and more comprehensible. Mlle Boileau has no recollection of hearing either version. – M.E.

unmanly adventures or my felonious plans. When I admitted that I had already formed a notion of impersonating the late Mary before proposing to her, Thérèse, she laughed in my face and said I was a goose to suggest that we should go out and 'do sums in the Antipodes amongst the rattlesnakes and the cannibals' when all the time I had a plan up my sleeve whereby we might live in the lap of luxury.

Two of the great difficulties which kept us in separate bedrooms were thus disposed of. There would, she believed, be no child and no scandal. For the rest we would live together as brother and sister, or rather, as sisters – for it seemed best that I should learn at once to play a convincing role. We would be chaste if not virtuous.

But, having gone so far, Thérèse began to look at her religious convictions in a new light. Unquestionably they were a bore, they spoiled such a very charming situation. Theoretically, she knew that she was damned, all she could do now was to remain as chaste as the circumstances would permit. But somehow the circumstances seemed to change. We lived in a bustle of tape measures and laughter. My memories of that time are dominated by a great evil-smelling vat in the boiler room. Into this, various articles of clothing which had once belonged to my cousin were thrust in the hope that they would emerge black – after all, I was supposed to be in mourning for a stepmother and a cousin. The patent dye failed to behave properly; the things emerged sometimes purple and sometimes a horrid green. I don't know why we should have thought this funny but we did. Everything about my metamorphosis kept us both in fits of laughter.

At more serious moments she still exclaimed at my wonderful generosity, in fact for several days she could hardly stop talking about it, how noble I was and she, how fortunate!

Then, somehow her good fortune seemed less apparent. Was it quite natural that we should both behave so well? When all was said and done, this conscientious chastity was a little absurd.

Dearest Thérèse, you were not made for chastity but for love. I robbed you of your virginity and of your faith, but at heart you wanted neither. Indeed, when you did lose your faith you turned against those who had 'told wicked lies' with too much violence. For some religion can be a consolation and can give meaning to the universe. You never worried about the universe, and when you needed consolation found it elsewhere.

THE CHANGELING: CHAPTER III

'A Garden of Eden just made for two with nothing to mar our joy.'

Commonplace words set to a bum-umpty-umpty sort of tune. In the hard winter of 1916/17 the soldiers stationed at Whitecross used to sing them as they came back from the Golden Ram across the park. The sound of their voices never failed to bring tears to my eyes. It was partly because the singers were so young and so far from any Eden, partly because so many of those cheerful voices would soon be silent for ever, but partly because I too have lived in Arcadia.

It was, to be sure, a rummy part of that province. Creek, on the face of it, was anything but arcadian – and what shall we say of a swain who spends his nights trying to play the man while by day he plays the woman? Yes, it was an odd business, but for the most part a very happy one. We had just enough to do to keep us occupied. We had a number of luxuries: good wine, good beds and, where food was preservable, it was of the best. We kept ourselves snug and looked out from our well-heated rooms at the desolate landscape. We made love, we made plans.

There were times when I felt panic. Could I possibly face and deceive Sir Amos and the rest? Everything would depend upon Sir Amos. If he were content and deceived then I might persuade him to let me study science at Imperial College. I could equip myself for a new life, perhaps with Thérèse at my side; I saw that I should have to depend heavily upon Thérèse. What I had at all events to resist was the idea of some kind of seminary – that would mean certain exposure.

Meanwhile, I had to train myself for a life of deception, and here a great many things were in my favour. Everyone would want to believe that Henry Brandon was dead, everyone save my brother, who would have in some manner to be told and put on his guard. No one now alive had ever seen the real Mary Porthow, or only when she was a baby. I had half a year in which to prepare myself for the task of deception. The fashions of that age were a help. They concealed the person completely. All that a spectator usually saw of a woman was her face, her hands and her feet. All the rest was muffled, engineered and reconstructed. A woman was enclosed within a carapace which, although it certainly proclaimed her sex in a most emphatic way, afforded no detailed information. I had only to hide within my shell. Nor with Thérèse to help me did I doubt my own ability to do so. Actually I overrated her abilities: I was a much less convincing lady than I at first supposed – but I did not know that until much later.

There were other tasks, a few of which may be mentioned. I had to develop a new handwriting, based upon the journals and letters in my cousin's writing-desk. I also went to the trouble of learning a new language which I called 'Maryanese', the language which one would expect of a person who usually spoke French and had borrowed some rather odd expressions from the servants. I learnt by heart and made Thérèse learn by heart an account of what we decided had happened when the boating party sank, and I used to cross-question Thérèse about it. All this was useful and made us glad that we had time to become perfect in our parts, not simply because it gave us confidence to face what might be a nerve-racking enterprise but also, it must be admitted, because it kept us occupied.

By an odd, and for me, a lucky chance, the library at Creek was well stocked with French and English books, most of them splendidly bound with uncut pages. I discovered Flaubert and Chateaubriand, also Humboldt and White of Selborne. Thérèse was not interested in printed matter and she became, in a way, jealous of those books. I for my part, although always amused by her conversation and always enchanted by her loveliness, was, all the same, in need of tougher intellectual exercise than she could provide. Sometimes it was hard to explain why I preferred the company of my books.

It was therefore with very mixed feelings that we awaited the boat that would take us away from Creek and, as we well understood, would present us with we knew not what dangers. We couldn't tell when it would arrive, that would depend on the weather. We spent a great deal of time making preparations and many hours on the battlements scanning the Sound.

Actually we did not see the *Brunswick* until we had heard her. She crept up through dense early morning mists bellowing like a stricken cow. We didn't know how to operate the steam fog-horn which should have answered her cries. At last the sun burst through the mist and we saw a large and very elegant steam yacht, immaculate in white and blue, gliding majestically towards the jetty.

They realised that something odd had happened: none of the usual servants was there, just two female figures, one in what was supposed to be mourning. 'Captain Arthurs,' whispered Thérèse. She thought the Captain a fool and easily bamboozled. It was Thérèse who with unexpected skill caught the line that they threw us. Within a few minutes a tall, shrewd-looking man was greeting me.

'Miss Porthow, I presume' (the phrase had only just achieved notoriety). The conversation which followed was momentous; it shaped the course of my life but I cannot recall it exactly, for one thing my part was in Maryanese.

I told my first lie: I accepted the Captain's presumption. But of course my whole aspect was a lie. He proceeded, stately, a little florid, as men are who are not used to speaking to women. He trusted that nothing was wrong. He had expected to see our servants at the jetty.

I told him that they were all dead.

He made distressed noises and asked after Lady Porthow.

I told him that she also was dead.

And Mr Henry Brandon?

Yes, he too was dead.

Seeking a more cheerful topic I asked after Sir Amos.

He replied, a little too abruptly, for he had been thrown by this catalogue of mortality, that Sir Amos was dead.

At this point I was seized by a horrible fit of the giggles. I bent my head and bit savagely into a black-bordered handkerchief. My shoulders must have been shaking with indecorous mirth. I felt a hand laid gently upon them and then timidly withdrawn. I realised that my emotion must have been honourably construed – indeed, there were tears in my eyes as I raised my head again.

I invited the Captain into the Castle. The little journey gave time for hurried reflections. Sir Amos was an old man and I should not have been utterly astonished by his death, but I was. I had thought of Sir Amos as being immortal. Now everything was changed. My first sentiment was one of relief: I should not have to meet him. On the other hand – it was all so bewildering – he would no longer serve as an excuse for our deception. And then, who was my guardian? Was there a will? We were in the hall; a decanter of sherry had been waiting for the Captain for a long time; there were social duties; the Captain wanted to know what had happened.

I gave him my version.

He listened attentively and then went straight to the weakest part of my story.

'You mean to say that five people packed into that little sailing dinghy? It was madness, sheer madness.'

I was exposed already and stood amazed at my own folly. But one learns to lie very quickly.

'I think that some of the men did raise objections; but my stepmother, when once her mind was made up, did not like to be crossed. She had her way, poor Maman.'

The shot told. Captain Arthurs had suffered enough from Lady Porthow's obstinacy. I fancy he felt a shade of satisfaction that it should in the end have been her undoing.

'Well, I am very glad that she did not persuade you to join this lunatic excursion. So you and your maid have been here all alone?'

'You may imagine how welcome you are, Captain.'

As I said this he fumbled in an inside pocket and drew out two letters. On one of them was written 'Henry Brandon, Esq'.

'Why that's for . . .' I had nearly said it and was indeed reaching for the thing when he cut me short.

'Yes, that is for your unfortunate cousin. It can hardly matter now.' He stuffed the letter back in his pocket. 'The other is for your stepmother and that too can hardly be delivered. The question is, Miss Porthow, what had we best do?'

'My cousin told me that his orders were to take me and Maman to Boston and thereafter we, or at least I, would be sent to England. Unless you have instructions which supersede mine, in which case I would of course obey them, I would suggest that we sail for Boston. We could put into port somewhere where there is a telegraph and let Mr Mellish know what the situation now is and what we intend. I know no one in England but do have some old friends in Boston and would rather stay there for a time as my father planned.'

He considered this and agreed. We agreed also that Creek Castle should be shut up and a few valuable things removed.

This was a great gain for I was afraid of returning to Aunt Martha and Mr Mellish. But I hardly had leisure to consider the matter for, while all this was being discussed and in a most amicable way settled, and while Captain Arthurs was quite evidently enjoying the prospect of never having to meet Lady Porthow again, I myself was the centre of a fierce debate, the outcome of which was still in doubt.

Twice during the past ten minutes I had come within an ace of giving myself away. My version of the accident was, as I now saw, improbable. I had diverted rather than removed his suspicions. It was his blindness which alone had preserved me from detection on the second occasion. Was it sensible, and with Sir Amos out of the way, was it right to continue in this perilous course of deception? Might it not be better to make a clean breast of it all, tell the Captain everything, ask him, perhaps, to marry me to Thérèse?

'Look, Captain Arthurs, as you may have guessed, I am an impost-er.'

These words were on the tip of my tongue. All I needed was a proper opening, some way of putting so fantastic a confession into words when Captain Arthur observed, 'One thing is fortunate in all this tale of disaster; I am glad, although it may not be right to say it, that you did not have to endure the winter with Henry Brandon for company. The fellow was, I am sorry to have to say it, a blackguard. The extraordin-ary thing is that your father left him quite a large fortune.'

I suppose that there are people who, after hearing that said, would have had the nerve to reply, 'As a matter of fact I am Henry Brandon. And, now that I know that he is well provided for, I don't mind admitting the fact.' I am not one of them.

But it was not that which silenced me. It was clear that Captain Arthurs rather liked Mary Porthow or rather, what he took to be Mary Porthow; unfortunately, it was equally clear that he detested the idea of Henry Brandon, and the absurdity of the situation was whereas he would listen sympathetically to anything that Mary might say, all that sympathy would vanish if he were to hear the truth. I should have made myself hateful. I must admit that the difficulties were too great for me, my resolve to be honest was blown like chaff before the wind. Taking relief in a kind of muddled indignation I began to defend Henry Brandon.

'Of course, you are a man of the world and I am only an ignorant girl. I don't know what Henry Brandon may have done during his short life, but he was only a boy when he died and he seemed to me a nice boy. Also, it surely says something for him that my father should have remembered him in his will.'

Captain Arthurs was a man who could not or, at all events, did not conceal his feelings. I had read his feelings about Lady Porthow, seen his genuine compassion when he thought me overcome by my father's death; now I saw in his face, first anger, then perplexity, then shame.

'Miss Porthow, I apologise. It was a stupid thing to say. Will you forgive me for having said it?'

I liked him very much then and gave him my hand. The gesture moved him to a further confession. 'Miss Porthow, I have to say something; it's rather embarrassing, but it must be said.'

My God, what now, I thought.

'The fact is that I hardly thought to be so kindly received by you; I did make a mess of things last summer. Can you forgive me for having sailed away without even seeing you?'

I had quite forgotten that Mary Porthow had a legitimate grievance against Captain Arthurs. Surely she could afford to be magnanimous.

'Captain, that's all ancient history and I know very well that you had an impossibly difficult task. Let us both forget all about it.' He took my hand again, with it a smile, and we were firm friends.

But thereafter it was clear that Miss Porthow must survive, at least until she got to Boston.

And now it was all plain sailing. I liked Captain Arthurs and he liked what he supposed to be me. His illusion brought happiness to everyone. I soon perceived that if there were anything dubious about my evidence it was ascribed to feminine ineptitude. He would report the matter to the proper authorities, everything would be all right and I was not to bother my head – I am not sure that he didn't say 'my little head' – about it. Having cleared those dangerous reefs and breasted the open sea I found that the most fearful of interviews was becoming the most charming and the most innocent of flirtations.

For him it was an unlooked-for delight. He had been nerving himself for dreadful interviews with the horrible Lady Porthow and her insufferable nephew, ending perhaps with another humiliating setback. Instead he was welcomed with every kindness and, while Thérèse dallied with the first mate, he made himself instructive, gallant and amusing at my side.

Everything was settled expeditiously, the Captain was anxious to get out of the Sound while the glass stood high. The cases of valuables were taken on board, the doors were nailed up and the last of the Rhode Island reds went to the galley. We left early on a summer's morning: nevertheless, ship's officers were at hand with parasols lest the morning sun prove too fierce. We were suffered to carry nothing heavier than a handkerchief and wherever our path was interrupted by the slightest asperity, gallant arms were at our service. Within a few minutes of daybreak Captain Arthurs was escorting us to our rather overdecorated staterooms and apologising for the imagined inconvenience of his ship.

I could not but reflect that I had arrived at Creek in a different fashion.

THE CHANGELING: CHAPTER IV

When we came to Boston it did not play an important part in our plans; it was to be a staging post. We would go there because we had a good excuse for going there and did not want to go to England – even with Sir Amos in his grave that was still my feeling. Also, Boston was the gateway to America, the ideal place to start a new life. With this in view I had written to Mr Mellish, posting my letter from Halifax, Nova Scotia, and asking permission to stay with my American friends; at the same time I dropped one very gross word which, I calculated, would make my presence in England an embarrassment. In this I was correct, but in fact I overreached myself.

Boston, then, was to be a jumping-off place and no more. But in deciding this I had reckoned without the Pullman family. We did not know America and we did not know the Pullmans. They were typically American in their attitude towards strangers. Their only vexation was that they had neither time nor means to enlarge their little house into a palace worthy of such guests. Everything that they could do for us they did and the reception committee, Mr and Mrs Pullman, Mr Alexander

Pullman and Miss Pullman — as handsome a collection of people as ever was seen — fell upon us with flowers, kisses, gifts and really thoughtful goodness which left me deeply ashamed of the equivocal nature of the role that I played.

I was not only ashamed but a little unnerved by the extent of their kindness. Mrs Pullman, benevolent, generous, enthusiastic and emotional, was at first almost too much for me. She implored me to look upon her as a second (or maybe a third) mother. She assumed that I was half-dead and half-starved; she thought that I needed to be 'built up', that I required absolute rest and medication. I have never known an odder mixture of real unaffected kindness and amiable absurdity. Mr Pullman, quieter in his manner, more truly thoughtful in his generosity, had much more common sense and was a far more interesting companion; there was an immediate sympathy between us.

Cecily Gordon once said that although he was a strikingly handsome man, he lacked 'distinction'. Certainly he lacked polish. Sitting in front of his house reading an evening newspaper, smoking a vile cigar and sipping root beer, Sandy Pullman, despite his noble features, was hardly elegant. He sat in his shirt sleeves with a disreputable-looking hat pulled low over his eyes, his much-patched trousers were supported by handsome suspenders (*anglice* braces) on which the stars and stripes were violently reproduced in Berlin wool. No, he was not elegant, but to me he was infinitely reassuring. It could hardly be said that he kept good order in his house, rather it was a home of good disorder, of worn, shabby comfort, of good feeling and goodwill where every kind of unpretentious hospitality was taken for granted. His son, his daughter and their numerous friends burst in or burst out again at all hours. It was Liberty Hall.

Mr Pullman kept me intellectually on my toes, but my emotional comfort, if comfort be the word, derived from another source, his daughter Kate.

At the age of nineteen I had an unbounded admiration for women. To my mind they were the best things in the world and in every important way superior to men. I even went so far, in my own private speculations, as to justify this feeling by an appeal to the biological sciences. They show us, I thought, that the only purpose of a species is to undertake the eminently feminine business of perpetuating itself. There are insects which, after a long preparation as larvae and pupae, live only for an hour, and in that hour lay their eggs. Here both sexes accomplish their work and die. But amongst the *arachnida* there are some in which the female devours the male; after he has ceased to be useful as a mate he serves as food for the offspring. Perhaps rather too economical an arrangement, but our own species has run madly to the opposite extreme: with us the perpetuator of life has been entirely eclipsed by her assistant and that assistant is actually allowed to thwart her in her task by the invention of celibacy and war. If some day, spermatozoa could be bottled and the whole clumsy business of preserving mischievous mankind for the sake of his one useful activity could be avoided, the world would no doubt be a duller place; but if the opposite arrangement were adopted and the world were divided between men and incubators, it would be intolerable. The fact that the arts, though practised by men, are so largely devoted to the celebration of women, while our ideal conceptions are commonly given a feminine personality, involves a tacit admission that women are not merely the sexual and maternal cynosure of mankind, but, although we may not consciously admit it, the representative of human life in its highest form of development. Our admiration of women is not simply erotic, it is an expression of our belief in the capabilities of the species.

As will be seen, my notions were not very clearly formulated and they depended upon a belief that all women are young and beautiful – an hypothesis which I have since found necessary to modify. But at that age it may almost be said that I based my opinions on observations. Bessy, our maid of all work, was no Cleopatra, but I wrote sonnets to her ankles; Mrs Borton, who exercised her dog before our window, was really quite plain, but I believed her to be formed like a goddess – in fact, she wore a very large bustle. I needed but the merest hint to suggest an enchanting reality: the momentary tension of a blouse, the caprice of a windblown petticoat, the escape of a mutinous lock, all these were favours granted by Aphrodite herself to the devout. Of real beauty I had no more than a few breathless glimpses until Thérèse gave me a first heady taste of what it could be – that was sufficient to leave me inebriated for six months. But Kate Pullman! Oh my.

She was the most beautiful thing I had ever seen. Her mother thought that she was in every way perfect, and I was inclined to agree, for at that time I thought that personal beauty must be accompanied by every other excellence. I suppose that a real 'connoisseur of the sex' might have called her beauty obvious: her eyes were almost too big, her neck too long, her waist ridiculous, her legs endless; she belonged altogether to the sixteenth century, to, shall we say, Parmigiannino? Or again, Bronzino might have formed her. There were times, looking at her, when I actually became dizzy with admiration.

And how the dear girl rewarded my wickedness. At our first meeting this heavenly creature took me in her arms, kissed me on the mouth and welcomed me as a long-lost sister. All the family loyally accepted the late Lady Porthow's account of what had happened in Mentone – the poor lady had been the victim of a wicked plot. Kate was the most enthusiastic in her sympathetic credulity. She almost believed that Thérèse and I had been chained back to back in an igloo, with nothing to sustain our spirits save pemmican and raw fish. Or, at least, if the facts had been a little different still I was a poor darling girl who had never spent a cent in a bonnet shop, had never enjoyed a ride in a street-car and, worse than all, had never stood up to dance with a gentleman. We were most profoundly to be pitied, most affectionately to be welcomed and most generously to be entertained. Kate would give me – oh my, anything on earth – the whole city of Boston, the entire heart of Kate Pullman. Nor, in sober truth, did there seem to be any limits to the good creature's open-handedness. If she could not give, at least she would show me the whole of her native city; we could leave no bonnet shop unvisited, no street-car unridden, no gentleman unintroduced. She regretted only that at that time of the year Boston had so few social delights to offer. All the same, she who ruled it could open the door of her parents' house and make me a present of those dear people, who indeed were only too glad to be given. As a final treat she took me up to her little bedroom to admire her finery and to hear – not, I am sorry to say, without severely repressed mirth – the extent of her information concerning the begetting of children.

One might laugh at some of the manifestations of Kate's generosity but not at the sentiment by which it was informed. That was a matter for serious joy and deep gratitude. Thérèse, partly because she was ill at ease with the language, partly because, for her, feminine beauty was not in itself an unending source of delight, managed after the first outbursts of welcoming friendliness softly and politely to withdraw. She, who had been taken from a not very happy home when she was still a girl, and who had indeed suffered grievously at Creek, was in truth a much more deserving subject. But she was content politely to waive her rights, preferring in her quiet feline way to curl up in a sunny place, take stock of her surroundings and maintain a tactful silence concerning the past. From her vantage point she might delicately stretch out a velvet paw towards anything which looked interesting – as for instance, Mr Pullman, Jr. It was I, the fraud, the totally undeserving humbug, who was rewarded. But then it was I who needed sympathy and guidance, someone to shore up the rickety façade that I had built, someone to be kind and helpful, to guide me and protect me. And there stood Kate with open arms.

Whenever I meet them – and they seem common enough in a certain type of mural decoration – those bare-bosomed nymphs sailing through the empyrean and dispensing goodies from a cornucopia remind me of Kate. Kate as I knew her in Boston. She was a natural donor, she loved giving and she gave me everything – except, of course, the one thing for which most men would have longed. For me (although of course I had other resources) her beauty, her good temper, good spirits and enthusiastic energy were enough. She was in no way a rival of Thérèse and Thérèse knew it. They got on well enough.

For me it was all delight. I was pleased with the Pullmans, with America and I suppose I must add with myself. It seemed unbelievable that I should fall so deep in clover. It hardly occurred to me that this was Capua, the place where resolution falters.

But now events were to complicate, though not altogether to dispel, my lethargy.

I had intended to repay a little of the kindness of the Pullman family by taking Mrs Pullman, together with her children to Saratoga Springs. It was a place which Kate longed to visit, a kind of social Compostela. In the end, she and Thérèse and I were the only pilgrims. There was no blessing on our journey. Kate discovered that, even in democratic America, you can come a cropper if you try to leap social barriers, while I found that I was profaning the shrine by wearing the wrong clothes, saying and doing the wrong things. I found myself sailing, like some impudent sloop, into an entire flotilla of stately old vessels and had to undergo an indignant broadside. In the end we slunk away in disgrace. Poor Kate was very sad and would have been quite miserable if some local rag had not reported our visit. The journalist raised me to the ranks of the peerage:

EARL'S DAUGHTER HELD CAPTIVE ON DESERT ISLAND
SENSATIONAL STORY OF SARATOGA VISITOR

This, for Kate, was a substantial consolation. All the world had now been told that she had been taking a holiday with a member of the British aristocracy. Being at Saratoga might not be such fun, but having been there was an achievement, better still to have it in print.

For her, I was glad. But in truth I was more profoundly depressed by this than by anything. Publicity was exactly what I did not want, for if it ever came out that Kate Pullman had spent the best part of a week in a hotel with a young man it would go hard with her. The girls of America, I had learnt, were very free in their behaviour; but there were limits, very precise limits, to what they could or could not do, and this was particularly true in the very religious community to which Kate belonged.

Unless I were to remain permanently in a false position I had soon to vanish. If I were to vanish, enquiries would be made and very likely the truth would emerge. There would be a scandal and one of the victims would be Kate. I had to try and devise some plan by means of which Thérèse and I could slip away and at the same time create no public suspicion. Nor did I feel that I could leave the Pullmans without some kind of explanation. It was not easy.

And then, when we were back in Boston I found that which made it particularly desirable that we should escape without delay.

THE CHANGELING: CHAPTER V

At my hotel I found a bulky and much-delayed package from England. It came from Mr Robert Mellish. He enclosed a copy of Sir Amos's will.

I found that I was an heiress and that a really enormous fortune would, eventually, be mine. For the time being I was penniless. I had nothing save the money and gems left me by Lady Porthow (that will was valid). Everything else, both capital and interest, lay in the hands of Mr Mellish, my legal guardian. He told me that he would make me a generous allowance.

My guardian attempted to explain the will, but it was not easy to understand. Sir Amos had wanted to give his daughter nearly everything that he had. But, if she were free to take it, he feared that she might be too much influenced by her stepmother. So there was a wilderness of amendments and codicils, which, giving with one hand, took back with another. I was to have nothing until I came of age, and even then under certain circumstances my capital might be withheld. It was a monkey puzzle of a will and I never fully understood all its provisions and contingency clauses.

Clearly Sir Amos wanted to die at peace with his relations. All the children of the late Sir Reginald except for me and Uncle Hector were made very comfortable. Then at the last moment Uncle Hector and I were given exactly as much as the others. It was maddening that I couldn't simply take my portion and leave all the rest to – I know not whom.

Mr Mellish wanted to know whether Mr Henry Brandon had left a will. He wanted to know about the servants at Creek and various other things. It seemed that my 'death' would make my brother William richer than his cousins, which was satisfactory.

But of much greater immediate importance were the instructions which Mr Mellish sent me. I was to remain at Boston. I was never again to use the word 'sod' when writing to anyone. Then a long homily. He had made enquiries concerning the Pullman family; they seemed respectable but, after mature consideration and in view of the fact that my wealth would inevitably place me in an important social position etc., something more than the tuition of the Pullmans would be essential. A Mrs Gordon, a widowed lady who had moved in the best society, would arrive with the least possible delay in Boston. She was invested with full authority and must be obeyed without question. If it were necessary, I must accept a form of training such as would not normally be employed in the education of a person of my years; that training would probably have to be continued until I came of age. It was essential that I should cooperate, etc.

So this was the result of my ingenious plan for keeping away from England and my Brandon relations. I had succeeded in shocking old Mellish – but to such purpose that I should now be treated as a child and kept under the control of a governess.

Better to fly at once, better to escape to Arizona or the Yukon than face so daunting a prospect. But that was just what I had decided we could not do. The letter from Mr Mellish had been delayed and Mrs Gorgon, as I mentally called her, might be upon us at any moment. I consulted with Thérèse. What lie could we tell that would convince the Pullmans? How could we prevent Mellish from pursuing us with enquiries? How to avoid suspicion? Nothing seemed possible. Thérèse took the view that we could only await the Gorgon and, having seen what she was like, make further plans.

During the next few days we speculated on Mrs Gordon's probable appearance and character. Tall, thin, flat-chested with *pince-nez* and a shabby umbrella – that was our general notion. Something comic, but potentially formidable.

The reality was rather different. Cecily Gordon was then about thirty, not a great beauty but with great charm and beautifully dressed.. She was intelligent, humorous and socially adroit. Her charm was not a sloppy vague sort of charm – in everything she was deft and deliberate: she moved with grace but also with care, her voice was lovely but always under control, her speech clear and precise, her manner easy and calm, her laughter musical and soft. In thinking of her, as I often do, I always come back to her appearance. I never knew anyone who dressed with more care and less fuss, who managed in so high a degree to be both casual and elegant.

She was, essentially, an amiable person; but she had cultivated the graces for so long and with such assiduity that her kindness, though real, could not be wholly spontaneous. When she came among us at Boston she seemed to know exactly what to say to everyone. In addressing Kate and her parents, who had expected her with some misgivings, she found just those smiles and those words which would best please them. Kate was altogether conquered and saw in her the perfect guide to those social territories which, as we have seen, she had failed to penetrate. The older Pullmans found her quite unlike the haughty Briton whom they had feared, she was so appreciative of their kindness to me, so unpretentious, so easy. And yet for Cecily, who was in fact dismayed by my hosts, it must have been hard to be easy.

On that first evening of her arrival, when all the welcoming business of the day was over, she came to my room and, having asked leave to do so, sat down.

It may sound absurd to say that she sat down beautifully, although veterans like myself will recollect that around the year 1890 it was no simple matter for a lady to be seated; but Cecily knew just how to manage a bustle. She sat with an enviable grace, and I knew at once that she was an expert in the art of behaviour.

'I fancy,' she began, 'that I am not quite the kind of person whom you expected. You also, if you don't mind me saying so, are a bit of a surprise. We are not at all alike, I think; I am sure you are very well read, certainly intelligent, know a lot but are, inevitably inexperienced. I, on the other hand, am ignorant, read nothing – nothing but novels – and am very experienced. We seem made for one another, also, I have come to the conclusion that I am going to like you very much. I do hope you will like me; it will be difficult if you don't.'

'Oh, but I do, Mrs Gordon, I do already although I hardly know you.'

'Whereas I feel that I know you quite well. You haven't always worn skirts I'll be bound. You have been brought up as a tomboy: fishing, sailing, climbing and above all reading, reading books a girl wouldn't be expected to read – be very careful how you quote from books – and, I imagine, hardly thinking of yourself as a young lady, not until quite recently.'

'You are very perceptive, Mrs Gordon.'

'So I am, my dear. Do I perceive in you a desire to talk about your life at Liberty Sound?'

'Well no, Mrs Gordon, please not. I would rather think about the future than the past, for the present at all events. There were things in the past . . .'

'Not if it makes you unhappy, my dear Mary, and obviously it does. Really, you have told me enough. It must be wonderful to be free.'

'It is like a rebirth. It is wonderful indeed.'

'And now here I am all ready to take it away from you once more. It is impossible that you should not feel that, because of course I do represent authority and it may be that I shall have to exert it, that is if we find no other way of teaching you. But my hope is that you will learn in the easiest and the best way, simply by being my friend and taking my advice. I think you are quite clever enough to learn without being subjected to discipline. But – I have to say this at once – if we can't manage it that way then indeed I shall have to become your governess and govern you, and it could be quite disagreeable for both of us. You see, I have a job to do and you must learn.'

'And what, Mrs Gordon, am I to learn?'

She laughed and blushed a little, although even her blushes seemed to be well under control. 'Well, in the first place – this was the first duty with which I was charged – you must not use certain words, words which would make a well-bred matron go into a swoon.' So saying she drew a paper from her handbag.

'These, my dear Mary, are words which you must never use. I hope you do not know what they mean. There may be others that are not on my list; I shall have to wait and see. It's rather terrible, I am continually wondering what you will say next.'

We both laughed and she continued. 'In fact I don't think we shall have much difficulty with the foul language. If you will imitate me, and if you read or reread Jane Austen, Thackeray, Trollope and George Eliot and imitate their ladies you won't go far wrong. The really important part of my teaching is going to be something rather subtler and much harder.' She paused, 'I was told that I had to make you presentable. I have to tell you that at present you are not presentable.'

'I don't think that I understand.'

'Well, put it like this. Within a few years you will probably want to marry; undoubtedly a great many people will want to marry you. With your looks, your wits and your money you could marry the eldest son of a duke. You may refuse him and marry a dustman, that's your business. What I have to make sure is that you can have the duke's son if you want him. Do you see what I mean? I want to put you in a position in which you can, if you so wish, disregard the world of rank and fashion, but in which that world cannot disregard you. I should hate to think of people 'making allowances' for you because of your money.

Your fortune makes it inevitable that you will come into contact with good society; you must be able to play the social game and you should be so well trained that you can tell the good money from the bad. This is an ability on which your whole future happiness may depend. In short, I have to teach you to cope with the world.'

'And is it then so hard?'

'Not when you know how to set about it. But there is a lot to learn, a lot of things which you will probably think futile, stupid, absurd indeed; but the conventions of good manners are not really more absurd than the conventions of grammar. No, it won't be easy, but I'm sure you can do it and you will find it's worth doing.'

'And how am I to begin, Mrs Gordon?'

'Watch me, copy me; I am not a bad model. I play a pretty good game. The Pullmans, admirable people, have taught you the elements of civilised living. I don't think they have very much to teach you now; in fact, from my specialised point of view they are not now good models. Thérèse Boileau will make an excellent lady's-maid, but she is not one yet. Of course at Liberty Sound she must have been a friend rather than a servant.'

'She was a friend indeed, Mrs Gordon.'

'No harm in that. But there is harm when she forgets her place in public. There must, in public, be a certain distance between you. If there is not it may prove an embarrassment, not only to you but to her.'

Cecily was being tactful; she always was. She treated the business of getting educated for the world of rank and fashion as a matter of expediency, because she had already sized me up so accurately that she could see that on any other terms I should find the idea unacceptable. But for her 'the game' was the grand business of life: good manners were an end in themselves and something of supreme importance; the arts and sciences, public affairs, and the pursuit of wealth were useful only in so far as they made 'the game' possible. She had loved, passionately and unwisely, but she could not have fallen in love outside her class. For this great purpose she was ready to accept or to demand heavy sacrifices, but it was a part of her good manners that her aims had, if possible, to be achieved as gently as possible. Thérèse had quietly to be put in her place, the Pullmans had to be cajoled and flattered; initially, at all events, she would impose no discipline to which I could not assent. It was not until much later that I understood how little we really had in common.

Thérèse disliked her at first sight, declaring that she was cold and calculating, a manipulator of other people moved only by a desire to dominate. This was unjust. Cecily could be entirely disinterested. Nevertheless, there was a scintilla of truth in it. From the very first, one of the feelings that she inspired in me was fear, fear that she would find me out, or if not that, that she would become too powerful.

Why then did I worship her?

'Worship' is, I think, the word. We not only love but fear our deities – and for me she was a kind of goddess. But what bound me to her was the fact that she liked me. It may sound like ludicrous mock-modesty, but at that time I was genuinely astonished when anyone liked me. As a boy I had admired many people but, except for my mother and my brother, no one seemed really to like me. That, I suppose, was one reason why I chose not to be a boy. When this superbly efficient, poised and elegant young woman showed by unmistakable signs that she did like me I found it impossible not to love her in return. I suppose I loved Kate upon the same principle, but half her love was given to a myth – she would have been kind to anyone in what she supposed to be my situation.

There was a kind of circular movement. I was conquered immediately by Cecily's charm, her deliberate grace and an air of composed authority which fascinated me. Feeling that I was hers, she made much of me. This further endeared her to me. I was dismayed when I discovered, as I slowly did, just how much she believed in her particular world, but the discovery did not weaken my attachment, although my feelings may in some ways have been changed. We do not cease to love our friends because we find faults in them – the Greeks worshipped

Zeus well knowing what a deplorable character he was. And of course she could make herself extraordinarily pleasant.

As I have said, she charmed the Pullmans. She charmed everyone except Thérèse. Thérèse had accepted my platonic attachment to Kate because she never took Kate very seriously. She took Cecily very seriously indeed, and saw in her a menace. Cecily was powerful, she held the purse-strings, she could dismiss Thérèse. She understood the work of a *femme de chambre* better than Thérèse did and this was galling. She believed me to be infatuated by the newcomer and she was jealous. She stood always on the verge of insolence or even of mutiny. She lost her naturally sweet temper and Cecily only smiled, which was an added vexation.

But it was I who bore the brunt of it. Every night Thérèse came to my bedroom and every night she had some new and usually quite absurd story about '*cette sale anglaise*'. I reasoned with her, laughed at her, explained, palliated, entreated; it merely increased her jealousy and led to further misbehaviour.

In the end the situation became intolerable. It was not only that these evening sessions became nightmarish, but that clearly Thérèse would soon go too far and she would be dismissed.

> Oh what a tangled web we weave
> When first we practise to deceive!

Anne and Jane Taylor? I think so.* At all events, such were my sentiments when, one melancholy evening, I retired to my room to face reality and, having faced it, to write two long letters. I hated it, but I had come to the conclusion that we must leave at once, while there was still time to do so. I should never see Cecily or the Pullmans again.

The problem was how to say goodbye to the Pullmans in such a way that Kate would remain uncompromised and her parents, as far as possible, unhurt by our departure. The truth would, I know, horrify

---

* Scott, actually. – M.E.

them. I had to discover some acceptable falsehood. In the end I thought I had it.

Building upon Lady Porthow's legendary account of her fall from grace, in which the Pullmans still firmly believed, I constructed a myth of my own. Lady Porthow's accusers had turned their attention to me. Their agents had appeared in Boston and were ready with a slanderous account of my stepmother's supposed crimes. My father, whom they had feared, was gone, so too my stepmother – and the dead cannot sue. They had documents, so-called 'proofs', of my stepmother's guilt. I knew no way in which I could defend myself or the others who would be hurt by their calumnies. They threatened and bullied, they demanded money which I did not have. I could see nothing for it but to vanish. I would seek my fortune in the west; Thérèse would come with me and would help. Some day I might perhaps marry an American citizen – I hoped so. I wanted them to be able to say truthfully that they did not know where I was so I would give no hint of my destination. I should never forget their kindness.

It was rather thin, but no thinner than the story which they had already accepted. I could think of nothing better.

A copy of my letter to the Pullmans was attached to another which I asked Cecily to read and pass on to Mr Mellish. In this letter I told the whole truth, concealing nothing. I admitted that my conduct had been very wrong. I was punished, and justly punished, by the loss of a fortune that would have been mine but for my own folly. I was taking the money that was in my hands, but hoped that I might soon be able to return it. Meanwhile, I implored both Cecily and Mr Mellish to leave the Pullmans their illusions.

When Thérèse appeared I showed her the letters. 'On Friday,' I said (it was then Monday), 'Mrs Gordon goes to Cambridge for the day. The Pullmans will also be out. Now, listen carefully. Tomorrow we must go out and buy some clothes for me; we will hide them here. I meanwhile will have sold my jewels so that we'll have enough money. On Friday morning, as soon as Mrs Gordon leaves, I shall dress as a man. We will leave the letters with the clerk downstairs, drive to the station and catch the 11.12 to New York. There we will find a judge and get married. Plenty of time to get the night train to Chicago.'

'Chicago?'

'The city of the future. They plan in four years' time to hold the biggest exhibition the world has ever seen. There must be an opening in one of the big hotels, the big expanding hotels, for a young gentleman with an English accent, good French, some German and Italian. It will give us a start. I can go to night school, train as a scientist, make good and become an American citizen. There now, doesn't that please you?'

'I suppose so.'

'I thought you would be enchanted. We shall never see Mrs Gordon again.'

'Or Europe.'

'Why do you say that?'

'We shall be known as thieves, how can we ever go back? And we shall be poor, very poor.'

'If one can work and has a little capital one can make money in this country.'

'But all that money thrown away.'

'It is not ours, it was not honestly taken. At any rate, it can't be helped.'

'But we have been so happy. Poor Kate will be heartbroken and her parents too. Mr Pullman is a good man and really devoted to you. It seems cruel.'

I liked her for remembering Mr Pullman as well as Kate. But she seemed unable to realise the nature of our predicament.

'Look,' I said, 'we have to face facts. You can never come to terms with Mrs Gordon, never – you have told me that repeatedly. This means that in the end she will lose patience with you. One day I shall be faced with a new *femme de chambre*. Then I am undone, as you well know. Since this must happen it's better to go now at a time of our own choosing. We can't afford to wait while you provoke her continually.'

Thérèse was for a moment speechless, her expression was tragic.

'Ah, now I understand you. You are doing this to punish me.'

'Punish you? My dearest Thérèse, is it then such cruelty to suggest that we might marry?'

For a time there was no conversation, only tears. Finally I did manage to repeat my argument. I was not blaming her. If she hated Mrs Gordon, that was that. It could not be helped. Only she must see that Mrs Gordon was in a position to destroy us – all we could do was to anticipate the blow.

'You said that there is no such thing as inevitability.' (This was an allusion to an entirely different argument.)

'Perhaps I did, but that's not going to help us.'

'Oh, but it is. You say that it is inevitable that I should hate Mrs Gordon and go on provoking her. I say that it is not. You say that it is inevitable that she should dismiss me. I say that it is not.'

'But my dear Thérèse, you yourself have said . . .'

'Of course I have! I say a lot of things that I don't quite mean. But I do mean this: I can make my peace with Mrs G.'

'I find that hard to believe.'

'Oh Henry, surely you know me by now? Yes, of course I have been cross and very foolish and it *was* true that I should always hate her; but it's true no longer.'

'But Thérèse, how?'

'It's easy now. I was jealous; but now I am not. So everything is easy.'

'Dearest Thérèse, where are we getting?'

'We are getting to a point at which I can make you a fair offer. I don't want to run away; later perhaps, if we had a little more money, but not now. Still I will run away, I promise I will, if Mrs G. and I are not good friends within a fortnight.'

'Are you serious?'

'Very serious indeed.'

'You can do it within a fortnight?'

'You shall see if I cannot.'

With this I had to be content, although I was quite sure that it would not work.

And then one morning when I was reading *Nature* in my room after breakfast there came from the adjoining room a sound of what I thought was tears but soon perceived to be laughter. I put down my journal and opened the connecting door. Cecily was sitting on a bed holding a package, Thérèse was standing beside her. They were exhausted by their mirth.

Cecily explained, not without difficulty. Mr Pullman had asked her to find an appropriate birthday present for Kate – Kate's birthday kept us all much occupied at that time – but he had then happened upon what seemed to him the perfect gift. He had sent it to Cecily for her approval, or rather, as his note made clear, that he might be congratulated upon his exquisite taste. It was an enormous brooch, a cheap-looking German imitation of Limoges enamel fashioned to resemble a nightmare butterfly. The unashamed vulgarity of the thing moved me to tears rather than to laughter.

'And poor Mme Gordon will be credited with helping him to choose the thing.'

Both ladies exploded again and Cecily, slipping an arm around the girl's waist exclaimed, 'Hold your tongue Thérèse, you must not add to the horrors of the occasion.'

Thérèse allowed me just half a glance, a glance of triumph. She had worked her miracle.

'But it was the simplest thing in the world,' she explained. 'I went down on my knees and begged her pardon. Of course, I couldn't have done that until I knew that you love me better than you love her; but knowing that, it was easy and it has made me very happy. She demands obedience, as you may find out for yourself one day, but when she has it she is as sweet as honey.'

The miracle not only worked, it endured. Cecily trained Thérèse and made a good servant of her. She did more, she made her proud of being a good servant. In public she treated us both with a new deference. But although in private she remained, as always, a charming, tender and amusing companion, she also became more exigent, anxious that I should do her professional justice, buy the right things, wear the right things and wear them properly. And of course the right things were the things that Cecily approved of. When, as not infrequently happened, I was too lazy or too preoccupied to conform to her ever-rising stand-ards, she was hurt and showed it. In fact, in making her peace with Cecily she had become her ally, so that at times she became an enemy, not of me, but of my comfort.

The immediate result of all this was, of course, that I had to postpone my plans for escape. I had made a bargain and felt that it was necessary to keep it. I was weak no doubt, very weak. I ought to have made no bargains, and when I did return to the idea of course I got the reply, 'Fly? What, now that I am getting on so well with dear Mme G. and she is teaching me so much?'

Then we came to a sort of crisis. It was suggested that we go to Europe. It had originally been suggested and agreed by Mr Mellish that we should remain in Boston until the spring. But Cecily, who was not happy in America, had proposed that we should leave at once. She might have insisted but, characteristically, was unwilling to do so; she canvassed opinion, finding Kate very much in favour while Thérèse, with a reticence which did her credit, secretly longed to see once more those who for all their faults were her parents and whom she had come to believe she might never see again.

This was too natural and poignant a wish to be brushed aside. She believed that her father was dying. How could I deny her the sad privilege of saying goodbye? Nor did she ask this of me, the demand came through Cecily, which made it doubly unanswerable. On the one hand it showed that Thérèse herself was reluctant to press me, on the other I could not reply to Cecily, as I might have to her, that we had already delayed too long and that it would be harder for us in Europe to start a new life.

The next morning I told Cecily that I would gladly come with her to Europe and as soon as she might wish.

THE CHANGELING: CHAPTER VI

'Rome in the autumn can be charming,' said Cecily.

For me, in the autumn of 1889 it was heaven. From the moment when we boarded the train at the Gare de Lyon everything seemed to go right.

In fact, I date this period of happiness from a time a little anterior to our departure for it was in connection with our journey that Cecily said a thing which although it may sound of trifling importance was, for me, joyfully momentous. There had been some question of dates and Cecily, who of course always had her way, made us reject the proposed day in favour of an earlier one. Later, in private, she explained that she had remembered that it was the 'wrong day of the month'; she would like to have her journey over before then, adding, in the most matter of fact way imaginable, 'Do you suffer badly from the curse?'

'Oh, hardly at all,' I answered, and the conversation drifted away in some other direction.

Now this was a happy event because, from the first, I had been afraid that Cecily, seeing so much of me and being so uncommonly sharp, would guess at the truth. I remembered our first conversation and that remark, 'You have not always worn skirts.' It was alarming to consider whither such a train of thought might lead. But when she spoke to me as she did about her menstrual period she did so in a tone of voice which convinced me that, clever as she was, she suspected nothing. The comfort of it was enormous; it was as though I had been in some way exonerated, as though I had been tried and admitted to membership of a sisterhood.

From a strictly moral point of view this happy reassurance was wholly deplorable. Not only did it make me rather smug about my own powers of deception, it helped to still my conscience.

Already, in Paris, the frailty of my moral purpose had become increasingly evident. That visit had had its pleasures but also its difficulties. I had met M. and Mme Boileau who were not dying, but were in truth very unpleasant people mainly anxious to intercept their daughter's wages. Cecily dealt with them very smoothly and efficiently. But my main difficulty lay in the fact that I had to pretend that I had never been in the French capital before, and in trying to explain why I refused to be quite so extravagant a shopper as my companions had expected that I would be. My careful, almost stingy proceedings were ascribed to inexperience with money – actually, they arose from a resolve not to spend more than had been left to Henry Brandon. I think that it was also about this time that I first began to make plans for disposing of the vast superfluity which would come to me when I was of age, or as I should then have put it, which would come into my hands if I were to persist in my present dishonest course of action. It will be seen that I was weakening.

Indeed my whole story up to this point is a story of temptation thrown in my way and, despite repeated half-hearted efforts, never rejected. I had been guilty, not so much of criminal activities as of criminal inactivities. I had let things wait, let things slide, allowed Thérèse to have her way. And the motive behind this culpable infirmity of purpose was of course that I was enjoying myself hugely. It was something, in fact, it was a great deal that I was able so triumphantly to 'carry the thing off' and deceive the whole world. But that private sense of triumph would not have been sufficient to make me adhere to a course of life which was not only dishonest but potentially vicious had it not been for the fact that I was, in spite of everything, outrageously happy.

There was I, then, ensconced in a most comfortable first-class carriage bound for Italy, with companions whom I loved and who seemed to love me. I, who a year before had been as wretched as a rat in a rickyard with cats and dogs and men with sticks all seeking to destroy me and nothing in my favour save my own utter insignificance, was now in the lap of luxury and as near to perfect happiness as any mortal can be.

And yet I was wrong, for the cornucopia of good fortune was not yet empty. When in the early morning the train came down from the Alps into the plain of Lombardy I fell in love, as many others have done, with dear Italy. That passion will never end. The journey was a series of delights, but the best was yet to come: Rome lay before us.*

Cecily used to say that I was in love with Raphael and would even refer to the Divine Urbinate as 'your young man'. I suppose that this was in a sense true – it was a rather one-sided passion.

But let no one think that I was incapable of attracting a living suitor. Fraud though I was, and still clumsy in all the arts of my adopted sex, I did once have a prince at my feet. Yes, and with every circumstance of romance. He proposed in the gardens of a Roman palace. There was moonlight, the scent of flowers, romantic music and although we were half-way through October the air was so balmy that arms and shoulders laid bare by fashion needed but the lightest of coverings. The Prince (admittedly his principality was small) pressed his fine moustache upon my glove, offering his heart, his hand, his princely name, in phrases which were melodious and eloquent, and he was quite young and very handsome indeed.

I might even have been a little astonished had I not been enlightened and forewarned by Thérèse. Ever since our arrival, the Prince had devoted himself to Kate; Kate, who was running around Rome like any Daisy Miller, with a host of young bachelors in tow – all exceedingly pompous, all sartorially preposterous – while Cecily was too busy dallying with the Hon. Freddy Kirkwhelpington to chaperone her guest properly. I was therefore scandalised when, returning unexpectedly to the Albergo Schweitzer one evening, I recognised the Prince of Negroponte as he fled gracefully from my suite – the suite I shared, of course, with Thérèse.

---

* About 1,000 words in praise of Rome and of its art treasures, together with a short essay on Raphael, are here omitted. – M.E.

Thérèse begged my forgiveness, not without tears and protestations. It was amazing that anyone should contrive to be so eloquent while keeping her tongue so visibly within her cheek.

'And what am I to say to Kate?'

'I hope that nothing need be said – Mlle Pullman would not understand.'

'I daresay not. I myself am not inclined to be very understanding.'

'Oh! But it meant nothing. He only came on business.'

'On business?'

'But yes, on very urgent business. The poor gentleman is in distress, he is in a state of dreadful perplexity, or at least he was – torn, he declared, by inward agonies.'

'What *is* all this about?'

'He is in a state of the utmost confusion; his entire future is at stake and now he discovers that he has been walking towards the abyss, guided thither by infamous companions. You see, he has very little money.'

'And what has that to do with his presence here tonight in your bed?'

'But everything! He believes that he has been betrayed, and in my opinion he has.'

'My dear Thérèse, you are driving me lunatic. I have had a very tiring day. Please begin at the beginning.'

'I beg your pardon. Well, yesterday, or rather, since it is now morning, the day before yesterday, you ladies went to "Norma", yes? Well, after you had driven back here, *la bande*, as I call them, strolled through the streets, as they often do, talking. And the one who talked biggest was the Prince; he was praising the beauty, the modesty, the purity of his Catarina. I imagine he was rather boastful, you know what young men are like.'

'Me? I haven't the faintest idea.'

'Well, he was telling everyone what a conquest he has made, he had plucked the fairest flower in the garden – no, he hasn't slept with her –

she was incomparable, wonderful, though in my opinion he and the rest are blind and if only Mlle Porthow would take a little more trouble with her appearance half Rome would be at her pretty feet.'

'God forbid! But go on about the Prince.'

'Well, he praised her beauty, he praised her character, and he was beginning, gently, to praise her fortune seeing himself as a millionaire, when the one whom they call Georges . . .'

'Giorgio Antonelli?'

'I think so. At all events, this Georges began to laugh, in fact everyone began to laugh, all except our poor Prince. He was very unhappy for he was struck by a sudden suspicion that his bella Catarina was not the one with the cash. Also, he remembered that it was Georges who told him, or at all events hinted, that it was Kate who had the money. If so, then Georges has done this to mislead a dangerous rival and secure you for himself.

'All that night he could not sleep. On the morrow he did not know where to apply for information. The people who keep this hotel would know who paid the bills, but they were Swiss and secretive. To ask Mrs Gordon might seem indelicate. So in the end he came to see me.

'Poor young man, he was beside himself. He wept with rage and chagrin. His distress was such that it would have been barbarous not to have offered consolation.'

'I am sure you were most humane, you promiscuous girl. When I think of the lengths I have gone to in order to preserve your good name . . .'

I tried to be stern and unforgiving, but it was no use. The pose of dignified anger is wrecked by laughter. We ended the conversation in merriment and embraces.

This explains why Piero Negroponte suddenly took an interest in art and followed me round the Capitoline for four days before declaring his passion in such a charming manner. But in truth, I did feel sorry for the Prince, and I felt worse for Kate. She had set her cap at that young man, yet I knew – for Cecily had told me – that an Italian of his class must either have money or marry it. Perhaps then, I could provide them with the wealth which they needed so badly?

Although I knew Mellish would never permit the use of Sir Amos's bequest for such a purpose, there remained the money from the jewellery I had inherited from Lady Porthow. But that account was my safety net, always there to give Thérèse and me a new start in life. At the same time, however, I felt so little desire to 'bolt' and things were looking so good, that I approached Cecily with my dowry idea.

At first, she was hesitant, and more inclined to send Kate straight back to Boston. But, rather to my surprise, she very quickly came round, although only on the conditions that Kate should never know and that we four should remove ourselves to Florence, from whence she, and she alone, would conduct negotiations with the Prince and his notary.

Florence, to my mind, has not the charm of Rome; it is a vast museum, but for me, at that stage of my education, an altogether wonderful and exhilarating one. I more or less lived in the churches and galleries, and every day seemed to bring me fresh and more astonishing delights. But not for Kate. Florence was 'a dump'; she was bored by the Uffizi, bored by the Pitti, bored by Michelangelo, bored by everyone and everything. She wanted her Prince.

'I hate you, I hate you, I hate you,' she screamed at me one morning, just as I was leaving for the Medici Chapel.

'What on earth have I done?'

'You're aiming to ruin my life. Oh yes! I know all about it. You're still crazy about Piero and because you can't have him—no, not with all your money — you are deliberately keeping him away from me. It's despicable.'

I told her she was talking nonsense, but she wouldn't have it. She had come to believe in her own fairy-tale. I was a hateful, cold-hearted plotter. I was a good many other things as well, and at one point I was a 'brazen harlot'; the absurdity of this last suggestion convinced me that, if she knew what she meant, she must be almost out of her senses.*

I had obviously underestimated the Prince. If I had been a girl this might not have happened. I had seen him, as I think most men would have seen him, as an amusing, handsome, but rather absurd creature. Now that I was better able to judge his effect upon women, I was obliged to admit that he was indeed a force to be reckoned with.

The spectacle of Kate's misery unmanned me – perhaps that's not the right verb. Anyway, I was deeply shaken, felt deeply responsible for what had happened, and longed to do something to set matters right.

What could I do but offer all my money to buy the Prince? I knew I should never be thanked by anyone, yet, all the same, I could not endure the notion that I was so mean a creature that I had to be paid for acting decently and with gratitude. I went straight out of the hotel, composing a telegram in my head, went to the Post Office and sent it off. I forgot what I said, but in effect I told the Prince how much I had to spend, told him that there could be no more and told him that Kate was miserable without him.

The next thing that happened was that I was nearly run over in the Piazza della Signoria by a cab. Cecily was in the cab and would not have been very sorry if I had been crushed by a wheel. Seriously, she was very cross indeed; I had never seen her come so near to losing her temper. It appeared that I had come out without putting on my gloves or a hat, I was smoking a cigarette and I forget what other sins I may have committed. Not unnaturally her temper was in no way improved when I told her what I had done. Having put her in charge of the negotiation I had gone behind her back and, as she said, had undone all the work that she had been doing for me. I must admit that she had a case but, if she had witnessed Kate's tears, she might have understood me better. As it was, she was frighteningly angry and for a moment almost at a loss what to do.

* Illegible paragraph. It would appear that Kate became violently hysterical and fled the room. – M.E.

However, it did not take her long to reform her plans. My part in them was to be purely negative. Within an incredibly short time I found myself bundled out of the hotel and driven to the railway station with Thérèse in attendance, there to catch the first train for Siena.

'Go away and look at Lorenzetti, you interfering little fool. And go on looking at Lorenzetti until I give you permission to return.'

It was in fact excellent advice. I was very glad to be out of the emotional turmoil of Florence and the Lorenzettis are well worth looking at, particularly Ambrogio; Beccafumi, at that time very little regarded, deserves careful attention and Siena itself is a delightful place. I was, of course, anxious to know what would happen to Kate and I felt that I was in disgrace. When Cecily's brief summons arrived I returned to Florence with very mixed feelings.

Cecily was all smiles when she met us at the railway station. The Prince had accepted my offer; Kate was happy and had gone to stay with her future mother-in-law and she, Cecily, had managed matters very well indeed. There was a brief note for me:

Dear Mary,
Piero and I are engaged. I am very happy. Try not to be jealous.
KATE

THE CHANGELING: CHAPTER VII

That day when I returned from Siena to find that Kate was gone was for many months to be regarded as a *dies nefastus*. Certainly, it marked the end of what had seemed an important friendship and the beginning of a very painful stage in my education.

The new regime came into being that very evening at the time then regarded as most suitable for feminine intimacies, the hour when hair was let down and daytime rigidities were exchanged for 'something loose'. In fact, it was my hair which provided Cecily with a target for her first ranging shot.

'It is a disgrace. How can Thérèse do anything with such a vile doormat? I have the coiffeur tomorrow and he shall come on to you.'

'But Cecily, the Poultons left a note asking me to go with them to Fiesole.'

'Then you must beg to be excused. Fiesole can wait, your hair cannot.'

'But Cecily.'

'No, this is an order. You are not to leave the hotel until your hair is properly dressed. Thérèse, you may leave us. I must have a word in private with Mademoiselle.

Thérèse dropped a frightened curtsey and vanished. Cecily turned on another tack.

'Mary, while you were away I met and talked about you with the Carpis.' (Carpi was something or other in the Pitti and supposed to be an authority on Fra Angelico.) 'I asked them, of course in an oblique way, whether you were to be taken seriously when you talked about Italian painting. They answered that you knew more than the average tourist who comes armed with *Mornings in Florence*, but that it never occurred to them to take you seriously.

'I tell you this, although I dare say that you already know it yourself, because it is relevant to other things that I have to say. The Carpis confirmed what I had already guessed: I have watched people who know what you are talking about, and the sad truth is that either you bore them or they laugh at you. Unless you were a prodigy of learning it could hardly be otherwise. You see, my dear, a girl who shows off her erudition in public must have something else to show with it if she is not to appear tiresome and ridiculous. Conversely, if she be a charmer, she can get away with very little actual knowledge – you, my poor Mary, are not a charmer, and your sins will not be forgiven. You *must* surely realise this. And yet you make no effort to appear to advantage, you dress ridiculously, you behave like a schoolgirl. Your appearance is an insult to whatever company you may be in – and it's no good thinking you can make up for it by talking grandly about art.'

'But after all, I do wear the clothes that you and Thérèse choose for me.'

'What's the use of that when you look as though you have stolen them from the shop and put them on back to front? I wish you could realise what Thérèse suffers when she sees how completely you undo all her work.'

'You are very severe this evening.'

'I have to be. It is high time you faced the facts. Socially you are a disaster. You need not be so utterly hopeless. If you had ever made an effort, if you had ever listened to me or to Thérèse you might by now have made something of yourself. Perhaps even now it's not too late. But you seem so completely unaware of your own faults; you don't realise what a ridiculous figure you cut.'

Then she began to tell me just how dreadful I was and how completely I had failed to learn anything.

Some of her accusations were, I had inwardly to admit, not wholly unjust. I *had* been slack, evasive and slovenly. I *had* taken things too easily, forgotten advice too readily. But some of the things she said were not just, her language was wantonly harsh. Everything was put in a way and with such a superior knowledge of social matters that it was hard for me to defend myself. And it went on and on, an endless procession of misdemeanours, until at length I felt a kind of numbed despair. Was I really so stupid, so childish, so completely unhelpful?

Presently she changed her tone.

'This is of course unpleasant for you, but I have told you again and again of your faults and you take no notice. I have to find some way of bringing them home to you. But have you any idea how unpleasant it has been for me? I had thought that it would be easy but you have made it impossible. You have not made the slightest effort and now I have to report complete failure. You remember that at our first interview I said that I would try to educate you without being dictatorial, but I added that if that did not work I should be obliged to govern you as a governess. You have forced me to that alternative. You leave me no choice for only thus can I do the job for which I was hired.'

'And that means?'

'It means that, having chosen to act like a child, you must be treated like a child.'

She then proceeded, with admirable clarity, to describe the regulations which she deemed it necessary to impose and to which I was asked to submit voluntarily. Every waking hour would be given to the business of 'education'. I should receive orders from her or from Thérèse which were to be obeyed promptly and without argument. There would be a great many simple exercises, simple actions to be repeated again and again until they could be performed with habitual ease and grace. My reading would be controlled; I should learn when to talk and when to hold my tongue; I was to learn the code and obey the injunctions of good society; my enthusiasm for art was to be restrained; I should have to acquire the techniques of polite chatter; Darwin would be replaced by Debrett; there would be no more cigarettes and half a glass of wine at each meal was to suffice. There was no visible activity not governed by regulations, none in which I did not require elementary instruction. In short, I was to become a kind of well-bred automaton whose every movement was planned and predictable.

I do not know whether I at all convey the dismay with which I listened to this programme or the despair with which I contemplated a life which would consist entirely of fashionable observances. I felt a rising tide of anger within me – surely these proposals went beyond anything which was just or reasonable?

Indeed, it was with some asperity that I answered, 'I see. And supposing I say that such exertions are beyond me and do not seem to me to be necessary?'

'In that case, we must say goodbye. I shall write to Mr Mellish, tell him that I have failed and that I resign. Fortunately there is a suitable establishment, a kind of finishing school for awkward cases. It is near

Sesto. I know the headmistress and have spoken to her already. I can leave you there tomorrow. I can give Thérèse a good character, but that is all I fear.'

An institution, a convent school, with no Thérèse to help me was a terrifying idea. It meant certain exposure. Achilles hid himself amongst the daughters of Lycomedes and had a good time with the girls, although even he was discovered and obliged to do military service. But he at least was not likely to be prosecuted for fraud and sent to penal servitude.

One slight gesture of resistance occurred to me. I had to submit, but I might still do so in such a way as to cheat Cecily of what she really wanted – a dramatic surrender, an expression of submissive love and perfect devotion. I did not take even that slight revenge. The thing was done in style, with tears and promises and embraces. I could see that she was both moved and pleased. In truth, it was a wiser and better course.

And yet when Thérèse came to me and it was past midnight and I felt utterly exhausted I did say to her, 'My life is going to be made intolerable. Shall we risk everything? Shall we fly?'

'Fly?'

'Now, at this very moment while there is still time.'

'But it would be insane. I beg you not to think of such a thing. Now we are penniless. We have nowhere to go. What would become of us?'

I let it go at that. Nothing more was said that night, nor on the morrow when the new regime began with a note from Cecily. She wished to see my polite refusal of the Poultons, in future she was to see all my letters. Then the whole day was mapped out; beginning with the hairdresser, then there would be lunch with the Burketts, a drive in the Boboli Gardens, leave cards, etc. etc. All subscriptions to learned journals were to be cancelled, all books collected for inspection. My *Tribuna* was already cancelled and replaced by a royalist journal, *La Fanfula*.

It was not until my hair had been reorganised and Thérèse had appeared with a new dress and new corsets to prepare me for lunch with the boring Burketts that we could discuss the revolution that had occurred.

'Oh Thérèse, she has taken my books, my cigarettes, everything – even my newspaper. What am I to do?'

'But surely Mademoiselle must do as she is told.'

It was Cecily, I knew, who had taught her to use that third person.

'But Thérèse, it is unreasonable, it is monstrous.'

'But Mademoiselle can hardly have expected anything else. We no longer have to consider the convenience of Mlle Pullman.

'I did not expect a state of slavery.'

'I think it was to be expected. To be a woman is, more or less, to be a slave, especially if you happen to be a well-brought-up young woman without a husband. So far Mademoiselle has been singularly fortunate; young women in America have liberties which are unheard of else-where and I suppose that as long as Mlle Pullman was with us you could not easily be asked to forfeit the privileges which she enjoyed. But now it is surely natural that Mme Gordon should exert the power which any European mother or any governess expects to have in dealing with a girl. It is not for me to question the enormous generosity that Mademoiselle has shown in thus, for my sake, accepting this role. But surely in doing so she must have realised that she was surrendering her liberty?'

'Perhaps not sufficiently,' I replied. I was a good deal struck by her words.

'And after all,' said Thérèse, pursuing her advantage, 'Mademoiselle did make that choice, that very noble choice. Madame is only con-tinuing the work that I myself began at Creek. I did not know how to do it, she does. And after all, she does love you. Personally I have known worse mistresses, far worse.'

'So you really advise complete surrender? Oh Christ, Thérèse, these stays hurt like the devil!'

'Mademoiselle has grown too self-indulgent; she will soon get used to the feeling. Yes, in my opinion the thing has to be endured, and the sooner the lesson is learnt the easier it will be.'

'I must take your word for it. Thérèse, how does one manage to breathe?'

'It is possible. Mademoiselle will please remember not to lean forward and put creases in the bodice.'

'Very well, lunch shall be consumed in a vertical position. Lunch indeed! Where the hell am I to stow it?'

For the next six months my life was devoted to a struggle with all-important trivialities. I was taught that there is a right way and several wrong ways of doing practically everything; even the simplest things – perhaps above all the simplest things – had painfully to be learnt, for my way of doing things was always wrong. You might have thought that to enter a room, to leave it again, to pour a cup of tea, to drink it, to return the cup to its saucer, to open a fan, to shut it, to lift a skirt, to pick up a train or a flower, to adjust a pair of gloves or to remove a veil were simple enough operations such as might be entrusted to anyone, even to a young unmarried woman. But no, these were exacting tasks, tasks for which I had no aptitude whatsoever. As Cecily put it, with greater truth than she knew, my upbringing had not prepared me for that which should have come easily.

Nowadays everything is very much easier: clothes, manners, conversation – they are looser, more rational. But in my youth, and in society for which I was being prepared, everything was rigid and regimented. I cannot tell you how hard it was for a well-conducted virgin to get in or out of a carriage without disgrace or indecorum. When at last I did master that almost impossible art we moved, exasperatingly enough, to Venice.

I think that the worst time was in Venice – I recollect Cecily actually shedding tears of vexation over my ineptitude in the hall of the Daniele – and it was many years before I was able to enjoy that delightful city.

The techniques of polite conversation were hardest of all (that was something which I studied in Vienna) but, though hard, conversation was more interesting. For a long time I was ordered to be mute and it was not until I had begun to master the simpler arts of behaviour that I was permitted to utter any but the most commonplace civilities.

When I could speak I was instructed never to express anything that could be classed as an idea. Young ladies did not have them. On the other hand, I was to be neither dull nor stupid.

Let me give an example.

A: Prince Apponyi has been made Ambassador to the Court of St James. What do you think of that, Mademoiselle?

B(1): The Prince is a stuffed shirt, but the Princess has been sleeping with the Minister for so long and has become so tiresome that something has to be done for her.

B(2): Indeed sir, I do not know.

B(3): Oh M. le Baron, how delightful, Kitty's friends will be charmed.

Needless to say (1) is wrong although both A and B know it to be the truth. (2) is better but not at all good: it gives no opportunity for further chatter. (3) is distinctly better for it allows A to suppose that Kitty's friends will be delighted to be rid of her. It is a bromide but gives some opening for malice. But (3) could be very wrong indeed if B were not actually on Christian-name terms with Kitty, that is unless B were so much Kitty's social superior that 'Kitty' became a sort of compliment, or again, if pronounced in a different tone of voice, a kind of insult.

It was an absurd but not a wholly uninteresting art. At the same time, and always, one had to remain alert for social disasters actual or impending. The disaster of the too-visible petticoat, a guest left unintroduced, an inattentive servant, an intelligent idea. All the time, while you were saying pleasing but not totally inane things, you had to be on your guard for such disasters and so much of a social automaton that you would at once take the correct action. I learnt the importance of this even before my long and painful tirocinium was over.

It was in the foyer of, I think, the Ring Theatre one evening in March

1890. The night's performance had been 'Trovatore'; we were descending a handsome staircase; I was with the wife of the Argentine military attaché, Cecily and the attaché were about thirty yards in advance; it was crowded. There are certain things that one says to a Wagnerite after a Verdi opera. I was saying them; but I was also glancing into a great gilded ornate mirror to make sure that I looked all right and that everything else was satisfactory. I would 'do' but everything else was quite dreadfully unsatisfactory: on the opposing flight of stairs was a handsome, red, happily excited face, the face of my Uncle Hector – the only person who would surely know me for what I was and who, if drunk, would hail me by name.

'No, Señora O'Duffy, I have never seen "Lohengrin".'

He had recognised me. He was very drunk.

'Yes, Señora O'Duffy, I have heard so little by the Master, I must surely defer to your judgment.'

Now it's coming.

'Henry, I say, Henry my boy, I thought you'd croaked.'

Remember that he cannot possibly be talking to you; you *must not* turn your head.

'But surely Señora O'Duffy, in melodic invention the Italian is unequalled?'

He must be close behind by now.

'Henry my boy, up to your old games?'

What would he do? What would happen? But the damned woman was still talking about music and some reply would be called for.

'Henry my boy, don't you know me?'

'Ah yes, of course, one cannot but admire the extreme ingenuity with which the leitmotiv is employed in "Die Meistersinger". No, I have not heard "Tristan" – Mrs Gordon does not think it quite suitable. Monsieur!'

A hot and sweaty hand was upon my bare shoulder. Now was the time for the amazed look, the maidenly recoil.

'Why Henry – I thought. *Entschuldigung.*' I think he must have seen my look of anguish and was sobered. With further muttered excuses he scrambled away through the crowd of polite music-lovers. I was in a panic until he managed to get clear of them, but there was excuse enough for some emotion and even Señora O'Duffy managed a few words of sympathy before returning to the music drama. I was able to say very little until we rejoined the rest.

'My poor Mary, who was that horrible person who ran into you on the stairs?'

'Someone who had dined too well.' (This was the correct euphemism.)

'Very distressing for you, poor dear. I only saw him for a moment, but he seemed vaguely familiar.'

'Altogether too familiar,' I muttered and meant it for, drunk or sober, the Brandons have a strong family resemblance.

By a very happy coincidence Giorgio Antonelli and two of his Roman friends called at our hotel the next day. We were out but someone had left a bouquet of white roses and a card bearing the words '*Perdono*, Ettore'.

'Ettore, who is he? One of your Roman admirers?'

'I knew him when I was free and wicked and I will admit that, just for a moment, I was in danger – but not now, I promise you.'

'Well, you are a sly thing!' Cecily was considerably taken aback. She felt that she had been caught napping and for that reason did not care to discuss the matter, as I had feared she might do.

I was both frightened and encouraged by the incident. It made me see that this social discipline could be really useful. I had been given a new personality, not a very interesting one but one which could be relied upon to keep its head in an emergency and present a solid face to the world. I had learnt to play the lady with conviction, and that education was to assist me enormously in one of the better acts of my life and, as you shall hear, in the worst. I was grateful that it had happened at a time when I was beginning at last to acquire a little social ease and it encouraged me to acquire more. In Vienna I became just presentable and, finally, 'quite an efficient player'. In truth I think that Cecily began to overrate my abilities: I never learnt to perform with anything like her own effortless grace.

When at last the time came for compliments and mutual congratulations Cecily began to allow a certain laxity, with frequent visits to museums and even to scientific lectures, although I was later to realise that certain essential freedoms had still been withheld. The circumstances of my education had been such that I hardly knew how far I still was from being a free agent. Between me and Cecily there was a complete and happy renewal of friendship. But between Thérèse and myself – the artist and the animated modiste's dummy – there was no change apart, of course, from the fact that she could attempt more ambitious confections with perfect confidence that the medium would now carry the full weight of her design. But in another way there was a very marked and very happy change in our relationship.

In her first desperate efforts to effect my transformation Thérèse had been so much in earnest that she did not hesitate to use every persuasive power, including that vested in her sex, to encourage me to persevere. The daily struggle to teach me was echoed in our most private encounters and sometimes in the most painful manner, so that there was no truce or comfort in the miseries of those first painful months. That time must have been hell for everyone. But it gave corresponding sweetness to my later achievements. Thereafter, life did become increasingly pleasant and Thérèse believing that much of the final success was due to her – and indeed it was – gained a further pleasure when she described her efforts as 'a little return for all that you have done for me'. I must, however, observe that this renewal of tenderness did not quite divert her from those little excursions, those illicit adventures of, let us say, the heart on which she so frequently embarked.

Her state of contented industry and my complete acceptance and dependence upon her services, together with the fact that we were now so placed that all immediate plans of escape were impractical, combined to make our rather strange symbiosis a matter of habit. From the time of my first success in Vienna our lives seemed happily interlocked.

As Cecily saw it, I became passable in Vienna and finally graduated *cum magnum laude* in the Faubourg. For myself, I never felt the glory of my brief excursion into those august regions. It was a matter of joining various gatherings in various respectable houses and remaining on my very best behaviour. It was dreadfully tiring. I suppose my memories are overclouded by my recollection of the last few weeks of that examination. To me it was all dust and ashes. I had got into a fix and could not see any way out of it.

How shall I describe the situation decently? It took the form of an irritating red spot which grew and became more and more inflamed. It was in the neighbourhood of the glans penis. It was persistent and it was very alarming and I am afraid I tended to blame Thérèse and her disreputable friends.

I could not see a physician as I was. I had to find some place where I could change my sex and find a good doctor. In Rome it would have been easy, but in Rome I had money of my own and time of my own. In Paris I was still very much supervised and Thérèse, as luck would have it, was out of funds. It would have had to have been done somehow if I had not at that very moment found that I was going to meet a doctor whom I could trust. Unfortunately, this raised problems quite as severe as those from which I hoped it would release me.

Here it is necessary that I should introduce my elder brother William Brandon. Billy was born in 1867. He had our mother's intelligence and nothing of our father's looks. Remembering the days of our youth I see him as a lanky boy who always seemed to have outgrown his clothes. His cuffs were near his elbows, his trousers ended six inches above the floor. Then, and later, he seemed to have had a fearful struggle with the suit he wore and to have won a very precarious victory: his pockets bulged with boxes and bottles, his waistcoat was riddled with acid burns. His hair seemed to be composed of a number of hostile factions each one resolutely determined to grow in the direction of its choice. His eyes, flashing behind glasses, were intelligent, his nose too short for beauty, his mouth was exceptionally wide and fell easily into a very pleasant grin.

At school he was brilliant. At home he kept a large array of flowerpots each of which contained a stinging nettle fed upon its own fertiliser and each of which supported a colony of caterpillars, small tortoiseshells I think. His hope was that the perfect insects would vary in relation to the fertilisers. The results were negative. He went to Bart's and was much surprised to find that his teachers thought him first rate. He qualified just before I left for Liberty Sound.

It was he who infected me with an interest in science – he knew nothing of the arts. His interests were limited, his sympathies were not. I remember him, while he was doing his midwifery course, coming home and exclaiming, 'We are pupae, we live in cases and complain that Uncle Amos gives us too little. I have just been helping to deliver the third child of people who think themselves very lucky to get three pounds a week.' He gave me the beginnings of a social conscience.

When one day we realised that Father's mind had simply faded away it was Billy who did everything. How he managed to look after us and still take his course I do not know. And then after all his sacrifices I had to go and disgrace the family. His conduct on that occasion was memorable. He thought my conduct 'rum', he thought that Uncle Hector had mismanaged matters, but he blamed no one.

As he put it, 'I can't see you're doing anyone any harm, so what's all the fuss about?'

During the past year I had, on several occasions, written letters to him in my head and sometimes actually on paper, but none were ever posted. There was a difficulty about writing; but I knew that, for my own sake, I must write, for if we met without a previous explanation he would surely recognise me and, since he had a positive genius for being tactless, he would hail me, 'Golly, it's Henry. Good old Henry, I thought you were dead.' I could hear him saying it – and with Cecily there too.

For the twentieth time I began to compose a letter. Before I could finish it there came another letter. This was from Mr Mellish. Mr William was coming to Paris on business. The very next morning we had a *petit bleu* telling us that he would call at our hotel that afternoon.

I had somehow to meet him alone, or at least with only Thérèse present. It involved me in some pretty hard lying but I got my way. Even so, it was worrying. I wanted to know the truth about my disease. And there was always the danger that Billy, although he would tolerate sexual oddities, might take a very severe view of embezzlement.

I was therefore depressed and agitated. He was late, but at last Thérèse announced him and left us. It was all I could do to offer my hand and make a polite noise of some kind. I did have time to observe that Billy had been dressed by Savile Row and had pretty nearly undone the tailor's work. For a little time we inspected each other in silence.

'Well Billy, I suppose you recognise me?'

'Recognise? Yes, Miss Porthow. Delighted, delighted.'

'You mean you don't?'

'No. Yes. I mean, I do, of course.'

'Billy, look at me hard. Don't I remind you of someone? Don't you penetrate my disguise? Don't you rumble me?'

'Rumble, Miss Porthow? I don't understand.'

'Heaven be praised! But don't you know my voice? Surely that has not changed so much? No? Then sit down and prepare for a shock.'

He sat nervously – clearly I was a lunatic whom it would be better to humour.

'Here's the shock, Billy. You think your brother is dead; he is alive and well – well, fairly well.'

'Golly,' said my brother; but he made it into quite a long word for, under stress of emotion, he stutters, and then, 'I must see him.'

'But he's here, Billy. Here in this room.'

Billy looked around wildly, as though he expected to find his brother concealed beneath a chair.

'Here,' I repeated, laying my hand upon the bosom of my dress. 'If I were to undo this you would find a birthmark that you know just below the solar plexus. If I pulled up my skirts you would discover an ancient scar, made by a broken bottle on the beach at Littlehampton. That was the summer we tried to dissect a dead cat and the smell was too awful. And do you remember the "Pondicherry Tree" and the picture of Moses in the hall?'

'Good God! I can't believe it.'

There was a pause. He touched my arm and said, 'Henry, you are real?' Another silence. 'I think you might have sent a postcard.'

'I might. The trouble is that I am the wrong side of the law. Very much so I am afraid. As things are, I couldn't let you know without asking you to stay mum. That would give you the pleasant choice of denouncing me or becoming an accessory after the fact.'

'Which I now have.'

'I do hope to put things right soon and with your help to live honestly. At present there's no escape from the consequences of my actions.'

There was another little pause and I began again. 'Billy, I have two begs.' (A 'beg' was a childhood word for a special plea.) 'Beg one: don't split on me, not until you've heard the whole story – then do as you think right. Until then let me be Cousin Mary. Beg two: I want to consult you professionally. I think I have clap.'

'Oh golly, you *do* get into trouble. As to the illegality, I should like to hear your story; but it's all right, I can't lose you again after all this. Now, as to this infection I had better see. Is there somewhere where I can wash my hands?'

He became the professional physician. 'How long since cohabitation? Any discharge? Is it painful to urinate?' etc. etc.

He finished, washed his hands and said, 'Henry, you are an ass.'

'You mean?'

After untold ages he managed to say, 'It's nothing, even you should have known that. A little ointment which I can prescribe and the thing will go.'

It was a joyous evening. I needed no extra glass of champagne to feel happily inebriated. Cecily was amazed by my good spirits and of course suspected that Billy and I were in love. Billy puzzled her; he was so obviously a gentleman and so utterly deficient in all the graces. Also Billy's conversation didn't quite suit her. I asked after our father and he replied, 'Perfectly well, but no mind left; took to eating soap, horribly incontinent – we had to shut him up.' But he watched his tongue. Only once did he call me by my real name; it passed unnoticed.

He asked me to show him the Louvre on the following morning. I turned to Cecily to ask her leave. 'Of course, my dear, you'll take Thérèse?'

I remember Billy's startled look and his unspoken comment when I answered, 'Of course.'

That night there was a glorious thunderstorm and in the morning Paris was charmingly refreshed. Billy called early and we set off across the Tuileries Gardens as happy as two sandboys.

'Do you really have to have a chaperone?'

'Yes, for the time being I have to be impeccably respectable. But Thérèse can hear what she likes, she knows everything.'

'It's a rum business.' Then, in another tone of voice, 'What happened yesterday has made me think furiously. I see it as a warning. Yes, a warning to me. You took me in completely. I saw a smartly dressed young woman and nothing else, even when you hinted at the truth and invited examination. Of course I did see the general Brandon type, but I was expecting that. That's the danger, Henry, that's the danger.'

'I am your Cousin Mary, please don't forget it. But what's the danger?'

'The danger to the diagnostician. I had been told I was going to meet a Brandon girl and there she was. I was simply incapable of seeing anything else. You had to force me to doubt my eyes. I suppose in the ordinary course of life one has to accept this blindness. If one looked to see that one's chair was not made of cardboard every time one sat down one would really waste too much time. But a physician must be suspicious. I suppose a doctor brought up in the Cartesian tradition would actually see the circulation of the blood in his terms. You have to accept Harvey before you can see properly. For of course, now that I know, there are all sorts of gestures and tones of voice that are unmistakably yours. Once one has begun to doubt, even so brilliant a piece of mimicry as yours fails to convince. The trouble is that one does not pause to doubt.'

I had forgotten how single-minded Billy could be and had expected that he would be impatient to hear my story; but it was not begun before we reached that triumphal arch which guards the approach to the Louvre and not ended before we had been at least a dozen times around the great courtyard. By then Thérèse had found a handsome *gendarme*; she enjoyed being in Paris. We sat in the sun and continued our conversation.

Presently Billy, who had lost his spectacles, they being at the end of his nose, wiped them and asked very kindly, 'Mary, are you very unhappy?'

'Not at all. I had some bad months in Italy, but on the whole since my transformation I have never been happier. Do I sound unhappy?'

'Not at the moment, certainly. But in a general way I should have supposed that you must be miserable. This metamorphosis is to me a quite incomprehensible thing. I see how you got led into it, but I don't see how you can endure it. Of course we are very different psychologically, but by your own account you have planned again and again to return to a normal existence. Surely so many attempts to escape and so many failures must mean that you hate this unnatural existence? You must therefore be unhappy.'

'To a logical mind such as yours that is unanswerable. Yes, I have tried to escape from my trap. But the trap was largely of my own making. I made it because, in a way, I wanted it. I shall escape from it, but I shall regret it.'

'But that sounds insane.'

'I suppose I am rather insane, but still not so mad that I do not know it. If one is mad as I am mad one has to live a rather mad life. Suppose one thought that one was a poached egg. Then it would seem both proper and desirable that one should live seated upon a piece of damp toast. One might wonder at intervals whether life has not better things to offer and at such times one would be unhappy. Nevertheless, there would be a rightness about the seating arrangements that would make them a source of happiness.'

'Well, I suppose you get something out of this business. No doubt she,' glancing towards Thérèse, 'is a source of great satisfaction; but it does pass my understanding that you should accept a state of affairs in which you have to ask that woman's leave before you can take a walk. Surely there can be no pleasure in that.'

'That is because, not knowing her or knowing her only through my description, you think of her as "that woman". For me she is Cecily. It is not or, at least, it is not now difficult to accept what to you looks like tyranny. Do you suppose that Hercules would have allowed Omphale to treat him like an incompetent housemaid unless he had been very sweet on her?'

'And are you very sweet on Mrs Gordon?'

'She is a respectable widow and I certainly am not Hercules. But yes, I am very fond of her and because of that and because, after all, she imagines that we are in a situation in which such "tyranny" is normal, I find, although I have not always found, that I can easily consent to her government. Also, I think that it is no bad thing that one sex should find out what the other sex has to endure by direct experience. I understand better what Mill meant by "the subjection of women".'

'I think you are destroying your own argument. You tell me that women are harshly treated, you test your theory by becoming a woman, only to discover that it's not so bad after all.'

'No, dear Cousin, I have discovered what we already knew. Where there is affection, servitude is supportable. But I have also discovered what I did not know: that is to say, the gravity of the wrongs which must often be suffered where there is no affection.'

'And this is to be the product of your adventure – a feminist tract?

"The Wrongs of Women By One Who Was One": it would sell with a title like that.'

'Now you suggest it, perhaps I will. But you know, Cousin Billy, I am in it for the cash. You get something out of this too. I get a lot. It's the greatest theft of the nineteenth century. I am the mute, inglorious Napoleon of crime. It's a pity I can't very well boast about it.'

'Seriously, Mary, you can't want all this money.'

'Seriously, no. If it be possible I would like to take as much as I would have had if none of this had happened. When I come of age and can have the money in my own hands I shall try to arrange that. I cannot see that anyone else will really suffer if I do that. As for the rest, the colossal, the indecently large rest. I have a plan for its disposal – but I need your advice and indeed your help in putting that into effect.'

'Well?'

'I had thought of a hospital, a hospital without wards; a place where instead of curing people who are ill, we would try to prevent them from becoming unwell. You yourself have told me how people live, how they suffer not only from poverty but from ignorance; the poisonous patent foods they buy and then, when they have poisoned themselves, the spurious medicines that they take. Why shouldn't we give people the chance to be healthy? Starting with the foetus, giving pregnant women the things that they need, and then children who would grow up eating the right foods.'

'It would be simpler if we knew what they really do need.'

'Well, I have thought of that too. Why shouldn't we begin with a survey of diet, housing and so on, and discover what relationship it has to infantile diseases and mortality?'

'We are very much in the dark. It would take a long time and a great deal of money.'

'With good luck and good management we could have a lot of both. I can supply the money, you have the ability. We are both young. I am very ignorant, but I can make myself useful. As I see it, you would really direct the whole thing. Won't you think about it? That's all I ask. We have time: I have only to lie low until I come of age, then, if you think it feasible, we would form a trust or tie up the money in some way. Then at an appropriate moment I would swim out to sea and never return. You would be in control of the fund. I should start a new life.'

'You have certainly mastered the feminine art of temptation.'

'And now I am going to tempt you into the Louvre – you will have to have something to talk about at lunch.'

After a few very enjoyable days Cecily came very near to asking Billy whether his intentions were serious. In the matter of my project they soon were.

Billy returned to Dainton, which was close to the old family home in Sussex. He left orders that I was to go into the country, rest and lead an unsocial life. His letters were our only distraction until another, from Mellish, brought us over to the English side of the Channel.

It was a strange excursion. We met my old antagonist, who at our last interview had been so horribly severe. Now he was all smiles and affability. In fact, it was I who had to put him at his ease for clearly he was alarmed lest I should greet him as 'a good old sod'. I refrained.

The Brandons, Sir Charles and his mother, were in Scotland so we were able to visit Ramsgate House, which was then still my property, unaccompanied. It was here that I had been scolded and lectured by Sir Amos. It was a severe neo-classical pile, as horrible as red plush and mahogany could make it.

But India Lodge, 'The Tartary' as they called it in the village, was another matter. Old Lady Brandon had removed herself to Hove, leaving some imbecile specimens of her embroidery together with the scars and smells of a pack of Skye terriers. The younger Lady Brandon wanted to demolish the place. I fell in love with it; Mellish said that I could certainly have it at a peppercorn rent; Billy pressed me to remain in the district in order that we might launch our project together and, without really considering the matter as I should have, I decided then and there to make it my home in England.

THE CHANGELING: CHAPTER VIII

I find it hard to recall dates. I suppose that we were in Paris throughout May and June. I remember that we were at Etretat on July 14th and had made our flying visit to Ramsgate before the end of that month. There was a good deal of work to be done at India Lodge and that work was not complete when we arrived at the beginning of September. There were still ladders and men with brushes about the house on that fine morning when two imposing figures – Lady Brandon, a tall woman, and her son, a giant – came knocking at our door.

Once I had feared to meet them, but since my encounter with Billy I had gained confidence. I felt pretty sure that Her Ladyship would not recognise in me the grubby, hot-faced schoolboy whom she had scolded so bitterly. Nor did she; I was offered a hand for pressing and a cheek for kissing and I was her 'dear Mary'. As for young Sir Charles, he had been a haughty Etonian ashamed of his grammar-school cousins. He would hardly have been aware of my existence. In this it seems that I was wrong.

When Lady Brandon had finished her salutations I found myself offering a hand to the young baronet. The hand went unobserved. Sir Charles was staring at me with the kind of cold, unblinking stupefaction, amazed and unwelcoming, with which one greets a slug in one's salad. This unfriendly observation was prolonged until I felt that indignation was colouring my cheeks. Aware that it was my duty to conceal or disregard incivility as best I might I turned to Lady Brandon with some tremendous banality upon my lips. Before it would be uttered she, addressing Cecily as much as me, observed that her son imagined that it was 'amusing to behave like a lout'.

With a visible effort the young man returned to the social world which, obviously, he had entirely forgotten.

'Cousin Mary, I beseech you to forgive me. I have been very rude. Not, I hope, unforgivably rude. The fact of the matter is that I was wool-gathering: you reminded me so forcibly of our poor Cousin Henry that, for a moment, he seemed to be brought back to life again. I have never known a sweeter nature, nor, until now, a more attractive face. That strong family resemblance struck me so much that I forgot everything including my manners.'

'Your manners, Sir, are quite atrocious. But I see you are the kind of person all of whose crimes have to be forgiven.'

I again offered a hand and this time it was kissed.

'Mary is too charitable,' said his mother. I could see that her son's manner of rescuing himself barely improved the case, for she preferred to forget the brief existence of Henry Brandon. So, to be sure, did I. Indeed, Sir Charles's propitiatory nosegay was for me so bewilderingly compounded of blooms and spines that I hardly knew how to take hold of it. For a few moments I needed above all things to be silent.

Meanwhile Her Ladyship was half-seriously suggesting that to bring such a boor into the house was altogether too much of an imposition. They would take themselves away until her son was in a better mood.

Hearing this, Sir Charles turned to me again and said, 'Happily my dear mother will save you the trouble of scolding me as I no doubt ought to be scolded; I can assure you that she will make an excellent job of it. Whereas you, Cousin Mary, are surely not at all adept in the art of making yourself disagreeable.'

'I may learn in time.'

'Let us hope not, it would not suit you at all. Your kind of beauty is made to be worn with gentle and magnanimous kindness. But now, may I learn something? Is that a Hiroshige?'

It was indeed, one of half a dozen prints that I had acquired in Paris and which were now set up against the wall. He was all enthusiasm: it was a lovely thing, just right for the Lodge, he admired the Lodge very much.

'Dear Mama with her exquisite taste wants to destroy the place.'

Sir Charles, I surmised, would have a very disagreeable walk home.

Wishing, at all events, to secure a cease-fire, I asked him what he thought of Japanese art.

He had thought a good deal, and had also thought a good deal about art in general. He had, as was to be expected, an unbounded admiration for Botticelli. I could not see eye to eye with him there and we wrangled, amiably enough, while Cecily and Lady Brandon found their own topics of conversation. The meeting ended much more comfortably than it had begun.

'Well, what do you think of our landlords?'

'I liked them both.'

'When I hear that you don't like someone I shall go straight to the police. But what do you think of them?'

'I thought her honest, trustworthy, sensible. I think perhaps a difficult life has made her rather stern. But we should get on well enough.'

'And how will you get on with the baronet?'

'I have been taught by my dear governess not to "get on" with young men, and I fancy that this one will get on very well without me.'

'Mary, you are an evasive hypocrite! And you haven't answered my question. What do you think of him?'

'He is decidedly decorative, very like Michelangelo's David: the same handsome rather sulky look, the same enormous hands and, I suppose, about the same bulk – but that may be an optical illusion.'

'He has the manners of a pig.'

'Even I noticed that. But then, so did he, and he apologised quite nicely.'

'I should think he must be used to having to apologise.'

'I dare say. That's how he learnt to carry it off with a certain style. Altogether an odd mixture; a poseur with a silly taste for decadence, but also with quite genuine feelings.'

'Have you seen so far so soon?'

'Well, he makes no secret of his foibles and when someone talks freely about art one can learn something about them.'

'Mary, what would be your honest opinion of Kate Negroponte now?'

'Kate? But we were not discussing Kate.'

'Let us do so, just for a minute. A year ago you thought her an intuitive genius, a miracle of womanly sympathy, a person of high intelligence. And today? Nice, sensible, a bit hasty, perhaps a little shallow?'

'Perhaps, but . . .'

'And allowing for the fact that when you met her you had met practically no one, is it not true that you credited her with more virtues than it was really fair to expect in anyone? And why? – because she is so beautiful.'

'Yes, but . . .'

'And did you not tell me that Thérèse was the perfect servant long before she was anything of the kind, largely because she is such a pretty girl? And am I not right in thinking that you engineered the Negroponte marriage not only because you are a particularly nice person, but because you liked the idea of marrying two such beautiful people?'

'Cecily, you are very acute. But is it necessary to cover so much ground in order to warn me against being too impressed by the appearance of Sir Charles?'

'I do it to ram home my point. He is much too handsome, you are much too susceptible to beauty.'

'So you think my god has feet of clay?'

'Of mud perhaps – it is too soon to tell. Oh Mary, don't throw yourself away. I could not bear it.'

'But Cecily, we have spoken together for ten minutes. Do I act as though I had been struck all of a heap? Do you really think me in danger?'

'Yes, I think that you *are* in danger, and not only from Sir Charles. The trouble is that you are so terribly well off. If you were poor do you suppose that the Brandons would have been on our doorstep before we had time to unpack our bags? Lady Brandon's a decent woman but I could see the intense anxiety on her face as she entered the room and the relief when she saw that you not only had a bank balance but are a lady. "There," she said, for her thoughts were quite audible, "there's the girl for my boy. How well the Brandon Diamonds will sit on her pretty shoulders."'

'Cecily, you're romancing, there are no Brandon Diamonds.'

'But there are my dear, only they happen to belong to you. Your father bought them when your uncle came a cropper and Mellish has them in safe keeping for you. That's why they've got to get you back, shoulders, diamonds and all. And they've only got to be a little bit nice to you for you to feel deeply beholden to them. I know it's your vice Mary, but don't give yourself away out of pure good nature.'

'I shan't marry to please Lady Brandon, I promise.'

'I wish they weren't so near. I think you know, that it would be a good plan if you were to have a *pied à terre* in London and make some friends there. At any rate, as soon as you are of age.'

This was no doubt very sound advice but it came rather late in the day. The difficulty was, although I had not yet met them, that I was prevented from leaving by Mrs Stevens and Mrs Denshaw.

Mrs Stevens and Mrs Denshaw were twin sisters – as girls they had both been employed at Ramsgate House – and they had married twins. Yet despite the similarity in their genetic histories, Mrs Stevens had normal, healthy babies, while the children of Mr and Mrs Denshaw were rachitic, so much so that one of them, Freddy, could be classified as a deformity. Why? We felt in the dark but at the same time tantalisingly close to the answer; and when one saw poor Freddy Denshaw hobbling around it became desperately important to find it.

After that momentous and exhilarating meeting in Paris, Billy and I corresponded continually. It became clear almost at once that he was deeply interested in my scheme but wanted to reshape it. He insisted on the need for research. The following letter may explain the nature of our debates, also it is a highly characteristic production.

Dainton Old House

July 10th, 1890
My dear Mary,

I agree with most of what you say, more in fact than you suppose. Yes, I do think that normal practice is important and certainly it is wrong to think of patients simply as statistics. My idea is to keep the practice, but to keep it small and to attend to patients who represent a cross-section of the population. I shall need to bring in a partner and know the right chap, Renshaw by name. He will keep me in touch with the 'real world' as you call it.

I have been wondering in a vague unsystematic way whether one might not make a map of the area, giving all possible information; natality, mortality, diet, drinking habits, incidence of common diseases, etc. We could use the records of schools and hospitals and local government and as the coincidence of medical and environmental information begins to show – if it does – we should begin to see promising lines of enquiry. What do you think? I believe something of the same kind is being done in York. If you think it worth while I would try to formulate my ideas properly. A thought occurs: if we went round talking to shopkeepers they might tell us what kind of filth their customers eat.

I came back on Monday from staying with Prof. Small, he full of ideas about appendicitis. The elder daughter could have been a useful secretary but is going to Leipzig for some reason. The younger one won't do, but a very pleasant girl indeed. I am suggesting marriage.

Yrs B.

P.S. Would farmers object to having milk analysed?

Billy seems to have found it easier to acquire a wife than to find a secretary. He did however appear to need my help and he implored me to take India Lodge. He was deeply committed to the 'survey scheme' and he also needed hospital records. He imagined that he had only to ask for them and they would be produced. Instead of that he encountered the natural sloth of the countryside, there were evasions and refusals. The opposition came from a Mrs Fairlight who controlled the Hospital Board. She was a local Lady Bountiful, rich, well connected and a bully. In some way Billy had offended her – he could be very tactless – and she had decided that he was to get no help from the hospital.

'Frankly,' wrote Billy, 'she terrifies me. She won't listen to reason and everyone is scared of her. It's infuriating to be thwarted by such an old (deletion).'

When therefore Mrs Fairlight's carriage came to my door I was at some pains to be polite and to say nothing whatever about my Cousin William. She was indeed a very overwhelming person. She wanted me to join the Unionist Party and, even more, to meet her son, the prospective candidate for the division who would soon be back from America, 'when we really must have you at Liverpool House'. I decided not to wait for Algernon.

'Algernon,' said Sir Charles, 'is a fat prig and very disagreeable.'

'You realise,' said Cecily, 'that Mrs Fairlight is not quite a lady?'

'Good heavens, you mean . . .'

'Only that at Liverpool House you will find too much gilt and too many orchids. One can't help smelling the vulgarity beneath the patchouli. Also she is a little too obvious: she told us twice that Algernon will be Prime Minister – perhaps he may, the electorate is wonderfully broad-minded I am told.'

'But surely she is socially acceptable?'

'She is accepted. Nowadays anyone with money is accepted. People say she has "character", which means that she is rude. Return the call by all means, but just think what a mother-in-law she would make.'

So I returned the call and there, sure enough, was a profusion of gilding, too many hothouse flowers, and a spurious Gainsborough. Even I knew that she would wear too much lace and be too effusive in her welcome.

Needless to say, we had to discuss Algernon and his perfections. One of Algernon's deeds of charity consisted of sitting on the Hospital Board. I saw my opening. I was 'awfully keen on hospital work' (a conscious vulgarism). Of course, I was 'pretty useless, but I would like to help'.

She snapped at the lure. 'But my dear, how angelic! When so many young girls think of nothing but tennis and dancing. But of course we must have you on the Board of Governors. We meet next Saturday, you shall be co-opted at once. *That's* where you would be really useful my dear, so much of hospital work is not suitable for a lady – we must not be *too* romantic, must we? But in your case Miss Porthow there can be no doubt, we need young people like you on the Board.'

'But the governing body?' I was genuinely amazed. 'Surely, Mrs Fairlight, a mere girl like me.'

'You must allow me to know best, Miss Porthow. You are in fact just the kind of person we want and everyone will be delighted to welcome you, if only for your poor father's sake – he did so much good you know.'

That certainly gave me a notion of why I might be welcome.

'Of course,' she continued, 'we shouldn't expect regular attendance at meetings; I know well enough that young people can't be expected to go to stuffy old meetings all the time – twice a year would be quite sufficient.'

'Mrs Fairlight, I am immensely flattered and grateful, but you do realise that I am not yet of age?'

'Oh, we can get round that, my dear Mary – you must let an old woman take a privilege – our secretary shall arrange that, you shall see.' She rang a bell and a downtrodden female appeared with magical celerity. 'Miss Simpson, Miss Porthow is to be co-opted onto the Board at our next meeting.'

'Yes, Mrs Fairlight, but . . .'

'But what, pray?'

'Mrs Fairlight, co-opted members have to serve on a sub-committee.'

'To be sure, what shall it be, Mary? Finance, Liaison, Publicity, After-care, Social, Records, Building? I think Social would do, eh

Mary? Miss Simpson, make Miss Porthow a member of the Social Sub-Committee.'

'Excuse me Mrs Fairlight, do you think I might be on the Records Committee?'

'Records?' Mrs Fairlight was considerably put out and astonished that I should be so impudent as to suggest anything. So far she had regarded me as a feather-headed chick with absurd dreams of becoming a nightingale. Now, for a moment, she looked at me with suspicious eyes; might I perhaps intend to be a confounded nuisance? As this was precisely what I did intend I felt it necessary to chirp a bit.

'I am afraid it sounds rather cowardly but on Social I think I might be expected to do things which, because I am new in this country, would be beyond me, and that would be rather dreadful. On Records no one would expect much of me and that would make an easier start.'

How effective such arguments would have been I do not know, but by a lucky chance Algernon was the chairman of that sub-committee. ('So useful in preparing parliamentary questions you know'; although why he needed to do this when he wasn't even an MP I can't imagine.) Algernon could instruct me, it would be nice for me to have a friend on the committee and Algernon was so good at explaining things. Mrs Fairlight gave her orders, the thing would be done, and she could continue with her favourite subject.

Poor woman, she little knew that her beloved Algernon was already married to Maisie Kartoffel, the belle of Babylon, North Dakota. He had gone to the altar with a shotgun firmly pressed in the small of his back.

I went on my way rejoicing. I was now entitled to examine any files that might interest me. Better still, there were a great many people who had made difficulties and whom I now discovered could be persuaded to co-operate. One major difficulty was Dr Mortall who was Mr Denshaw's physician and who had firmly resisted all our enquiries about his medical history. He was an obstinate man, but after two dinners at India Lodge – at the second of which I was able to produce Professor Small – he capitulated and became very helpful.

Cecily had taught me that a lady is one who can ask a favour and seem to be conferring a privilege. With the right clothes, the right accent, the right manner you could nearly always get your own way. It was odd, and rather amusing to discover that the precepts which had so painfully been imparted in Venetian and Viennese drawing rooms could be adapted to the collection of statistics concerning the diet of the rural and the urban poor. It was delightful to be able to help Billy, to see our store of data growing, and finally come to the exciting moment when we believed that we could see a shape emerging from the mass of information.

But of course it was all crazy. I was tying myself hand and foot so that, if I were really to help the Denshaws, I had to remain in a situation which might become dangerous. To make matters still more absurd, at the very time when I was getting myself involved in research I was looking about for means of escape if they should be needed.

Through Billy I got in touch with Uncle Hector, now back in London. He could help me in this matter, but I knew that there would be trouble if it were known that I met him, and to go up to London alone for that purpose was out of the question.

Then Professor Small and his daughter came to stay at Dainton. Billy found this delightful; he could make love to his Augusta and he could talk to the Professor about the alimentary canal (the Professor had never been known to talk about anything else). Augusta couldn't even talk about that. At Ramsgate the Smalls were a decided failure and knew it. Nor were they altogether a success at the Lodge. Cecily found that a little of the alimentary canal went a very long way; she never much cared for Billy, his bride she described as 'a middle-class mouse from Wimbledon'. Unlike the Ramsgaters she did try hard to welcome them, but there was not much that they could talk about. As a natural result, they turned to me and pressed me to come back with them to Wimbledon. Gussie was sure that I could help her to choose 'the right things' for her trousseau, the Professor gallantly promised me a sight of his greatest treasure – 'a really lovely thing' – which turned out to be an ulcerated rectum preserved in alcohol.

It was not these delights which brought me to London. I had an ulterior motive which was realised on the last day of my visit when I managed to get rid of Gussie (Thérèse was her truly useful guide) and, in front of Pollaiuolo's 'Apollo and Daphne', I contrived to run into my Uncle Hector.

My uncle had not been on the stage, but he had been so much in the wings that he had acquired something of the old thespian's manner.

'Miss Porthow, by all that's charming.' He swept off his hat and bent over my hand. 'Seen enough pictures? Let's go and get a drink.'

'Of tea? Thank you.'

'Tea!'

'It's bad enough to be seen with you here – to be caught hobnobbing in a saloon bar would be my undoing.'

'Jesus marbles, what a life you must lead. All right, I know a place where people can swill tea without being observed amongst the potted palms.'

He was as good as his word and, a few minutes later, we were tête-à-tête in a forest of tropical vegetation.

'Henry, my boy.'

'Mary, please. And please make a habit of it.'

'Mary then, I owe you a thumping apology for what happened in Vienna. It was a cad's trick – or at least a fool's. I was drunk as Davy's sow. I'll tell you an odd thing: if it hadn't been for the liquor I wouldn't have known you. Just now, in the gallery I found it hard, even knowing what I know, to believe it was really you.'

'Uncle Hector, you can repay me for that blunder. I have two questions to put to you.'

'Fire away me . . . Mary.'

'First of all, if I were to want to vanish – and it might be necessary to do so at very short notice – could you help me? Could you tell me how to transform myself into a young gentleman in, say, Milan?'

'Nothing easier if you have the spondulicks. You can become someone quite different simply by taking a train and going to the right address.'

'You're sure of that?'

It seemed that he was. He gave me enough detail to convince me that he knew what he was talking about. I turned then to a more immediate problem. 'Tell me, do you know anything about Cousin Charles?'

'Charlie-boy? Hardly know him. But I have my spies and from what they tell me he picked up some rather unsavoury friends in Oxford. There's nothin' definite against him but, but – this is hardly a matter that one can discuss with a young lady.'

'With such a paragon of morality as my dear uncle anything can be discussed. Tell me seriously though, do you suspect what they call "the worst"?'

'Could be. But I think he's like the fellow in the play: "mere prattle without practice".'

'Cassio?'

'I shouldn't wonder. He got sent down, but I think it was for some monumental piece of nonsense rather than for anything really vicious. He talks big, likes to be thought a real live hardened sinner, a decadent, a diabolist, all that kind of rot. Probably mere swank, but if I were you I should keep Charlie-boy at arm's length.'

'In my particular situation everyone has to be kept at arm's length.'

'Heavens, I don't envy you, not with all your millions. I see why you want to bolt. Or do you, Mary? You're such a queer cuss, I believe you more than half enjoy the business.'

'Well, it's no great sacrifice to keep Charlie at a distance.'

'I'm glad to hear that. But in that case why do you live in his pocket? He and his horrible mamma will snap you up if they get half a chance.'

'She's not horrible.'

'Well, she's a prude and a whore – offered to sleep with Sir Amos if he would pay for Charlie's schooling.'

'Uncle Hector, that's pure invention.'

'Maybe a little exaggerated, but I have my spies and they tell me things about that virtuous woman that might make your hair curl.'

I only just caught my train. Uncle Hector was a disreputable old roué, but when he got onto the subject of human depravity he could be very entertaining. It made a pleasing change after three days of the alimentary canal.

I returned to a very different scene. Colonel Buxton Russell was at the Great House. Lady Brandon considered him the most respectable of Charlie's friends. The youngest colonel in the British Army, he had done remarkably well in Burma and the Black Mountain Expedition, V C, D S O, all that sort of thing; he was now home on leave. He was some kind of cousin of Lady Brandon's and had met Cecily in Poona or some such place. She had invited the whole party over to India Lodge.

She was enthusiastic about her friend; he was a very good sort and I should like him immensely.

I rather doubted whether he was my sort of good sort. It happened that Sir Charles and his mother were pre-engaged so we should have the gentleman to ourselves. I anticipated a pretty tiresome evening – nor did the appearance of the Colonel reassure me. He was beautifully turned out, his face was brick red, he had handsome moustaches and a handsome monocle, a shrewd eye and a pleasant voice – nice but limited, I thought. Naturally he and Cecily had a lot to say about old so-and-so and Major Thingummy; they seemed to know half the officers in the British Army. Then the Colonel, noticing I suppose that I found this rather tedious, politely suggested, 'This is a little unfair to Miss Porthow.'

I was in a naughty mood. 'It is natural that you should want to discuss old friends after so long a separation. I only regret that so many charming people make it their business to kill their fellow men.'

'You must forgive Mary, she wants to abolish wars and armies.'

'No one who has seen war at first hand ought to disagree with her.

But, Miss Porthow, it is not we, but governments that start wars. We kill, certainly, but we do so at the command of others.'

'Like the hangman.'

'Mary!'

'Yes, like the hangman, but at some risks to ourselves.'

'I grant you that; but still I agree with the poet: "war's a brain-spattering, windpipe-splitting art".'*

'But you forget, Miss Porthow, that he goes on, "unless her cause by right be sanctified" – and, as you will also recollect, when he died at Missolonghi he was on active service. Also, let me ask you, did you ever hear of a monarch or a government which did not consider that whatever war it happened to be waging was thus sanctified?'

'That, I must concede, is undeniable. But Colonel, are you not proving too much? That war is a murderous business can hardly be denied, you are now pointing out that it involves not only murder but hypocrisy.'

'I am not denying that for a moment. I am merely trying to defend myself and my profession. It is governments not armies which tell lies and invent excuses. Yes, we are like the hangman; if an innocent person suffers it is the court, not the executioner, who is to blame. Even if we know that we are being told to kill and be killed for very bad reasons we cannot protest. Surely you would not have us defy the civil power?'

'No, I suppose not.'

'Mary, you have not a leg to stand on.'

'Then, like Sir Richard, I will fight upon my stumps. For I am sure that there is something about the Colonel's profession of which I do not approve. I think really it is this: he is altogether too impressive a figure. All right, I will grant that he is not responsible for wars, neither are we unless they give us a vote; but he or, at least, the traditions of his profession are responsible for making bloodshed seem positively desirable. His banners and trumpets and uniforms make war palatable.'

* Byron, *Don Juan*, Canto IX, iv. – M.E.

'Again, Miss Porthow, I would say that governments and popular opinion and even, if I may say so, nurse-maids, do nothing to discourage military display. Indeed, in my view we spend far too much time in trying to look splendid, and far too little time in making ourselves into an efficient instrument for the prosecution of wars. But, even so, one may argue that if one must have wars it is better that they should provide a little aesthetic satisfaction.'

'But I don't believe that one must have wars.'

'If you mean that one ought not to have them then I entirely agree; but doesn't this bring us back to our point of departure?'

I seemed to be getting the worst of it and hoisted a white flag – it was embroidered with lace. 'Colonel, you have outmanoeuvred me; if your strategy is anything like your dialectic I am very sorry for your enemies.'

I glanced at my opponent and saw neither amusement nor complacency. He had treated me as an intelligent adversary and had taken my first impudent sally very well. Beneath the 'correct' exterior there was, I discovered, a lively and well-informed mind and, as I perceived before the evening was over, a degree of clarity and intellectual honesty which I should never have expected when he entered the Lodge.

Cecily was a great deal amused by my reverse. It was not hard to see that she had found in him an alternative to Sir Charles, a thing for which she had been seeking but which she had failed signally to produce. And the next day she followed up that victory with another which pleased her immensely.

She had managed to be compelled to go over to the Great House very early and had met the family at breakfast.

'My dear,' she declared on her return, 'you have made a conquest. The Colonel is going to lay siege to you.'

'Having routed me so completely last night I doubt whether he will spend much powder on such an engagement.'

'Stuff and nonsense. You wanted to be taken seriously and you were – you got exactly what you asked for.'

'I certainly got it.'

'And liked him the better for it, I'll be bound. He certainly liked you for the way you took it. But listen to the latest bulletin from Ramsgate House.'

'Well?'

'Well, as I think you know, for Martha Brandon the Colonel is Charlie's good genius, an antidote to all his other friends. Naturally, when the Colonel arrived she was all over him, pressed him to stay for as long as possible, hunt with the Southdown, etc. The Colonel was polite – he always is polite – but he had a lot to do, his leave was short, might he have a little time to arrange, etc. All natural enough. Well, then, this morning at breakfast, just as I arrived, the Colonel explained that, having thought things over he had come to the conclusion that he could allow himself the pleasure of accepting their kind invitation, that is if they were sure he wouldn't be in the way.'

'Tableau! Of course they would be delighted. Oh, no, of course he wouldn't be at all in the way, they would be overjoyed. I am afraid that it may have been something in my eye which disturbed the poor woman, but Lady B.'s overenjoyment seemed a bit overdone. As for Charlie, he looked dreadfully hipped. It seems that the Colonel had been talking about you with enthusiasm, and they were ruefully putting two and two together. The Colonel is here to stay. He's bringing his hunters over from Leicestershire – and if you knew what that means you really would be flattered.'

I don't think that I felt the flattery of it, but in a way I was pleased. The Colonel, I anticipated, could give me something that I had not had since I left Boston: an intellectual sparring partner, someone with a mind sufficiently practical and political to keep my own mind in training; neither Billy whose interests were purely scientific, nor Charlie, who wanted to talk about painting and poetry, quite filled the gap. Billy wanted to talk about what was fast becoming the real business of my life, research and the prevention of disease. Charlie, I discovered, could be enormously amusing on his favourite subjects and did feel very deeply about some works of art.

But now I was to see another side of him.

> Sweet Prince of Night, thou shalt prevail
> Lovesome, narcotic, Astradale.

The poet who wrote these appalling lines, and indeed many others, was called Saxton Filbert-White. He was a friend of Charlie; they were sent down from Oxford together. A queer little tadpole of a man whose relations had decided to send him out to South Africa. He came to Ramsgate to say goodbye and he brought, as a parting gift, this epic, or whatever it was, of which I have quoted the only lines that I can remember. It was written in celebration of one Astradalius or, as in the example provided, Astradale, a person who seemed to have been compounded from the more pleasing traits of Jesus Christ, Hector, St Francis, Alcibiades and Shelley. I was tactful enough to see that this could only be Charlie.

Charlie himself, who had to listen to the entire work, was not quite insensible to its flattery but he had taste enough and sense enough to see how awful it was and was sufficiently unkind to tell the poet. In fact, Charlie made such excellent fun of the whole thing that it was impossible not to laugh, although Flibert, as I called him, was reduced to tears.

Charlie was very unkind to Flibert and so was everyone else – all except the Colonel who treated him very decently and, having been in Africa, could give him some advice and introductions. Aunt Martha practically froze him out of the Great House so that he came and moped in my drawing room. Cecily snubbed him severely. I tried to be sympathetic, but I did not try very hard. Charlie treated him like dirt, but then he rather liked being treated like dirt.

This was what I tried to point out to Cecily who, while constant in her detestation of Flibert, was equally harsh in her judgment of Charlie. She was anxious, as always, to extol the superior virtues of the Colonel, and I had to admit that his greatness of mind put the rest of us to shame – but I couldn't blame Charlie as much as Cecily would have wished. It was true that Charlie played the tyrant with his friend; but in truth it was no more than play, and the game was one which Flibert himself enjoyed. The world, I opined, was full of natural slaves, and Flibert was one of them. That Charlie was a natural slave-master I would not admit, although I was ready to agree that he fancied himself in that role.

'And what are you Mary, a natural slave or a natural slave-mistress?'

I was a good deal astonished by that question and wondered how serious Cecily was in asking it. I answered in Hamlet's words, 'Oh what a rogue and peasant slave am I', at the same time informing her that she 'Her Majesty, the Queen of Prussia', was by nature a tyrant, at which she pretended to be indignant.

My quotation was not taken at random. The game – I shall continue to call it that although with how much playfulness it was being played I do not know – offered a spectacle which Cecily, honest, womanly woman that she was, observed with a disgust which was all the more profound because she half-understood its erotic nature. I from my peculiar vantage point could see further and, being like so many young people inclined to find in myself some likeness to the Dane, recognised affinities which were interesting and not entirely comfortable. Was there not in Flibert's predicament, unheroic though he might be, a certain nobility? A kind of passive or, as some might say, a feminine grandeur which enabled him to suffer the slings and arrows of an outrageous fortune with a becoming grace? And in the demeanour of his friend was there not an ability to take arms against a sea of troubles so that, unlike Flibert, he might at the very least cleave the general ear with horrid speech? Between them they seemed to exhibit both sides of Hamlet's personality while I, more Dane than either, felt both impulses at once.

But it was not the spectacle of my own hesitant and two-faced self that really worried me at this point. What distressed me was my own inability to feel as I felt I ought to feel for Flibert in his misery. He was absurd, pathetically silly and a dreadfully bad poet, but he was not in any way nasty. He was being punished, as I had been punished, for not conforming with the accepted picture of what a man should be. He was too gentle, too submissive, too Christian if you like, and for this he was, I believed, being sent to his death. Why then should I dismiss him with unkind laughter? Why could I not treat him with the same tolerant decency as the Colonel? Why, and this was the really disconcerting question, should I feel something like envy, like jealousy when I saw him tormented by the Charlie?

The whole business made me re-examine my feelings for that young man. No, I was not in love with him, but I did consider him, despite faults which were glaringly evident (but all I felt superficial), with a kind of sympathy and admiration. I could not dismiss him as Cecily could – for her he was simply an affected braggart. For me he was all that but also something else, something much finer and more interesting, more noble, but which I could not describe even to myself.

Charlie was soon to die, and whatever the law might or might not have said about the manner of his death – if the law had been in possession of the facts – I have always known that it was I who killed him. Because of that, and because today there is hardly anyone who remembers the fourth baronet, I would like, if I had the art, to bring him back to life in these pages.

The first thing that comes to mind is the aspect of the man. I think of him whenever I see the great cats – the panther, the puma, the leopard, formidable strength melting into elastic fluent grace. He reminded me always of Michelangelo's David in Florence – which someone has called 'an adolescent of colossal proportions', which describes Charlie very well. The hands in that masterpiece have been seen as a fault – 'too big,' they say, 'and hence ungraceful' – but to me, both in the statue and in Charlie they seemed and seem very splendid, they are hands of godlike power and most beautifully welded to the arms. Also, when he was moved by beauty, a real grace of mind, at all times a majestic ease.

And he could do things, rearrange the flowers in a vase, find exactly the right phrase with which to describe a picture or a friend: then he could be impressive. He made sketches and wrote verses and knew that he had failed, knew that they did not describe the real feelings which lay beneath his nonsense, hoped one day that he would find himself as the artist whom he wanted to be and who would have been a fine artist but who could never scramble out from beneath the nonsense. And most of all, I felt that he must be, at heart, on the side of the angels, my own particular angels.

He once wrote a short story, he called it 'The Fable of the Good Shepherd and the Black Sheep'. It was very carefully written in the highly scented prose of that time, which I don't much care for. It might not be readable today. But the story itself did interest me. It concerned a shepherd who was very much distressed by the black sheep in his care; he thought that their colour derived from a kind of moral dirtiness. So did the white sheep who formed the majority of the flock. They despised and bullied their darker brethren. The good shepherd did not quite approve of their attitude, especially when they turned from passive to active hostility but he said to himself, 'They are good white sheep; it is natural that they should resent uncleanliness in their midst,' and, when the white sheep became really violent, 'Well, at least they have sound instincts.' Then, one by one the black sheep began to disappear so that soon none were left, and thereafter the maculate sheep, which, without being totally black, had some blackness in them, also vanished. Soon the whole flock was white as driven snow and the good shepherd rejoiced.

The time came to bring all the sheep to market. The good shepherd knew that his flock would be the whitest. He knew that he would be embarrassed by much praise and perhaps a little jealousy; he prayed to be delivered from false pride. His prayers were answered for, when he came to town, no one stopped to congratulate him; shepherds and sheep alike took to their heels and fled. 'Alas,' said the good shepherd, 'their hearts are struck with envy.' Then he caught sight of the old master shepherd, his teacher. The master shepherd was sitting on a rooftop laughing.

'Master,' said the good shepherd, 'why do you laugh?'

'I laugh for two reasons; firstly because I am in a place of safety; secondly because it is so funny to see a shepherd with a flock of white wolves.'

I found this story sympathetic. It combined high morality with irreverence, and that seems to me a healthy combination. In fact, it was the irreverent side of Charlie that I liked best. He laughed at pomposity and humbug. If he had lived he might have used that ability to some purpose. At the same time, it must be said that his satire could be exasperating, and perhaps in justice I ought to record a conversation which shows Charlie at his most maddening.

We had been to Brighton, Cecily, Charlie and I, to hear a concert. There had been a lady harpist who delighted everyone with her playing and who, as it happened, was very pretty. On the way home Charlie remarked, 'Has it ever occurred to you, Cousin, that women have been playing the harp for centuries (since Shakespeare's time at all events) and in all these centuries can you recall a single piece of music written for the harp by a woman? Why is this I ask you?'

'You do nothing of the kind, you are about to tell us.'

'I will not be deflated by you, Cousin. I am far too resilient.'

'You certainly bounce, Sir Charles. Take care less you become a bounder.'

'Mrs Gordon, I will not be diverted by such feeble pleasantries.'

'Come on Cecily, he wants to tell us. We must let him do so.'

'I shall tell you, ladies, although you have already shown that you are afraid of what I am going to say. Women can't compose music because music is too much like abstract thought for their charming but limited minds. But they go on playing the harp, and will I hope continue to do so, for the very excellent reason that it gives them an opportunity to display their pretty arms.'

'What a monster you would seem if one were to take you seriously.'

'Cousin, I am a monster and you ought to take me seriously for I tell you monstrous things which you know in your hearts are true.' Etc. etc.

There was a mixture of cleverness and silliness about Charlie which could be very tiresome. And yet at other times he was so right and so reasonable.

THE CHANGELING: CHAPTER IX

Many years later Billy wrote something which, although inaccurate, gave me such pleasure that I cannot forbear to quote.

Already, in the autumn of 1890, when our work was hardly begun I went abroad and, in my absence my cousin Mary Brandon, then Mary Porthow, went through my papers and put them in order. Then she wrote a memorandum concerning the proper direction of our research and hazarded a guess at what we might find. When one considers how little we, or anyone else, knew at that time, it is a breathtaking feat of clairvoyance. Before we were properly started the Brandonian Theory was foreshadowed in the Porthow Hypothesis.

Billy always did magnify my contribution to the work of what became the Institute: it consisted mainly in stealing cash and giving it to scientists. But I did occasionally do some guessing and for this I sometimes had a gift, shall we call it 'feminine intuition'? And thus it was, while Billy was on his honeymoon and I was tidying his desk, I suddenly became aware that the evidence pointed in one particular direction. One evening I believed that I knew, more or less, what had happened to poor Freddy Denshaw.* I could prove nothing and years of research might be needed before we could be sure of anything, but I was convinced that I was on the right track and I lived in a state of euphoria. I longed to talk about it with someone, but Billy was away;

---

* Mary Porthow's paper on diet and bone formation has been very fully discussed by Sir John Frend, *Mary Brandon, a Memoir*, London 1943, pp. 5–11 and by Professor Dawson, *op. cit*, pp. 83–115. 800 words are therefore omitted. – M.E.

Cecily regarded my work as a form of charity which might fittingly culminate in a bazaar; Charlie disapproved; the Colonel was sympathetic but knew too little to share in my rejoicings.

All this is relevant to my story only because it added to the confusion of my mind and the infirmity of my purpose. I still planned to leave my loot in Billy's hands and vanish from the scene. Meanwhile, a little very mild flirtation with Charlie and with the Colonel was, I thought, permissible. I was living very pleasantly with my friends and with my work. Only when I contemplated my eventual flight – which would mean separation from Charlie and my other friends and which Thérèse would not like at all – was I depressed. Now I was still more depressed by the idea of leaving my research in other hands. Muddled thought is the child of easy living. I did not think because it was more agreeable not to think. All through September, October and the beginning of November my mind was pleasantly amused.

Then, in the middle of November things began to happen and, when Gussie asked me to go with her 'to choose some things for the sitting room' I accepted willingly and made my way after lunch to the usual place very full of news for Uncle Hector.

'Well,' he said, 'what have you been up to?'

'I have been a success, a tremendous and unqualified success.'

'Done something quaint to a white rat?'

'Oh yes that too, but this is a more womanly triumph.'

'Well?'

'I've had a proposal of marriage.'

'Charlie?'

'No, the Colonel.'

'What colonel?'

'Colonel Buxton Russell – surely you've heard me talk about him?'

'Colonel Buxton Russell, VC, DSO, etc. etc., the "hero of San-dang"?'

'The same. I was sorry to refuse him.'

Uncle Hector whistled like a steam locomotive. 'Well I must say, for a pure, modest, well-conducted maiden you sail uncommon close to the wind.'

'Oh come now, Mrs Gordon thinks him *le preux chevalier sans peur et sans reproche*, Lady Brandon prizes him as dear Charlie's one wholly respectable friend. You surely haven't the brass to suggest . . .'

Uncle Hector guffawed so loud that it shook the greenery by which we were surrounded. 'My dear sister-in-law is a fathead. Thinks she knows everything. But your Uncle Hector has . . .'

'His spies; I know.'

'As it happens I know the whole story. It's rather sad. Brilliant at Sandhurst, great career before him, stationed at Dover – donkey's years ago it was – then "there ariseth a little cloud out of the sea, like a man's hand". It belonged I gather to a corporal of marines. It blew over, but there was talk, nasty talk. Like a good strategist, the Colonel mounted a counter-attack.'

'Whom did he attack?'

'His colonel's wife. That made quite a noise, but the *ruse de guerre* worked. The first scandal was forgotten in the second and people were confused.

'"This fellow Buxton Russell, some hanky-panky wasn't there?"

'"Yes, a married woman."

'But that's all right you know, dreadful mashers all these subalterns and if an officer can't play a game of puss in the corner with his superior's wife, well, what's the army coming to? So he went to India with hardly a stain on his character, and then he's such a decent cove no one wanted to think ill of him. Then he spiked the enemies' guns, or hoisted his petard or something and became a public hero. The *beau idéal* of the Ramsgate ladies, bless their little hearts; good-looking I'm told, well-connected, well-heeled, rides straight to hounds and all that, and really a very likeable fellow. And then . . .'

'And then? You're breaking my heart.'

'Then a poor Indian.'

'Oh dear.'

'I gather that the poor Indian has been disposed of – no, I don't know how much he cost – but of course people started talking again, things began to be remembered. So what is our hero to do? What did he do last time? But this time he needs a wife.'

'I say, you might consider my feelings.'

'Men were deceivers ever, my dear. I take it that you won't actually drink poison?'

'No, but he has taken me in.'

'But who's in deepest? Look at it from his point of view. He's got to go back to India with a wife, he discovers a lovely girl with oodles of tin and a thoroughly nice disposition; just what he needs. He marches in, trumpets blowing, flags flying, and what does he get?'

'Fortunately he doesn't know.'

'Of course, if he did know and you wanted to set up a partnership it would be the very ticket. You could have done worse: unlike your Cousin Charlie, he's a gentleman.'

'What makes you say that?'

'My spies have been at work, my dear. They have been investigating that precious nephew of mine. I know he's not in the running, but it's right you should know the form and I can tell you, I've heard from the stable boys. Charlie's a bad lot. No, I mean it, an election egg,* a real bad 'un.' He paused to light a cheroot.

'No one,' he continued, 'could call me straight-laced. I've taken my fun where I've found it, romped with the girls and maybe had a bit of fun at the back door. Sometimes, I won't deny it, I've had a bit of rough and tumble, but never really to hurt anyone, never – unless the other party was asking for it, and hollerin' pretty loud and clear. But your Charlie. Ever heard of a party by the name of de Sade? That's Charlie's style, and it's dirty and it's cruel; in fact the sort of thing that gets vice a bad name. Mary me dear, you steer clear of Charlie.'

'I will. But although I've no doubt he talks like a disciple of de Sade –

* An egg useful only as a missile. – M.E.

I've not read any of the books but I have a pretty fair notion of what that implies – still, can you really trust your spies?'

'I tell you, I have it from the stable, and it's not pretty. He has a little pad near Brighton; the butler's a male prostitute, the other servants are out of the stews. They lure boys in, make 'em drunk, tie 'em up, beat them and you know what. I tell you, some of the things I heard made me blush.'

'So I am pursued on every side by perverts.'

'That's about the size of it, me dear.'

'Uncle Hector, life is too complicated. I thought when I settled in the country I could lead a quiet life and wait for my majority and everything would be all right. I had not thought that England, let alone Ramsgate, would be such a hot-bed of unnatural vice and that the complications of society would be so unmanageable. Now I must go to Victoria to meet my cousin-in-law; she at least is not complicated.'

'Bred in Lesbos, ten pounds to a tanner, and loves you madly.'

The next few weeks were devoted to argument and preparation. Arguments about my hypothesis, against which Billy, very rightly, threw all the objections he could find; preparations for a programme of experiments and, of course, for Christmas.

Christmas and the New Year were, it seemed, to be celebrated in great style. In fact, the Christmas dinner at Ramsgate House was not a very brilliant affair. Our party was small and dull and elderly. Cecily was with us, having chosen to put off dim relations in Shropshire, the Colonel was doing his duty elsewhere; there were some old and tedious Strand cousins, Billy and Augusta and that was all. We ate and drank more than was good for us, we exchanged presents which, for the most part, we did not want. The only person who came out well was Charlie – he, who might so easily have been bored and sulky, was charming. He did his best to enliven us; he succeeded in being funny without making the kind of joke that would distress his mother.

When our enormous meal had been disposed of we removed to the drawing room. Some of us were more or less comatose. Then, quite without warning, something happened, an incident every detail of which I was to revolve in my mind for many years to come.

There was an argument, an argument that could be settled by reference to a book. I went to the library, found my book, glanced to make sure that I was in the right and hastened back to the drawing room. I ran smack into Charlie. He flung his arms around me, kissed me repeatedly and began, unskilfully, to undress me. He was very large and strong. He picked me up and carried me to a leather sofa, there presumably to rape me. I dropped the book, which I had been clutching as though it had been my virtue, and attempted to free myself. It was no use. He flung me down upon the sofa and flung himself on top of me. But at this point that hideous and apparently solid piece of furniture lost a leg. We spilled out on to the floor. Before Charlie could pick himself up (he was not quite sober) I was behind a mahogany table.

For a moment we faced each other panting and amazed. When I could I spoke, 'Listen Charlie, if you try that again I shall scream. I shall scream the house down; people will come; it will be very unpleasant and embarrassing and I shall have to find a house in another neighbourhood. That,' I added, for it had occurred to me that I ought to have been screaming all the time, 'that is why so far I have been silent. But if you start again I shall yell like a slaughtered pig.'

He stared at me, angry, dismayed, crestfallen. 'That damned woman has put you against me.'

'My dear Charlie, no one has put me "against you", not even yourself. But did you really suppose that I should welcome violence? Or that, even if I had, I should have been so imbecile as to consent to a session of violent love-making in the library while the rest of the company waited for us in the drawing room?'

'All right,' he said, and his air was that of one who accedes to an absurdly unreasonable objection, 'I will play the little gentleman. Miss Porthow, will you marry me?'

'Sir Charles, I will not.'

'It's that damned soldier.'

'I have no intention of marrying the Colonel if that's what you mean.'

'Listen to me, I know our Dickie, he's . . .' I noticed with sympathy that he was checking an indiscretion, 'he's after your money and nothing else.'

'Like enough. He's a man of sense and knows that there's little else to be after. But let me assure you Charlie, that I am not in love with the Colonel and I have good reason to suppose that he's not in love with me. I promise you that I shan't marry him.'

We were still on opposite sides of the library table. I was doing my best to repair my dress and to make sure that Charlie in his enthusiasm had not discovered too much. At that time a woman, even when wearing evening dress, was so completely encased that her sex could not easily be ascertained. It seemed all right. He, for his part, was scowling with his hands in his pockets like that man in the picture by Degas.

'Look Mary, what have you got against me?'

'Well, the last five minutes for a start.'

'But don't you see. I love you, I want you, I've got to have you. I'm perfectly willing to behave myself – this shan't happen again – but you simply must marry me.'

'Charlie, I'm sorry. Really I do like you very much when you take the trouble to be likeable. But, for reasons which I cannot discuss, I can marry neither you nor anyone else. That really must be the end of it. Now be a dear and go and tell them I have had a little accident with my dress and have gone to find a needle and thread. I'll be back in a moment. If you don't they will send a search party.'

I made to leave, but he intercepted me, snatching my wrist with such violence that I thought for an instant that there was to be a renewal of hostilities.

'No, you need not scream. I shall let you go in a moment. I know what you think, Mary: you think that I am just a foolish boy who can be rebuked, dismissed and forgotten. You are wrong; this is not the end of it and I shall oblige you to marry me. All right, you can go now.'

I left him feeling that he had recovered the initiative. He had spoken with intense conviction and seemed quite sure of himself, and I must admit that I was frightened. Not without reason.

The very next day, Boxing Day, we had to return to the Great House, this time for the servants' ball. Does that phrase mean anything to the present generation? It is years since there was a servants' ball at Ramsgate House, or anywhere else I fancy. Those decorous saturnalia of the British upper classes, classes then so sure of themselves that they could pretend for an evening to forget about class, are but a memory. Aunt Martha insisted that I come bringing Thérèse who, I must say, looked very well.

There was Charlie dancing with a housemaid, and Lady Brandon standing up with the butler.

I found myself waltzing with Mr Selmersham, Charlie's valet. He danced admirably, far better than his master, and was perfectly at his ease. I had already had a few words with him from time to time and had not much cared for him, but now I found him repellent and frightening. He perceived my fear and, as I could see, enjoyed it. When, as we danced, he whispered, 'Excuse me, Miss Porthow, please excuse me, but there is something very important that I ought to say to you in private – would you be so very indulgent as to grant me five minutes of your time?', I wanted to say no, but said yes.

The housekeeper's room, to which he led me with exaggerated deference, was well chosen for his purpose; although one could just hear the music and the scrape of feet, it was quiet and could not be approached without notice.

Mr Selmersham began with elaborate apologies, almost dancing up and down. His countenance, like his speech, was respectful, servile even, but his attitude of evil, mocking joy was quite perceptible. Never once did he say anything which could not easily have been repeated in a court of law.

He asked my pardon for mentioning such a matter, but Sir Charles told him everything. His master admired me very much. So far, he believed, Sir Charles had not prevailed in his suit. If he were wrong he would say no more and beg pardon for the intrusion, no one could feel the intrusion more deeply then he.

He paused. I was silent. He continued: if his master were to be disappointed a 'situation' might arise, 'annoying for you, Miss, disastrous for Sir Charles'. Clearly he was pleased by that phrase and repeated it.

'If thwarted,' he continued, 'Sir Charles might say things, very foolish things, very outrageous things, that everyone would regret.'

He paused again, and I began to see what he had in store for me. 'Sir Charles does get ideas, very, very strange ideas. He fancies himself very much as a fascinator of ladies and, in this case, because he has failed to be fascinating, he will have it that you are not a lady, I mean not a woman, that you are – I know that this will sound ridiculous – a boy disguised as a lady. Preposterous is it not?'

I agreed, with as much assurance as I could summon, that it was indeed preposterous.

'That, in a manner of speaking, is the trouble. He will make a laughing-stock of himself. But of course it can be tiresome for you too: people love gossip, don't they, Miss? They love to pry and peer, and with nonsense of this kind it is hard to know what to do. I have said all I can to put the nonsense out of his head you may be sure, but if he's disappointed again there will be no holding him – I know him, Miss, there will be a lot of silly, annoying whispering.'

'Once one has begun to doubt, even so brilliant a piece of mimicry as yours fails to convince . . .' Those had been Billy's words and they returned with horrid force. I managed to observe that this would no doubt be the case. It could be tiresome. But I could not be expected to marry a man because he might threaten me with ludicrous gossip.

'Oh, believe me, Miss Porthow, nothing could be further from my thoughts. My idea in asking for this interview was quite the opposite from that. I want to kill the notion before it can come to life. I want to make it impossible for Sir Charles to say such things, things so disrespectful to you and so injurious to himself.'

He paused to let me speak, but I remained silent, guessing that he had some other engine to use upon me and that the worst was yet to come.

'I am hoping, Miss, that you will be ready to disprove his accusation before he can make it.'

'To disprove? But that's not so easy.'

'Not on the face of it, Miss. But I have given the matter some thought and I have found a way by which, if you would be so good as to offer your assistance, we can make an end of the scandal at once and quite without saying anything embarrassing, or unpleasant.'

There was another pause and he continued. 'On the 29th you are invited here. Dr Brandon will be staying with Professor Small. I suggest, Miss, that after dinner you should be taken ill, you can whisper to Her Ladyship — I don't know what, but whatever ladies do say when they are suffering from some female disorder, some ladies' complaint — of course, you will know what to say. As a natural result, Dr Brandon being absent, they will send for old Nannie Weller; whenever anyone in the house is ill Nannie has to be there anyway. So there will be some kind of medical examination and then, very soon, you will recover and in half an hour the whole business will be forgotten.'

'And then?'

'And then, Miss Porthow, I can go to Sir Charles and tell him that the whole thing is absurd. Nannie, the biggest gossip in the county, found nothing — nothing unusual that is — and so the whole story falls down and so will Sir Charles kindly forget it, and he, obviously, would have to do so. What I am suggesting, Miss Porthow, may seem tiresome and and a bit impertinent, but I can assure you, Miss, that no impertinence is intended.'

'The assurance is supererogatory, Mr Selmersham.'

'Quite so, Miss Porthow. The point is that it would put a stop to this unpleasant business before it can begin.'

'And when if it does begin is it likely to begin, Mr Selmersham?'

'After the New Year's ball, Miss. I believe that Sir Charles will, er, "pop" the question again on that occasion. If he is again disappointed he will I fear be very cross and quite unmanageable.'

'That is in five days' time.'

'Exactly, Miss. That's why the 29th seems such a good opportunity.'

'Thank you, Mr Selmersham.'

'Thank *you*, Miss, for listening so patiently to what I had to say – what had to be said. Believe me Miss Porthow, it has been a most distressing task.'

He looked about as distressed as someone who has picked a sovereign from the pavement.

I made my way back to the party and there, after a few minutes of empty conversation, I thought to ask for Thérèse. I was told that she had walked home across the park. There was snow on the ground and she had been assured of a place in our carriage. A hideous thought struck me. I persuaded Cecily to desert the second footman and go home with me. There were maddening delays and I had to conceal my anxiety. At last we reached India Lodge. I ran upstairs to my room. No Thérèse. She was lying on her own bed. She had taken thirty sleeping tablets.

I made her take an emetic. Fortunately the pills had not begun to work; she was sick again and again; I sat up with her until, at last, day broke and she slept.

Her story was what I had thought it would be. Selmersham, a very successful lady-killer, had 'made up to her'. He hadn't actually seduced her, but he had achieved his main object. On Christmas evening he had made her drunk and she had talked. When she saw me give him a private interview she realised that I was betrayed, and by her. She did not think that she could face me and sought the only refuge that she could find.

We had several long talks that night and again on the following day. I made her promise never to do such a thing again. I told her, truly I think, that I should have to follow her out of life. I had not realised, until then, just how important she was to my happiness. I told her also that it might now be necessary for us vanish and this time she must not make difficulties. To this she agreed. Also, because I had the first inklings of a plan, I asked her not to break with Selmersham. She was to procrastinate, she would have him when Sir Charles married me. She found this harder to accept – not that she doubted her ability to keep him dangling, but because, as she put it, she could never again feel really happy until she saw the handle of a knife sticking out of his belly.

THE CHANGELING: CHAPTER X

'You must do a bunk, Mary, these half-measures are no use.'

Uncle Hector and I were in our teatime lair amongst the rubber plants and the potted palms and I had been trying to persuade him, and myself, that I knew how to stand firm and deal with Charlie. Uncle Hector wouldn't hear of it.

'I know it's a dirty shame that you should be driven out of your comfortable home and have to say goodbye to all that tin, and all your good works, and even the life you lead, for I see you like it. I know all that, and I know it's very hard to leave it all; but you must face facts: Charlie has you by the you-know-whats. You simply can't afford to be suspected; once you're suspected, you're cooked; you will be found out and then, you know, things could be really ugly for you. If, on the other hand, you go to the God-shop and get spliced you will be in his power, and I can assure you that my spies *are* telling the truth when they tell me he's a proper swine. The mere fact that he's ready to bring you to heel with blackmail gives you his true phizog.'

'I'm not sure that he is blackmailing me.'

'How, not sure?'

'I am not sure that he knows anything. Talking to him I cannot believe it. I think Selmersham may have told him that he knows how to coerce me, or something of that kind, but without giving full information. It would be like him to keep his own counsel and then, probably, try to blackmail us both.'

'That could be possible but it doesn't make much odds at present. What you have to bear in mind, me dear, is that there's nothing that you could call affection. He's simply after your tin – that, and a key to your back door perhaps. It's no good thinking otherwise, so I say you must run. What does Billy say?'

'Poor Billy is split in two: half of him thinks as you do; the other half needs me, me and my cash, says that we stand on the verge of great things, great medical discoveries that are worth any risk.'

'Yes, but it's *you* who take the risk – and the risk is too great. Be sensible, Mary me girl. All you need to do is to send me a telegram, come to London with your girl and I'll have everything ready for the grand transformation act.'

'You're very kind and I am most grateful. But there is another possibility.'

'The Colonel?'

'Yes, I could tell him everything. He would listen.'

'He might tell you that he had troubles enough on his own plate.'

'He might, but he would be sympathetic. Besides, I wouldn't go to him empty-handed. I could offer myself, and I should in some ways be a convenience. He would probably let me help Billy with his work.'

'And Selmersham?'

'If anyone knows how to deal with Selmersham, he would. Probably he could tell as many tales about Charlie as Charlie could tell about me. If I married and went to India the blackmail would lose much of its force.'

'Do you like the Colonel?'

'Yes, well enough to accept his protection. And he needs a wife.'

'Well, it's an idea . . .'

I did not hear the rest, for I had become aware of a couple sitting not far off, but almost concealed by greenery.

'If you look through the zareba,' I said, 'you will see a very smartly dressed woman wearing a black bonnet with a white feather. It's Mrs Gordon.'

'And the chap with her?'

'The Colonel.'

Uncle Hector peered for a bit then, very sadly, said, 'Mary me dear, you're pipped to the post. The Colonel has found his wife. You really *must* do a bunk.'

I just caught my train, bundled breathless into a first-class compartment and found Cecily. There were other passengers, so we fell silent. She had the *Standard*, I had Wallace's *Malay Archipelago*. We both stared at our reading matter. I wonder how much either of us read.

What on earth was I to do? I could refuse him. I could tell him the truth about myself and offer to buy him off. I could bolt.

To refuse, to tell the truth – both would leave me open to further blackmail; the second was particularly dangerous because I should, in effect, be bringing the blackmail down upon my own head; but neither option really seemed feasible as things stood. If I could be quite certain that Charlie knew nothing I might just possibly have risked it. Selmersham on his own was not very formidable: he had servants' gossip with no atom of proof – I felt sure that I could disregard him or, with Charlie's help, silence him. But for that very reason I could not believe that Charlie did know nothing; it seemed far more likely that Selmersham was acting as his agent.

Now, Selmersham backed by Charlie was very formidable indeed; a few half-uttered hints from Charlie and I was done for. If refused, he would strike me down. If appeased he would demand Danegeld. I knew well enough that he would come back again and again for more and more money. In the end he would ruin me and, what was worse, he would ruin the research. The mere idea of being blackmailed was enough to fill me with horror – anything would be better than that.

And what if I bolted? That was defeat. Worse still, it was a defeat in which the research would be sacrificed, and our research was the most important thing in my life. To abandon it without a struggle would be too shameful a course.

There remained only marriage. And Charlie, for all his faults, was very attractive. Of course, the risks were great. I might lose my money, the research and, if Uncle Hector's informants were to be accepted, something else, something very unpleasant. Was it, however, too humiliating and too painful an ordeal if I could stop the blackmail and save my work?

Then I saw that I could accept. Charlie wanted the cash but he knew nothing about the intricacies of Sir Amos's will, and if Mellish would help me I could keep the money in my own hands – there would be nothing that he could do about it. Under these circumstances, I could bargain with him and silence Selmersham. As a last resort I could even threaten to bolt, leaving a confession that would ruin them both. Better still, in marrying me Charlie would become my accomplice. In effect, I could become the blackmailer.

My safety, indeed my only hope, lay in audacity: I had to surrender myself to him at the altar, garlanded, presumably, in orange blossom. If I kept my head I could save the research.

The Colonel then was really an irrelevance and, considering the matter less selfishly, I saw that he had chosen very well. Cecily was the girl for him, since there had to be a girl. It was not I but he who needed looking after, and Cecily would do it beautifully. She would be the perfect wife for a very unconventional soldier. With such a wife, even the War Office would forgive him for being intelligent.

And so when we were properly installed with hot bricks for our feet in my carriage I was able, warmly and sincerely to congratulate her. I did take her unawares! I'll swear her jaw dropped. We kissed with real affection and all that evening we planned the fine things that General Sir Buxton Russell and his lady wife would do in the years to come.

Ay de mi, how could we know that he would die of the cholera in '98?

It was that very evening – no, it was the next – that I was supposed to go through this charade at Ramsgate House. I pretended to be ill and left my enemy to wonder, but this was merely a delaying tactic. The New Year's ball had to be faced and I had made up my mind. In fact, it was all quite simple when it came to the point.

Those were the days of programmes and I was already engaged by Charlie for the first and second waltz. The first we danced badly – he was nervous and ill at ease. The second we 'sat out'. In fact, we stood in the library, the scene of our previous encounter, and there, having invited me to sit down, he simply observed, 'I am again asking you to marry me. I will take no denial.'

'Very well, I will marry you.'

He kissed me and said that he was very happy. I replied that I too was happy. He led me back to the ball and then indeed he became almost boisterous in his joy. It was as though we had agreed to play a game together: we were playing at being engaged.

There was, of course, a great deal of buzz and bustle. Aunt Martha shed tears of joy; Cecily and the Colonel made beautifully polite noises; Billy made a dreadful speech. But naturally it was Charlie's behaviour which engaged my attention. He was immensely proud and happy, and of course I had to dance with him again and again and tell him that he danced divinely and how proud I was to be his. He longed to be flattered, above all by me. And he was.

'Is it wise?' asked Thérèse.

'I am not sure. We still have time to bolt. But it does give us our one chance of getting even with Mr Selmersham.'

That, for her, was sufficient.

I rose early, as I sometimes did when the morning was lovely and I had serious matters to consider. My walk took me, appropriately enough, to a little neo-classical tempietto known as the Temple of Hymen and there, coming through the trees I saw a man. Charlie, I thought, and felt slightly agitated, but it was the Colonel.

For a moment we were both confused; then, simultaneously, we began to congratulate each other. The Colonel had already performed this duty but it had been in public. In private mine was the easier task, or so I felt. I therefore held out my hand, said that I wished him well and believed that he had made a very wise decision. It was easy to expand on this theme and it gave him time to meditate his own speech.

'You are,' he said, 'marrying a very remarkable man, a man of taste and intelligence who may go far, particularly with you at his side. I think you will both be happy, indeed it is impossible that he should not be happy with such a bride. But Mary, do you realise that it is not going to be easy? He is very young, very impetuous, you will need to conduct yourselves with wisdom and perhaps some forbearance. He sees only condescension in compassion, and can become roused when checked. In the beginning I think you may have to be wise for two.'

We were walking down the path which meanders gently towards the Lodge. For a time we were both silent. Then he resumed: 'We are old friends, he and I. You will find him, as a husband, passionate and proud – passionate by nature, proud of his conquest, and rightly. But very young and sometimes blundering. In some ways you are much older than he. As you know, and as he will learn, pride and passion are splendid things, but in a marriage wisdom and loving kindness are far more important. Mary, do you love him? Forgive me, I should not have asked that.'

'I feel that you are privileged. Yes, Richard, I do; I believe I can make our marriage happy. I love him well enough to save him, if need be from himself.'

'He is indeed a fortunate man. But Mary, you do realise that there is no more difficult operation?'

We were silent again and then, in quite a new tone of voice he said, 'I know that you are a classical scholar.'

'Hardly that.'

'But you have read some Livy?'

'Livy? I once tried him and found him a bore.'

'Look again Mary, look at the story of Cannae. With superior forces the Romans thrust the Carthaginians back, making a great dent in their centre, almost breaking their line. Intoxicated by success they pressed on, forgetting their flanks until suddenly the Carthaginians swept in upon their adversaries' wings so that the Romans found themselves surrounded and were destroyed.'

We had reached the garden gate. The Colonel put his hand on the latch. 'Allow me to go on boring you for a moment. Hannibal had enticed the Romans into a too impetuous attack. Cannae should have been the end of the war. It was not, because the Carthaginians in their turn lost their heads in the moment of victory. If they had been mag- nanimous the two nations might have lived in peace. Instead the war went on and, in the end, it was Carthage which was destroyed.'

'What are you two discussing so earnestly?' It was Cecily at the window.

'The Colonel is telling me about the Punic Wars.'

'That's a fine thing. You ought to be discussing my perfections.'

So we came inside, broke our fast pleasantly enough with conver- sation which was agreeable but forgettable until we heard a visitor arrive and, for the second time that morning I prepared to meet my fiancé. In fact it was Billy.

We left the young lovers alone and went to my 'stink room', the room set aside for scientific business. Here Billy sat and said, 'So you decided to go through with it.'

'It's the only chance of carrying on the research. Have you done those sums?'

The conversation became financial: we had to find out how much we could do and for how long without using my money. We discussed that matter at some length until I returned to the immediate situation.

'You realise that Charlie will tell me to stop work?'

'That's tiresome, but surely you can persuade him that this is something really important?'

'No Billy, I can't. He knows how much I value the work and how bitter it will be for me to be out of it. That is precisely why he will tell me to leave you. It will be demanded as a proof of affection. I shall do as I am told.'

'Mary!'

'Yes, Billy, I shall and, for the time being, you will have to find another assistant.'

'But it's absurd. I need you.'

'Look Billy, you must understand my situation. It is in the highest degree dangerous. If I quarrel with him he can break it off; if he breaks it off he can give a thoroughly good reason for doing so; and what will become of the research then?'

'But if you give in to him now you will find that you have to give in to him later.'

'That's what you think and that's what I'm very anxious that he should think. If you will consider the matter carefully you will see that I am doing the only thing that I can do. You should read Livy, my dear.'

'Livy? What on earth has he to do with it?'

'Never mind. Let it suffice that until he takes me to the altar, I intend to submit to my lover in everything.'

There was a good deal more discussion and it was some time before I could persuade Billy that I was not being foolish. But in the end he was more or less convinced, which was just as well for my strategy had to be put into effect at once and in his presence, for soon the bell rang and it *was* Charlie.

He found his way up to the stink room and, after an enthusiastic salutation, justified my prudence and foresight by remarking, 'Mary, my sweet, now that you have said that you belong to me I am going to give you an opportunity of showing your sincerity. Not that I am really asking much, only,' here he glanced around at my books and bottles, 'only that you should leave all this dreary nonsense to our gifted cousin. It suits him well enough, but all these ghastly statistics and scientific slumming doesn't suit you at all.'

'My lord, you know how much this means to me, are you really insisting that I should abandon all my lovely work?'

'Yes Mary, from now on you take your orders from me. I will not marry a lab-girl.'

'In that case I must stop being one. Billy, anything that you may need shall be sent over to Dainton this afternoon. The rest shall be sacrificed on a votive bonfire.'

'And is poor Mary, who loves this research, to have no choice in the matter?'

'My lord, may I answer him? There is no choice in the matter. I do love the work but I love Charlie a great deal more, and I trust him to know what is best for me.'

'Oh damn!' said Billy, and went out slamming the door.

When he had gone Charlie laughed, put an arm around my waist and said, 'Mary my sweet, you exceed my expectations. I had feared that you would argue.'

'What's the use of arguing when one is helpless?'

'A very sound maxim. Let us go out of this nasty room and enjoy the beautiful day.'

He was in high good humour and chattered aimlessly but amusingly until we reached the Temple of Hymen. Then he became a little more serious.

'Mary, don't think I undervalue your sacrifice. I know that we do not yet think alike; you may even be a little cross with me. But I shall convert you. You are far too modest but I shall make you vain, vain and happy. I shall make you see yourself as something precious and wonderful and remote from all the ugliness of life. Mona Lisa might have made an excellent hospital nurse, who can tell – she was content to exist and to be immortalised beautifully. So you are destined to be fine and remote and wonderful. Not yet, but when I have forced you into the exquisite mould that I have wrought for you. I am the artist; your consummate fate is to be the perfect medium.'

Translated out of the original nonsense this meant: 'Will you let me do as I please with you?'

The answer had to be yes, all the answers had to be yes. It was my first big gamble and I won it. For having asserted his rights he did not insist on them. It was my acquiesence rather than my person that he now desired. Of course, he took some liberties but although he had the licence, he was not licentious. I became almost sure that he knew what he would find if he were vigorously to resume his search and for that very reason he was anxious not to extend his enquiries too far. As yet he did not want a show-down, although of course that magnificent body would demand its plenary rights eventually. His pleasure lay, for the time being, in the assertion of power, I was to acknowledge that he was the master. I was ready to oblige.

But it was hard and indeed shameful work. He needed to be assured continually of the reality of my surrender. To this end he issued incessant demands and prohibitions and I had to suggest that these entailed a real sacrifice on my part; even when, as frequently happened, his regulations were trivial and unimportant he had for ever to be flattered by a show of sacrificial obedience.

There were times when he forgot to play the tyrant, times when he could be excellent company and I did not need to make a Flibert of myself, but during the period of our engagement they were too few.

Here let me append the report of a conversation between lovers.

He: I have been talking to Mellish about your settlement. I do hate this legal business, they use such vile prose as to be virtually incomprehensible and when Mellish explains he darkens counsel. But I don't know that I care for it: as far as I can see everything remains in your hands.

Me: Does it matter, surely we'll have money enough?

He: Oh yes, but it's the image that is wrong. The wife should not hold the purse-strings.

Me: But my lord, I could no more hold a purse-string than I could hold a whip. Mellish imagines that by tying my money up so that, theoretically, it is in my hands, he can prevent you from spending it – and you do have a reputation for glorious extravagance – on race horses, yachts, Monte Carlo and, I dare say, actresses . . .

He: Mary!

Me: But even if it were actresses, do you think that I should give even the feeblest twitch to the purse-strings? You have only to say "Mary, I need twenty thou' ", or whatever it is and I shall give you the money, and you will give me the exquisite pleasure of showing my obedience. Poor old Mellish doesn't know me; he thinks I should stand on my rights. Whereas you know perfectly well that even if I could find a right to stand on, I should immediately tumble off it.

He: Well, I suppose I need not really worry about arrangements which will exist only on paper.

Me: Indeed, my lord, you need not. You have won me, Charles, and I don't give myself by halves.

Chorus: Oh black and deliberate falsehood.

I wanted to grasp those purse-strings in the tightest of hands. I was glad to make Charlie a rich man, but equally I fully intended not to let him ruin us – and, above all, not to starve our research. There really was a lot of money and that did not seem too difficult a programme. My trouble was that I did not know how to find a legal mechanism which would make my position secure. The difficulty was rather unexpectedly solved.

Charlie was off to Newmarket. I had a day off duty but was summoned by Aunt Martha. I found her in her ugly sitting room with Mellish. They were uneasy, they had something difficult to say. In the end it was Mellish who, with much stately beating about the bush, came to the point.

'Miss Porthow, we are in a difficulty. You are marrying a man who has every gift and every virtue but who suffers from, what shall I call it? – an hereditary disease, an illness of the temperament. Like his father and like his grandfather he simply does not understand money.'

'Like pouring water into a colander,' observed the fond mother.

'Even so great a fortune as yours would be at risk.'

'But if I understand rightly, and I must admit that I am a child in these matters, the estate remains in my hands.'

'What's the use of that,' said Aunt Martha, 'when you do exactly what he tells you to do? Oh, I've seen you together, and you can't deny it – he'd have every penny out of you for the asking.'

I reflected that I had rather overacted the part of slave-girl. It was hard to correct that impression. I temporised.

'What then is to be done? If Charles is not to be trusted with money and I am not to be trusted with Charles, what *can* be done?'

'Your father,' replied Mr Mellish, 'was a very far-sighted man. He was anxious that you and your fortune should not fall into the wrong hands. Amongst the provisions of your father's will there is one which, while it makes you absolute mistress of your father's income, would for a number of years leave the capital in the hands of your guardian. I do not feel that I can use this instrument without your consent Miss Porthow, and when you attain your majority I shall need that consent in writing.'

'So the capital would be in your hands and I could not give it away because I should be powerless to do so?'

'For a period of five years.'

'I should make it ten,' said the fond mother.

'At the end of five years there might be a family to consider. Also I think that there is one thing that you may have overlooked. My future husband may want to be extravagant and you may need to restrain him, but there is also the possibility that I myself may want to be extravagant.'

'You have not given that impression, Miss Porthow.'

'Until now I have not been tempted to extravagance. But now I believe that my cousin's scientific work is really important and may become really expensive. I shall try to persuade my husband to let me assist it with a very large endowment.'

'Very well, Miss Porthow. If he agrees so will I.'

'That's a bargain then. Aunt Martha and Mr Mellish, I know and trust you both. I will do what you ask.'

'Bless you Mary, you are a good girl.'

'Since I have been so good may I ask you, Mr Mellish, for a little money? I want to buy something for Mrs Gordon, and perhaps for my prodigal fiancé.'

Mr Mellish mentioned a sum so enormous that for a moment I thought he must be joking. In fact, he never joked about money. As a result I was able to buy something really nice for Cecily; it was my only grand extravagance. An eighteenth-century Polybius for the Colonel and a little Monet for Charles were both dirt cheap and I was still rich enough to open an account with a foreign bank, just in case.

That was in Paris and Paris was delightful. Charles did not come with us – for some reason Aunt Martha thought it improper – so there were Cecily, the Colonel, Thérèse and me; it was like a revival of our best days when Kate was still with us in Italy. There was a little shopping and a lot of picture-gazing and some theatre-going and everything was delightful. But the best thing was that I could stop telling lies, I could forget that imaginary Mary Porthow, the one in whom Charles wished to believe. I never could understand how he tolerated that tedious young woman.

It seemed only a few days after our return that I was watching closely to see how a bride should behave as Cecily went to the altar. A few hours later I was saying goodbye as the P. & O. liner sailed out upon the Thames. I think we both wept.

Very soon there came that rainy afternoon when I sat with Uncle Hector's postcard before me:

STILL TIME TO ABSQUATULATE. HERE AT YOUR SERVICE IF NEEDED.

I had only to invent an excuse, take the train to London and, instead of being a married woman, become a young man with a girl on my arm strolling through the Galleria in Milan. My whole life would have been different and Charlie would have avoided an early death.

But I dressed in white satin and Nottingham lace and went to Ramsgate Church and what Billy called 'the usual lies' – only they were rather unusual lies – were proclaimed and there was Mendelssohn and champagne and a lot of silver paper and my going-away dress laid out by Thérèse and everything had gone splendidly. Then I went and put my foot in it.

The carriage was waiting, Charlie and I were standing amidst a group of young men and Charlie was extolling his property. He was coarse and offensive, pointing to my neck, my eyes, my hair, as though nobody had ever had such things before, and then he ran his big hands over my body and bade everyone admire it. I asked him softly but urgently to desist, but he was too drunk and was enjoying himself too much. Despite some raised eyebrows and astonished mutterings he continued to be, not only gross but poetical.

> See, when she walks, a miracle of grace,
> Divine in balance and divine in pace.*

'Oh Charlie, do stop making a fool of yourself. Everyone knows that it's only my bank balance that interests you.'

I have never seen a man so disconcerted: it was so long since I had spoken to him in such a manner. But why did I say it? I had drunk too much champagne, but I was further intoxicated by fury and exhilaration – exhilarated because now, after months of perfect dissembling, we were safely married; I suddenly saw that I could discard this odious and servile personality. Nevertheless, I should have held my tongue and would have, had he not seemed to be deliberately provoking me – treating me like a prize sow in a pen. Unable to contain my long-pent-up rage I continued to tell him what I thought of his behaviour as he led me to the waiting carriage.

I realised too late that I had gone too far. I attempted to apologise. It was no use. He had been horribly shocked by my tone. He had forgotten that I was capable of opposing him in any way and was beginning to realise that the new situation held disagreeable possibilities. In fact, he had become that dangerous thing, a frightened

---

* Unidentified. Possibly a very free translation by Sir Charles of Virgil, *Vera incessu patuit dea, Aeneid,* 1.405. – M.E.

tyrant. I could see that he was meditating some tremendous reassertion of his authority as he sulked all the way to Penny Villa.

Arriving at that horrible place I had hoped to be greeted by Thérèse; she had gone ahead by train. Instead it was Selmersham who stood at the door. Charlie took him aside and whispered something. Selmersham took my overnight bag, conducted me up two flights of stairs, opened a heavy door, ushered me in, dropped the bag on the floor and locked me in.

After a few minutes a tearful Thérèse was thrust in together with a good deal of luggage, both hers and mine.

It took me some time to calm Thérèse. She was overflowing with information.

'They are criminals down there, Mademoiselle – I mean Milady. The cook is out of a brothel I am sure of it, and the scullery-maid little better, the "buttons" is a male prostitute and I think an assassin. As for Mr Selmersham . . . They all want to know whether you have brought money with you; it seems they never get paid and hardly dared to face the tradesmen until the engagement was announced. Sir Charles lives on credit, the servants get paid by being invited to their master's table, that's their "fun". Milady, we have fallen into the hands of miscreants.'

Thérèse had learnt a great deal during the short time in which she had been at liberty. Amongst other things she already knew where everyone in the house slept, a piece of information which was later to be useful.

At length the door was unlocked. Selmersham put his head in, and told us to dress. He gave us half an hour – what was more to the point, he gave us a candle.

Then came another long wait. Almost an hour elapsed before the door was again opened. We were cold and tired and very hungry by then. Three men came into the room, my husband, Selmersham and the buttons. Charlie was armed with a whip, Selmersham with some lengths of cord. I perceived that we were about to face circumstances which, although they had been

CHAPTER 3

[Maurice Evans's Investigation
concluded]

This is all that remains of the manuscript. Ten pages have been cut out of the minute-book in which it was written. It seems likely that the author found the rest of his story too painful to be preserved.

The only hope of completing my knowledge lay in a further interview with Thérèse Boileau. With this end in mind I returned to Amboise. I told her how much I already knew and let her see a copy of *The Changeling*. I also gave her a letter from Sir John Frend in which he answered for my discretion and encouraged her to be quite frank. She was at first very angry and distressed and came near to sending me away *re infecta*, as Henry Brandon would have put it. But after many hours of discussion the atmosphere improved and she asked me to give her a week in which to think the matter over. When I returned I found that she had occupied her time in drawing up a very full statement.

Mademoiselle Boileau's statement was, of course, written in French. In places she attempts a rather grandiose style, in others she is barely literate. There are many repetitions most of which have been excised. I have in places rewritten the text in order to make it more readable. The answers to a number of supplementary questions have also been incorporated in the text; with these I bring our story to an end.

The events at Penny Villa, April 7th and 8th, 1891
Statement by Thérèse Boileau

Monsieur,
Finally I have decided to tell everything.

I begin where Milady broke off. Three men entered that poor room where we were shut up as though we had been criminals. There was Sir Charles, the buttons and that dirty animal, Selmersham. Sir Charles dominated the scene like a Mephistopheles between two smaller devils.

They had been drinking. They looked bad and dangerous. Their breath stank and I admit that I was horribly frightened of them. Milady remained calm. In a dry, even an authoritative tone she demanded of Sir Charles that he explain himself. He replied, with the utmost brutality, that he was the master and that we were to be tied up and brought downstairs. Without for a moment losing her dignity she argued with him. For reply he cracked his whip. She fell silent, indeed I do not think that she ever spoke to him again.

Selmersham set himself to his odious task, not without obvious pleasure. You cannot conceive how infamous it was to see that low scoundrel, that beast, setting himself to insult and to humiliate so beautiful, delicate and distinguished a person as my mistress. Me too he tied my hands behind me with a cord, but for me that was less painful, less odious, there was some measure of equality between us. I knew, or thought I knew, what he wanted of me. I had to endure it still hoping for a time when I could thrust a knife into his belly. But Milady, so good, so lovely, she should not have had to suffer such an outrage. It was abominable, but it was only the beginning.

Well, we were taken down to the 'theatre', it was a little auditorium which served as a dining room. There we met the 'ladies' that is to say the cook, the maid, the 'scullery'. They greeted us with ironic cheers, laughter and indecent jokes. They too had drunk. The meal was far advanced. They had finished a piece of pork, a big knife and fork remained on the table amongst the debris, they also had had chicken, vegetables and salad, there were a great many bottles on the table. Coffee and brandy had already been served. The table was empty towards the stage so that the diners could see what was going on there. Sir Charles was at the extreme left, facing the stage, he put Milady on his right, then there was the maid, then, nearest the kitchen, Selmersham, with the cook on his right, next to her the buttons with me on his right and next to me facing Sir Charles, the scullery.

Amidst all that rabble Milady remained calm and dignified. She said nothing, not a word, even when refusing to eat, for although she must have been hungry, she would take nothing, she simply pursed her lips and turned her head away. Sir Charles poured some wine and pressed the glass to her lips, but still she would not drink and he, with almost incredible brutality, dashed the wine into her face. Remember that she could not defend herself at all but sat like some ivory statue with the wine trickling over her bare shoulders. Me, I confess that I was not so proud and when the scullery – she was I think one of those little tarts who specialise in abnormalities – gave me food and wine I could not refuse. Anyway that poor creature was less nasty than the maid and the cook. She was very much afraid of Selmersham but nevertheless whispered a few sympathetic words in my ear. My torment was the buttons, an overgrown boy, a male whore. Seeing that I was defenceless he took disgusting liberties.

They continued to drink, to sing and to laugh – the noise was unbearable. At last Sir Charles rose and walked awkwardly up on to the stage. Then he called for silence and made a speech, intended I think to be witty. The others of course applauded their master, but I couldn't understand half of it. Perhaps it was for this reason that I was dumbfounded by what followed.

Monsieur, I have agreed to tell you the whole truth about that terrible night, but it is hard indeed to tell you what happened now. It was something which I would not have thought possible amongst the most degraded cannibals.

Well, Sir Charles came down from the stage and took Milady – his own wife, sir – untied her and then fastened her again to the column that supported the proscenium arch, that is, quite close to me. I have to be exact in giving these details for, as Milady was to say later, 'they were all important'. He made her put her arms around the column, as though she were embracing it, and then tied her wrists together. He also put a cord around her waist. He then tore away her skirts so as to leave her buttocks – such exquisite buttocks, Monsieur – quite naked, but not so much that her sex might be observed.

Then the filthy pig called for his whip. It was not to be found, they searched everywhere. So he took a napkin, soaked it in wine and used that. I had the tiny satisfaction to see that he was too drunk to do as much harm as he wished. But this, you will not believe me, was only a prelude. The dirty beast, let this be swiftly written, raped my poor mistress, there on the stage in front of everyone. But I still have to be exact, it was not a normal rape, such as might happen at any time, it was, how shall I put it? – the rape of sodom.

Finally, and here we sink to almost incredible depths of horror, and it is frightening to think that even the vilest of men can sink so low, but it is true, having violated his wife in the most degrading manner that can be imagined, this sorry individual withdrew and invited its valet to follow and take its place.

Even there, amongst those brutes without honour and without conscience, there was a murmur of protest. The scullery cried out as though terrified by such an enormity. I would have done likewise if I had not already expressed my disgust with such energy that a gag had been put in my mouth. Selmersham cowed them with threats which I did not understand. He did everything, and with enthusiasm. He deserved a far worse fate than that which awaited him on the morrow.

Then there was a kind of lull. The cook and the maid still sang, but with less force, and I had the impression that after the intervention of Selmersham there was a little reaction, perhaps even a little stirring of conscience in their souls. As for Sir Charles, quite drunk and fast asleep he lay back snoring in his chair. Selmersham went on drinking a mixture of brandy and champagne.

But from where she sat by my side the scullery looked at Milady who was still tied to her column and, I think, weeping. The girl took the large knife which had been used for the pork, crept up discreetly and cut Milady's bonds. Then she returned to my side and made herself as small as possible.

I remained where I was, still gagged, still bound. Morally I had suffered atrociously but physically I had hardly been attacked. It was the buttons who decided that my turn had come. He began to undress me. Naturally there was practically nothing that I could do, but Selmersham, who regarded me as his legitimate prey, woke up. He rose, walked round to my side of the table and ordered the buttons to desist. The two gangsters exchanged the compliments habitual in such company, that is to say they exchanged abuse, and then suddenly came to blows. I was badly placed to see what happened But I gather that Selmersham smashed a bottle and jabbed it into his opponent's muzzle. The young man had time to kick his adversary in the stomach. They both staggered back. The buttons seeing his shirt covered with blood ran into the kitchen. Selmersham held the field but his face was livid, he tottered away towards the lavatory, but fell, and to save himself, clung to his master. By the happiest chance the food and liquor, urged by that kick in the stomach, erupted. He still clung to Sir Charles and at the same time he vomited, but copiously, like a tap, like a fire hydrant, like the fountains of Versailles and his half-digested outpourings deluged the head, the hair, the face, in fact the whole person of the baronet.

It was my first happy moment since I had entered that house. The best of it was that Selmersham remained as though glued to the body of his employer, who woke up in a great state of bewilderment, even of fear, while this animal continued to spew filth straight into his face.

It was not a very pretty sight, but it was funny. I did not have a chance to enjoy the spectacle at leisure for I was seized from behind, my bonds were cut, and I myself was pushed out of the theatre and up the stairs into the little room which we had left – how long ago? It seemed like a week.

It was Milady. When the scullery set her free she remained as though dead at the foot of the column. Little by little she regained her strength and restored the circulation in her wrists. Then she waited for her opportunity. It came when Selmersham fell upon his master, all eyes were fixed upon that comedy. It was so easy to leave unnoticed that she had time to collect the carcass of a chicken and a bottle of wine.

You, Monsieur, who knew him only through the modest pages of his novel, imagine no doubt that Milady (I have used this title for so many years that I cannot change it now) was a feeble creature, a cowardly weakling. Monsieur, it is not true; there was a sweet and timid side to his nature; but he could be proud and strong.

But you know she was amazing. When we were back in our room I had but two ideas: firstly to comfort her as best I might; then to fly, no matter whither, but at once. Instead of that it was she who had to comfort me, and when I proposed flight, she replied, 'Fly? From those imbeciles? They had made a trap and caught themselves.' I told her I was frightened lest they should come back and she had the spirit to laugh, 'Those gentlemen hardly have the strength to get upstairs.'

She lit the candle and by its light showed me the big knife that she had brought from the dining room and then, tearing the chicken to pieces and eating it with her hands, she gave it me. 'Not too much zeal, be careful not to use it unless you really have to, for me there is this whip which my husband thoughtfully left on the bed. And now,' she said as she finished the bird, 'to bed with us. We have work to do tomorrow and must be up early.'

In effect she woke me at five. 'Thérèse,' she said, 'dress me with care. I have got to be very much the lady, very severe, not at all frivolous.'

I did my best and I know my job. While I worked she explained her plan of campaign.

We went down to the kitchen to get ourselves breakfast. Everyone was still asleep. We breakfasted in Sir Charles's study and having found writing materials Milady drew up two documents. I woke the other servants, all except Selmersham whom we allowed to sleep. I found the buttons in bed with the maid. I told them all to come to the study if they wanted to be paid.

The four of them, the cook, the maid, the scullery and the buttons came in together. Milady did not look up from her work. But the difference that a few hours sleep and reflection can make! The night before they had been four demons who sang and danced and we were their victims, entirely at their mercy. Now they were four poor devils, uneasy, unwell and fearful. The buttons had one side of his face covered with sticking plaster, one eye red and the other black. They were all very pale.

Milady spoke like a magistrate, without pity, without anger. The things that had happened the previous night would interest the police. For herself she did not want to bring in the police at all; but if there were proceedings they would find that the penal code – she cited the relevant articles – had very severe punishment for such crimes. If any one of them had already attracted the interest of the law, it might be very disagreeable indeed. It depended entirely on them.

'I have a document,' she said, 'which you must sign, if you do not sign, and I must have all your signatures, then you give me no choice. I go straight to the police. As I say, it is in your hands. If you don't sign or if you whisper one word – one word will be enough – the intervention of the law will become inevitable. The document which I will now read is intended to reduce your sentences, it cannot secure acquittals. Let us hope that it will never have to be used.'

Then, in a very clear voice, she read out loud that which she had been writing. Recently I burnt that document, but I can give you a fairly exact account of it.

We, the undersigned (then the real names of the four servants) saw the following things on the night of April 7th, 1891 at Penny Villa.

Sir Charles Brandon, assisted by his valet George Arthur Selmersham forced Lady Brandon, wife of the said Sir Charles to take part in a celebration given by Sir Charles to his servants. Lady Brandon and her maid Thérèse Boileau were threatened with a whip, bound with cords, Mlle Boileau was gagged during the séance; both ladies were molested in an indecent manner by Sir Charles and his valet.

Sir Charles beat his wife, inflicting superficial wounds, he then raped her. This rape took place in our presence and was visibly an act of sodomy. Sir Charles then invited his valet to do that which he himself had done upon the body of his wife. We heard this invitation given, we saw it accepted, the act of sodomy being again performed in our presence. Later Mr Selmersham attempted to rape Mlle Boileau, but did not succeed in doing so. The fact that these two ladies were later able to escape is in no way due to Sir Charles or his valet.

While admitting that we, the servants of Sir Charles, were obliged to witness these crimes we would make the following observations.

(1) That we had been assured by Mr Selmersham that these ladies were consenting parties, that they were taking part in a kind of comedy agreed upon in advance by all concerned, that the beating and rape were to be simulated but not actually performed. It was too late to take action when we perceived that there was nothing feigned in these crimes.

(2) It became clear that there was no play-acting when Sir Charles committed sodomy; but we were unsure whether a husband had not the legal right to act as he did.

(3) When Selmersham took a hand in the business we did protest, but Selmersham and his master were able to overrule and threaten us.

(4) One of our number (the name of the scullery is given) set Lady Brandon free and assisted her to escape together with Mlle Boileau.

(5) Another (the name of the buttons is given) intervened in order to prevent the rape of Mlle Boileau and was in so doing, wounded by Mr Selmersham.

(6) When the ladies had escaped we, all of us, intervened and prevented Sir Charles and Mr Selmersham from again molesting them.

So far as their knowledge goes (i.e. on points 2, 3, 4 and 5) Lady Brandon and Mlle Boileau are ready to declare that the signatories are telling the truth. They hope that proceedings will not be instituted against these witnesses, or, if a prosecution is inevitable, they plead for clemency. In sign of this they affix their signatures.

Penny Villa, April 8th, 1891

The buttons spoke first, he was very ready to sign. The scullery and the maid followed suit. Only the cook refused but in the end she was compelled to yield to the arguments of the others. In the end they all signed.

Milady then told them that when the dining room was cleaned up – properly cleaned up – she would pay their wages and that they could then have the rest of the day off, until three o'clock. She ended with a final injunction: for their own sakes they must be discreet.

Nine o'clock struck. The scullery was the last to be paid off; she left with a little present. Milady recopied her second document.

We heard Selmersham in the kitchen shouting angrily for his breakfast and went to meet him. I admit that I was still afraid of him, he was a wild beast with a wild beast's cunning and a wild beast's ferocity. I did not know what would happen. Nevertheless, in the interview which followed I foresaw, and foresaw rightly, that Milady would have two advantages. In the first place I had used all my art in dressing her and I am an artist, I gave her an appearance which was really impressive. In the second place Mrs Gordon had trained her to be, as you put it 'a gentlewoman', and if she had seen her pupil in that hour she would have been proud of her. She knew how to make Selmersham feel the dirt that he was. But at the beginning of our encounter I was still fearful.

We found him astride a chair. He looked ill, a kick in the belly can be uncomfortable on the morning after. He looked at us with a bored expression, he didn't move.

'On your feet, Simmons.'

It was his real name and he was so much disconcerted at hearing it that he rose and, in a slovenly way, stood.

'In my presence, Simmons, you will stand.' Milady sat down.

His air remained contemptuous and he replied, with a touch of irony, 'Let us hope that Milady,' in his mouth the title became an insult, 'has brought plenty of cash with her. Milady is anxious to please her husband I'm sure, very anxious I dare say. Milady has learnt to be prudent, hasn't she? Also we shall need quite a lot of cash: Sir Charles owes me above a hundred pounds.'

'I am not interested. Even if I were, you would get nothing from me for in fact I have no money. The other servants had to be paid. Later on Mr Mellish will be here. If your master agrees to the terms that I offer some money may be available, there might even be some for you if you behave yourself. I might as well tell you that one of my conditions is that you shall leave for good and at once.'

'I think that Milady knows better than to give herself airs. I'm sure she doesn't want to put the master in a bad temper again, nor me either, Milady. I think Milady will have the sense to pay me now . . .'

At that moment he caught sight of me standing behind him. I

watched his face in the mirror, one of those looking-glasses that you find in big houses put there for the servants to see themselves before they go into the dining room. Thus too he could see me. I was close behind him sharpening my big knife, it shone in the morning light bright as a razor. I think he knew how much I longed to use it. Already pale, he turned green and his assurance left him. He continued, but in an uneasy voice, 'Sir Charles will never dismiss me.'

'When Sir Charles discovers that his lackey is an imbecile who has made a mess of everything he may change his mind. But,' she continued with a happy smile, 'supposing that he is so foolish as to reject my offer, you may leave together and perhaps even share a cell in the police station.'

He was still looking at my knife. 'But Milady, you wouldn't dare squeal on us. It's not possible for you.'

'If you will reflect a little you will discover that it's not merely possible, it's highly probable.'

'But, to begin with there's no proof, no evidence.'

'Poor Mr Selmersham. You get up too late. It's a fault in a servant, and in a criminal a fatal weakness. Allow me to read this.'

In a gently mocking voice she read out the deposition. It was a pleasure to watch Selmersham's face.

'Did Kitty sign that?' – Kitty was the cook.

'They all signed. Your Kitty sold you an hour ago. Really Mr Selmersham, you don't seem to have much talent for making friendships last. All those witnesses against you, not to speak of Thérèse and of me. Then of course there is your own criminal record to consider. When Mr Mellish and the police know about it, well, I shall be sorry for you. Your only hope is to make peace, the very fair peace that I offer.'

He had lost his confidence but not his courage. He turned to bite: 'You, I can ruin you. You and your rubber bubs.'

I prepared to strike, he was so near to violence. But Milady exploded. With rage? No, Monsieur, with laughter. With such laughter that it was some time before she could continue. Selmersham, who had been astonished, now began ruefully to understand.

'Is it not wonderful, Thérèse? He still thinks he can blackmail. And we had thought him clever.' Then, to Selmersham, 'You want money? Well then, repeat these words until you can understand them: "No Miss, no marriage, no marriage, no money." It's not really hard, and in the end even you will perceive that if your master hasn't a wife he hasn't a penny.

'But now, since last night's happenings my little secret has become a spring-gun which will blow off your legs unless you're very careful. What you did last night was a punishable offence. Are you really stupid enough to think you can do yourself any good by saying that your victim was a boy?

'Obviously, if you are indiscreet it will be tiresome for me. But, after all, I've had plenty of time to make my plans. I have friends, I have a nice bank account overseas. I shouldn't be so terribly put out. It will be a lot worse for Sir Charles. You would certainly make an enemy of him. Still, even for him there would be possibilities. He can get away, he has influential relatives. He would have a good barrister to say, "This poor young man has been led into trouble by his servant, a criminal, a gaol-bird. Sir Charles knew nothing, he had no notion that he was committing an unnatural act." No, the villain of the piece will be Selmersham, alias Simmons. Sir Charles is young, he is amiable, he is distinguished; but his lackey, who is neither young nor handsome nor pleasant is from the lower dregs of society, he shall serve as a useful scapegoat. Everyone will be against him. How old are you Selmersham? You won't come out of prison I think.

'Now I'm not looking for revenge. I want everything hushed up; I want it so much that I'm even prepared to see you pensioned off. You will take this letter to Sir Charles and you will persuade him to accept my terms. If he agrees then a great deal of money will be available, and a very generous portion will be yours. If you fail to persuade him you are finished.'

She handed him a letter. He took it without a word and turned to go. But, Monsieur, I had an account to settle also.

'One moment, M. Selmersham, I have something for you.'

He turned and looked me in the face – he looked as though he were in hell. I spat in his eye and he left like a viper broken by a wheel.

He went to the larder, no doubt to get his master's breakfast. We returned to the study. Later we heard him knocking on Sir Charles's door.

Monsieur, I am not vindictive, mine is not a vengeful nature. Ask anyone about here and they will tell you that old Boileau is a decent enough sort. For a moment when I saw him go, old and miserable and broken, I was almost sorry for the reptile. But later, when we were alone I rejoiced. Milady had been superb. It had been a famous victory.

Milady did not share my feelings. 'Yes, it was right, it was just and necessary that you should have your revenge, but . . .'

'But what, Milady?'

'Wellington said that the only thing worse than a victory was defeat. And, well, I hit too hard.'

'But think what happened last night.'

'It's over, I don't want to think about it. Yes, Selmersham is abominable and much stupider than I had supposed. But Sir Charles is a child. I wrote him a letter which he will hate; it will wound him terribly although I don't see what else I could have said.' She heaved a great sigh.

It so happens that I have that letter. I provide a copy, let Monsieur decide whether it is too hard.

April 8th, 1891   *Penny Villa*
My dear Charles,

I do not want to discuss last night's events, not more than I have to: but unfortunately I do have to say a little about them because it is in the light of that incident that I have to dictate my terms – I have made them as generous as I can. I have decided that we must live together, for a time at all events, but we have to live with the memory of what happened and we have to take precautions in the light of your conduct.

As you may have observed you made me cry last night. I cried until I could cry no more; but with my tears I shed some other things – illusions, day dreams, childish stupidities. At the end of it I found myself strong and exhilarated, I had become aware of the realities of life and aware that I could deal with them. You did indeed teach me a lesson, it was like growing up very painfully and very fast, a most salutary lesson. It would show base ingratitude on my part if I did not try to teach you the same lesson, Heaven knows that you are even more in need of it than I was. If you are to cease to be a third-rate poseur you must be able to understand that what happened was the result of your childish need to translate rather unhealthy day dreams into facts, nasty, squalid, ludicrous facts. I believe when you *do* grow up a little and become less irresponsible, you will learn – you must already be learning – that this kind of folly brings no real pleasure to anyone, just headaches and legal troubles and vomit on the floor. I felt, all the time, your desperate need to be taken seriously. The only answer to that craving was to behave like a pig. It doesn't make you impressive only, in a very sad way, ridiculous. Perhaps it began to dawn on you that neither your victim nor your servants could see in you anything but a spoiled child with dirty habits, trying to play a 'demonic' role in which even you could not quite believe. The practical result of all this is that, for the time being, I have to treat you as an irresponsible adolescent.

Other practical considerations arise from your insane and infantile need for an audience – for it must have been some kind of puerile vanity which led you to invite witnesses and make an exhibition of yourself *coram publico*. That really was the height of irresponsibility and you may thank me for having, I hope, shut the mouths of these witnesses. (I cannot think that you will be so unwise as to force me, by refusing my offer, to institute proceedings against you, but you might as well know, in case such a lunacy did occur to you, that the servants have put their names to a full and complete account of last night's events.) These servants, if the matter did come before the courts, would be accessories before the fact. I have made them realise this and they will, let us hope, be discreet.

Altogether I think that, provided you and Selmersham are capable of acting rationally and in your own best interests, the thing can be hushed up. I certainly don't want a public scandal and you two have far more to lose than I.

We both have to face the fact that you have brought us all to the verge of disaster.

The offer that I am going to make seems to me, under the circumstances, pretty generous. I make it partly because I feel that a little of the fault lies with me. I have been dishonest; I must admit that. On the other hand, I was virtually obliged to be dishonest because of the much greater dishonesty of Selmersham. As I hope you do *not* know, he has been blackmailing me. Like all blackmailers he wanted money, but he realised that I being a minor and a spinster had very little. In order to lay his hands on really large sums he had to enable you to marry it (I mean money); his blackmail therefore took the form of compelling me to accept you. Of course, I realised almost at once, as he did not, that this was a fool's game. Once we were married, the weapon which·he had used in order to drive me to the altar would break in his hand. (I think, however, he will understand that by the time you read this letter.) From my point of view, therefore, the sooner we could be married the better. What I could not anticipate was how completely you would destroy your own position and place yourself in my power by last night's stupidity. Obviously you cannot have seen the situation at all clearly and, as I hope, never realised what Selmersham was doing.

My only real difficulty lay in finding some method, when we did marry, of preventing you from ruining us both by your childish extravagance. To this end I had to convince both you and Selmersham that, even after marriage, I should give no trouble. You had to be made to suppose that I should always submit to your will. I am afraid that I did take you in rather completely, so completely that you were ready to put your name to documents which left us both powerless to touch our capital for many years. Mellish has therefore been able to construct legal barriers which keep my money safe from your innocent but profligate hands.

Yes, I admit that it was wrong to defend myself as I did; I can only plead that circumstances left me no choice. I could not have dreamed that you would deliver yourself into my hands so completely.

Well now, here are my terms of peace.

(1) Selmersham must go at once. It is impossible that he should remain under this roof for another night. He has behaved abominably to me and still worse to Thérèse.

(2) We will dispose of Penny Villa and its staff. There is to be no more horse racing: it is a philistine way of losing money.

(3) As you know, I shall have a large income when I come of age. I had thought to give you half of it. But I have observed that you and Mr Selmersham like to share and share alike, so 25% each seems more appropriate.

(4) My capital remains in trust. This is not a stipulation, it is a fact. For

the time being neither of us will touch it unless to pay debts already incurred.

(5) Two thirds of my capital shall be earmarked for scientific purposes. I shall, of course, do as much research as I please. We shall live at Ramsgate in order to make that possible.

(6) For six months we must remain, outwardly at all events, on good conjugal terms. This is vitally necessary for both of us. There is bound to be some gossip; this is tolerable so long as it remains mere servants' talk and so long as it is consistently belied by our public union. If this means that I have to go on playing the tiresome role of your devoted slave, then so be it; in public I will submit. I can't help feeling that by now even you must be bored by that performance. At the end of six months we will decide to separate or to remain united. I won't insist upon a union unless at that time it seems too wildly imprudent not to do so. But it is my hope that we may remain together and that you will come to see in me not a puppet to be used in joyless orgies, but a real person whom you can love and who loves you and that, one day, when you have grown wiser and I am in a better temper, we shall indeed be happy.

For the time being, I cannot but remain apprehensive of what you might do if your impulses remain unchecked. I must have real, cast-iron safeguards and, when Mellish comes, as he will this morning, we must be in agreement, you must support or, if you like, advance as your own the financial propositions that I have listed. If for any reason you were to refuse my offer, or if you were for a moment to be indiscreet – but no, I don't want even to consider that possibility. I cannot bear to think of destroying you for, in spite of everything, I am, yours affectionately,

MARY BRANDON

Surely, Monsieur, you cannot call that a 'hard' letter. Think what he had done to her, the unspeakable brutalities, the gross humiliation that she had suffered and then not a word of reproach, not a trace of anger and she even thinks of offering him half her income, an enormous income. At that time – that morning I mean – I had not seen what she had written and I imagined it to be something very severe indeed.

She was depressed, anxious, altogether at a loose end. In order to be doing something we went up to the third floor and inspected the servants' bedrooms. There was dirt and dust and disorder everywhere.

In the buttons' room we found great quantities of sugar which he must have been stealing.

From below we heard a cry, a shout rather. It was not very loud but it was clear that Sir Charles was very angry about something.

Then came the first shot.

Milady was leaning over the banisters listening intently. We heard the second. She ran down. I was not quite sure what to do, but decided she might need me. I followed, still holding my knife.

In the theatre I found the body of Selmersham and cried out — Monsieur, I must confess that it was a cry of joy. That black heart beat no longer and I was glad.

But my joy was short-lived. In Sir Charles's bedroom I found Milady livid, with terrified eyes, almost fainting. She had fallen into a chair. On the bed was the body of Sir Charles, a Herculean figure and still beautiful, beneath his chin a little hole which hardly bled; but the top of his skull was broken up like a soft boiled egg, a veritable *pâté* of blood and brains was mixed with the feathers of his pillow. There was blood on the floor, also the remains of breakfast. From this I extracted Milady's letter.

I helped her out of the room and put her on a *chaise longue*. I found some brandy in the kitchen and we both drank a large glass. Then in a most remarkable fashion she regained her strength and, as always at moments of crisis, began to think clearly and to act swiftly.

'What is the time?'

'Twenty minutes past ten.'

'Time enough. Go upstairs and get my luggage, put it in Sir Charles's bedroom. I will go and see if I can find that letter.'

Like a good captain she made me share her *sang froid*. I remembered that I had the letter and gave it her. I brought down her luggage and so arranged matters that anyone would have supposed that Sir Charles and his wife had slept together all night. I put away the carving knife and found that Milady had written out the answers that I was to give to the police. I went off to fetch a constable, at the same time repeating my lesson to myself.

The police came, the doctors came and then M. Mellish. He was a good deal put out as you may imagine. He questioned me a little, but he spoke in bad French and could not really understand my replies. Milady was too distressed to say very much; she really was distraught, and M. Mellish did not keep her very long. For my part I am convinced that from the first he scented a scandal of some kind and did not want to know too much. As for the police, he was determined that they should know nothing at all. He was present when they questioned us, he seemed to know them very well and the interrogation was little more than a formality. M. Mellish was mainly interested that we should have somewhere quiet to lie down and remain undisturbed while he sent a messenger to Ramsgate. He got rid of the police, the doctors and the bodies. When the servants returned he saw them privately. I do not know what passed between them. In fact, I think that by then we were on our way back to Ramsgate. Milady the mother of Sir Charles was, as you may imagine, in an indescribable condition. The next day Milady and I returned to India Lodge and there we remained.

As I said, M. Mellish asked very few questions. He managed matters in such a way that we were, as far as possible, spared any inconvenience. For me who had expected a terrible inquisition it was an enormous relief. Not for Milady. She wanted to be doing something and he carefully left her nothing to do. He seemed to know what questions would be put at the inquest and rehearsed us in our answers. Everything seemed to be in his hands and we had merely to do as we were told.

While we were waiting and still felt ourselves to be in danger Milady remained calm and self-possessed; but when the inquest was over and it was clear that we were safe, she fell into a terrible melancholy. She felt that she was a criminal. For her everything was over. She did not know what to do with herself and did not want to live. She could not sleep, and when she did she was visited by horrible nightmares from which she would wake up screaming. Yes, Monsieur, it was a black time – but it did not last forever.

What happened between ten and ten-twenty on the morning of the 8th? We never knew.

Milady formed two hypotheses. It had always seemed to her possible that Sir Charles had been completely in the dark, that he had believed, until a few moments before his death, that Milady was indeed a woman. Selmersham knew better but did not tell his master, as this would have helped him later on to blackmail Sir Charles. But then Milady's letter would have aroused his suspicions, he would have cross-questioned Selmersham who, seeing that further concealment was impossible, and indeed dangerous, would have admitted everything. Then Sir Charles would have seen that he had married a boy, that he had been the dupe of his own valet, a mere pawn in the game that was being played out between Selmersham and Milady. He would have been seized with anger, hence that terrible cry, and in his anger he fired.

The other hypothesis was more disagreeable and, according to Milady, more probable. Sir Charles did know, and knew all along. At their very first meeting at India Lodge he had been struck by her resemblance to Henry Brandon. He had been made suspicious and, having once suspected, he would have noticed all those tiny things others never saw because they did not look for them. Then, at Christmas, that terrible Christmas, he made what Milady called a 'reconnaissance in force' that would have left him with few doubts. That pig Selmersham discovered the rest through my folly. His last doubts were removed when Selmersham challenged Milady and Milady could not call his bluff. He knew then that he could force her to marry him and could make himself a rich man. Her conduct during the engagement seemed to show that she would be as governable as that other young man* and he imagined that his violence on their wedding night would cow her altogether. That his wealth would be magnificent, that he could practise who knows what enormities on my mistress – all this he devised with Selmersham.

Imagine then his feelings when he read her letter. He expected a

*Saxon Filbert-White – M.E.

violent expression of distress and perhaps of anger, probably of despairing and terrified submission. Instead he found himself treated as a schoolboy who has made a fool of himself, an urchin whom one might punish but whom one spares because he is so young and so foolish. Milady made fun of him, gently and with condescension. And now Selmersham, who had led him into all this, urged surrender. They had as you put it, 'caught a tartar', and there was no choice but to submit. And now Selmersham was actually going to profit from the disaster. Selmersham was to be richly rewarded; he and Selmersham were to be treated as equals. It was intolerable. His valet and his wife had combined to outwit him and now they were laughing at him. He seized a pistol, because at least you can't laugh at murder, and he let fly at the bearer of bad tidings. If he had succeeded in dispatching Selmersham the other bullet would have been for her; in fact it was Selmersham who saved her life.

I don't know, perhaps it was like that. The motives of those two wild beasts hardly merit discussion. The world was well rid of such gallows meat.

No, Milady could not see it from that point of view. She called herself a thief, an impostor and a murderer.

Yes, it was M. William who saved her. He set her to work, he gave her her 'rats'. I have never understood these things, all this fuss about this food or that food — for me good cooking is sufficient. But Monsieur, I have blessed those rats. They gave her the occupation that she needed, they cured her, and it was for them that we stayed at the Lodge for half a century and were, in the end, so very happy. She came back to life. She went out, but not very much, she even had a few flirtations, although she had learnt not to think of any kind of marriage. She kept her beauty for many years and I knew how to make the best of it, there were evenings when she left my hands as beautiful as Venus.

Was her life a happy one? Yes, and she deserved to be happy. She had her rats and then, you know, she had me.